The Golden Thread

The Golden Thread

STORIES BY

Ann Copeland

VIKING

VIKING
Published by the Penguin Group
Viking Penguin, a division of Penguin Books USA Inc.,
40 West 23rd Street, New York, New York 10010, U.S.A.
Penguin Books Ltd, 27 Wrights Lane, London W8 5TZ, England
Penguin Books Australia Ltd, Ringwood, Victoria, Australia
Penguin Books Canada Ltd, 2801 John Street,
Markham, Ontario, Canada L3R 1B4
Penguin Books (N.Z.) Ltd, 182–190 Wairau Road,
Auckland 10, New Zealand

Penguin Books Ltd, Registered Offices:
Harmondsworth, Middlesex, England

First published in 1989 by Viking Penguin,
a division of Penguin Books USA Inc.

1 3 5 7 9 10 8 6 4 2

The following stories have been previously published in slightly different form:

"Taking the Discipline" in *Southwest Review*; "Obedience" in *Matrix* and *Journey Prize Anthology* (McClelland & Stewart Inc.); "Cloister" in *Western Humanities Review*; "Angels of Reality" in *Canadian Fiction Magazine*; and "At Peace" in *Canadian Fiction Magazine*, *Best American Short Stories 1977* and *77: Best Canadian Stories*. "Higher Learning," "Cloister," "The Golden Thread," "Jubilee," and "At Peace" appeared in *At Peace* (Oberon Press).

The author thanks the National Endowment for the Arts and the Canada Council for their support during the writing of parts of this book.

LIBRARY OF CONGRESS CATALOGING IN PUBLICATION DATA
Copeland, Ann.
The golden thread / Ann Copeland.
p.   cm.
ISBN 0-670-82977-3
I. Title.
PR9199.3.C647G6   1989   88-40629
                                                              CIP

Printed in the United States of America
Set in Garamond No. 3

For Thomas Gavin Furtwangler
and Gavin Copeland Williamson

Contents

Sins of Omission   3

Taking the Discipline   31

Obedience   49

Higher Learning   61

Cloister   87

The Golden Thread   107

The Nature of Love   149

Angels of Reality   173

Jubilee   191

The Perils of Translation   219

At Peace   249

The Golden Thread

He who finds his life will lose it,
and he who loses his life for My sake will find it.

Matthew 10:39

Sins of Omission

When we were young the nuns impressed upon us that there were ever so many ways to sin. These included omission as well as commission. It was easier, though, to number and arrange in hierarchical order sins of commission as you knelt in the church pew once a month on the Thursday before First Friday, let out from school an hour early to go to confession. Public school kids had to wait until three o'clock and give up part of their afternoon if they wanted to confess. On Tuesday afternoons, moreover, they also had to sacrifice free time for religious instruction, whereas we had it integrated into school time, a lesson first thing every morning. To say nothing of weekly visits from the pastor, Father Donlon, and sermons from our classroom teacher, Sister Whoever-it-was-that-year.

Daily, inexorably, in ways subtle and overt, the good nuns

were training us to delicacy of conscience—even as they assured us that ours was, ultimately, a benevolent God.

After eighth grade, to complete my religious formation, my parents sent me to the one Catholic girls' high school in town: Holy Angels. Here classes began at eight in the morning. We were allowed sixty seconds to change rooms (in perfect silence), ten minutes for lunch, and dismissal came at one-fifteen, early enough for girls over sixteen in the commercial program to hold down afternoon jobs. We enjoyed certain other advantages as well: holy days of obligation plus our annual retreat netted us a full week extra out of class. The public high schools might feature boys, but we had the shortest school year in town.

Holy Angels was an old dark building in a run-down section of town near Scovill's factory and the Catholic hospital. Though the school had been there for years, I was unaware of it until I entered those doors in 1946. I was quite aware, however, of the two girls' prep schools outside town, schools nestled in against their own cultivated hillsides and approached by winding drives, schools to which I would not be sent—although my older brother had already been packed off to their respectable male counterpart. The girls' schools were not Catholic (nor was his, for that matter), but Episcopalian.

For a brief few weeks midway through eighth grade my parents did consider sending me as well to a prep school. But we were not rich, just (as my mother put it) "comfortable." Unlike my brother, I had no learning problems that needed special attention. I was clearly college material, whereas he would need help to get there. Moreover, I had flourished so far under the nuns and no doubt would continue to do so. My father, whose pure tenor voice I loved to accompany, was eager that I continue with music, and the nuns were always good in the arts.

For years I carried a lingering sense of the difference that one decision may have made in my life. When my parents took me out for a drive on a beautiful October day and we passed those handsome stone buildings and tennis courts, it seemed to me that the lives within must be so much more rarefied than mine, more traveled, more experienced, more secure, more everything—except religious. Too young to value delicacy of conscience, I yearned to explore landscapes as yet but dimly sensed.

Holy Angels might lack boys, science labs, tennis courts, a football team, and cheerleaders, but it had music.

Our annual spring concert was a sellout for three consecutive nights every year: people traveled distances to hear us sing. The head of the department—or, one might say, *the* music department—was one nun: Mother Magdalena. She was energetic, feisty, critical, homely, and French. (I mention nationality here because living in an immigrant factory town made one aware of names, backgrounds, sections of the city that held the French church, the Italian church, the Irish churches—rich and poor—the Polish church, and so on.) Her glasses were so thick that the pupils behind them looked like pinheads. She moved fast, rocking her stout figure from side to side, and had a habit of rubbing her lips together, and sometimes her hands, as she moved. She often scowled and looked as if she were about to erupt. No one knew a thing about her except that she'd come from Canada. She took no nonsense and hated small talk. Because their headdresses rose to a peak in front, the nuns' hair showed, offering a clue to their age. Her hair was still brown, but to us she appeared at least sixty. She always wore a black apron with a large pocket in front where she stored Kleenex, in case a student began to cry during her piano lessons. This could happen.

Mother Magdalena taught piano in a small studio on the ground floor behind the auditorium stage. High windows lined one side of the room, and along the sills stood various plants: trailing Swedish ivy, impatiens, dormant geraniums, wandering Jew, and a gnarled Christmas cactus that burst into bloom every Advent and Lent. One corner of the narrow room held a dark, open-top desk crammed with papers and music. Here she kept track of accounts. You paid her directly at the end of each lesson, four dollars an hour. Above the desk hung a dark crucifix and a small, round silver-framed photograph of an elderly woman with a soft expression about the dark eyes and her white hair in a bun. I sneaked several close looks at this benign face, always wanted to know who it was but never got up courage to ask. Personal questions were taboo. The nuns were dropped into our lives dressed and complete, unencumbered by personal history.

Naturally, this tantalized our adolescent imaginations. The younger and more beautiful the nun, the more mysteriously appealing. Who knew what fascinations her obscure past might have held? What drama, what pain, what heights? What reaches of experience now so effectively concealed that we could but vaguely imagine them? Such mystery—combined with the thrill of the absolute, incarnate and present to us in their very beings—drew more than one high school girl into a crush on the nun of her choice. Certain girls were always hanging around certain nuns. Though I did my share of it, I wouldn't have dared "hang around" Mother Magdalena. She knew what it was to waste time.

Along the inside wall of her studio stood two upright pianos. Behind them, along the wall beneath the windows, were bookshelves crammed with sheet music and yellow G. Schirmer albums: Bach, Beethoven, Weber, Liszt, Debussy—all the greats whose musical heavens I strove to enter. When she'd turn away from me during a lesson and begin to rummage through those stacks, my heart would lighten. It meant I'd done well enough that she'd decided to give me a new piece. On top of the unused piano, between two metronomes, stood a plaster-of-Paris bust of Beethoven I coveted.

For my first lesson with Mother Magdalena I was in terror. I'd already heard she was terribly strict. Since second grade I'd studied with an old German musician who'd made no secret of the fact that I was his best pupil. Now I had a new teacher to please. What would she want? Would I be able to do it?

That first morning she sat to my left, her black form just visible to my peripheral vision, hands folded in her lap, as I worked my way through Chopin's "Valse brillante."

6

"*Mon dieu*," she murmured when I finished. She got up and walked about the small room, chewing her lips.

I didn't have a clue.

Then she turned suddenly and came over to the piano, resting her hand on my shoulder, the weight of her long black sleeve falling against my back.

"Now, *mon petit chou*, you play well. But you must practice your scales, your arpeggios." Somehow I'd thought, now that I'd switched to the nuns, I'd be let off that. "Your little finger is too weak," she went on. "We must have you trill. And the movement, the movement . . ." She waved her hands—small, firm, freckled hands with trimmed nails—in a large arc to indicate the desired design my fingers and wrists were to trace. "You must always be loose, *ma petite*, loose, wrist like this"— she shook her wrists in midair, "the fingers firm. So you will never be tired as you play, never. Your fingers will grow nimble. *You must practice.*" She sat down. "Now go on. Let me hear more."

Mon petit chou. It was a while before I understood it as a term of affection. By the end of the first year I'd grown more confident. I knew she liked me, saw promise. In April she started breaking me in to accompany the Choral Club the following year, for the senior accompanist would graduate that June.

Choral Club met two mornings a week, during the eleven o'clock period, in the auditorium. As girls raced down three flights to make it on time, Mother Magdalena would be standing in the middle of the stage rubbing her lips together and calling, "*Vite! Vite!*" She detested tardiness.

Once the girls were in their places on the stage steps, she'd vocalize them chromatically, "*aaa, eee, iii, ooo, uuu,*" waving and pulling at them, seeming to shape their voices in midair. She'd stamp her foot, wave her hands, shake her head in disgust, cajole them into producing the sweet, pure sounds that had won her reputation. They must stand erect, firmly on both feet. They must maintain eye contact with her. "*Attendez!* Here! You look at me! Not at the music! You must memorize the music, all of it. So you are free of it, so you can feel it."

When they finished a number, she would clasp her hands behind her back, stride up and down in front of them, muttering in French. Then, with surprising agility for her size, she'd wheel and face them. "Sopranos, you sound like a barnyard full of chickens. Blend! You must hear the person on either side of you. Listen! Altos, you missed the F sharp in line three. First it's sharped, then natural. Second sopranos—too soft. Build. Like this." She'd sing their part quickly, perfectly, in a thin, shaky voice. "And you!" She'd point at some poor girl who might have yawned or blinked. "Any more of that, Miss, and you're out!"

They hated her and loved her.

The night of the concert they loved her.

By my second year I was regularly at the piano for rehearsals. She'd raise her hand, pause, then start. I learned to interpret her sighs and "hrumphs," her shrugs and silences. She might look over at me, suddenly waving the singers to stop. "Play it a step higher." I learned to control my panic. She did everything from Palestrina to Bach to Gilbert and Sullivan. I grew to love it all: the accompanying, the fact that she counted on me, my privilege of sitting down. She kept her singers standing for rehearsal always, even when they practiced two hours at a stretch for spring concert.

By third year my position was secure. Whatever rewards eluded me in algebra, Cicero, or world history, I more than made up for in my time with Mother Magdalena. Leaving the upper floors and hurrying down the back stairs to the auditorium when I had a free period was my great escape. I went whether I was supposed to or not. I had only to say, "Mother Magdalena wanted to see me," and my homeroom nun would nod. No one crossed Mother Magdalena if she could help it.

Once in a great while, when no one else was around after school, she'd suddenly emerge from her studio, rubbing her lips together, her brow contracted and those small eyes alight. "Come, *ma petite*," she'd say. "Let's play. *Vite!* I don't have all afternoon."

We'd open the stage curtains onto the empty auditorium, push the grand pianos from the wings onto center stage, turn up the overhead lights, and she'd raid her pile of two-piano arrangements. We'd settle at our pianos and, watching each other across the raised polished mahogany, feel our way into the music, sight-reading. It could be anything: Gershwin's "Rhapsody in Blue," Beethoven's Fifth Symphony arranged for two pianos, a Mozart sonata, Schubert Variations. We played undisturbed. To my knowledge, no one saw or heard us. By four-thirty the nuns would be over on the convent side doing whatever they did there, and the students would have left their side of the building. We were alone with the music.

In the empty auditorium on those late afternoons I discovered the exhilaration of making music with another. It was a dialogue, a challenge, a friendly competition. I raced to keep up with her, straining not to default. If one of us got lost, the other would go on. Before long there would again be two voices arching over the raised pianos, asking and answering.

At the end of such a session she sometimes spoke brusquely. "Come, *ma petite,* let's erase the traces." We'd lower the covers over the keys and shove the great pianos back to the wings. "Push, don't pull," she'd admonish. "Don't strain. A girl your age must be careful of her insides. You could injure yourself." All this said with a scowl, as if to hide her concern.

We'd spread the heavy dark green cloths over the glowing mahogany. Then she'd lock her studio.

"*Eh, bien.* You'd better go home now. Scat!"

She'd swing through the door to the cloister.

All the way home on the crowded late afternoon bus the warmth generated by our music would remain with me.

In late November of my third year, I went to school one morning and discovered Mother Magdalena had disappeared. Her studio was empty, the door locked. Someone had drawn a curtain across the glass window in the door. No one was around in the practice rooms. She was in the hospital, we were told. Only that.

The first Sunday of Advent was upon us. Time to prepare for the Christmas pageant, a predictable affair: the usual manger scene, selected freshmen as live angels, aching arms extended. Mary and Joseph were reserved for seniors. Jesus would be a plaster doll, though invariably some girl lobbied futilely for her baby brother or sister. The student body would sing carols, and the principal, Mother St. David, would address us. Usually Mother Magdalena would train a special group to sing. I would accompany them. Not this year.

Our Christmas pageant had one unusual addition. Because the feast day of the foundress of the order occurred during Christmas holidays and we mustn't miss celebrating it, the nuns added a few figures to our tableau. The foundress, Blessed Marguerite, and her original band of followers, occupied an appropriate space in front of the angels and behind the shepherds.

This aspect of the pageant was of some significance, for it gave six girls (upperclassmen only) the opportunity to don the religious habit. They would stand on the stage near their foundress and pose for a few moments to remind us all what sacrifice and toil in seventeenth-century Quebec lay behind our thriving eight-hundred-strong Catholic girls' high school in twentieth-century Connecticut.

Who would get to dress up as nuns that year? A far more burning question than which seniors would play Mary and Joseph. Although the honor carried with it the suggestion that the nuns had spotted you as a potential vocation, many of us coveted the chance just once to look out at the world from inside that cloth, from within that stiff frame of starch. And if, as I had for years, you nursed the secret hope that you might one day be found worthy of that very commitment, this chance was all the more compelling.

On the other hand, for me it might complicate. To stand before my schoolmates garbed in the cloth would work against a certain secretiveness I even then strove to maintain. Some girls in our school seemed destined to be nuns. They set themselves apart by a premature dowdiness, an absence of makeup, a lack of interest in boys, and a tendency to parade their piety. Labeled "Father Carthy's girls," they could be seen every Saturday afternoon lined up outside his confessional. They called him their spiritual director and periodically went on trips and retreats with him. Every year six or seven of them entered right after graduation.

I wanted no part of that. In my view, these girls needlessly cut short their chances for fun. If, in the end, God answered my heartfelt prayer and called me to this highest of all womanly vocations, I wanted first to experience what I could. Not that I imagined all pleasures came to a halt with the putting on of the cloth. I was not suicidal. Many nuns at Holy Angels seemed quite happy. Talented, too. Particularly, as my father had rightly judged, in the arts. Occasionally some of them appeared small-minded, and that would disturb me. But my mother, always sympathetic to nuns, would remind me of what I perfectly well knew: nuns were only human, after all.

How deeply I grasped the immensity of their step: entering. It was total, irrevocable. No looking back. Its very immensity, its absoluteness, attracted me. The most wholehearted response one could make to God Himself, the God Whose love and care I believed in and trusted. The God Who had given Himself so utterly for me. What higher call could there be than to respond to Him with one's entire being?

It would mean sacrificing many things, cutting ties with a world whose provocative beauty and possibilities for adventure drew me. There was beauty and love in my home, as well as much understanding. Fresh roses on the piano, mellow moments accompanying my father as he sang through favorite Irish ballads, less mellow but nonetheless fun hours when my brother (whose drum set graced one end of our large living room) would put on a record of Mugsy Spanier or Harry James and drum to their beat or, better yet, deign to drum with me as I turned into

Hoagy Carmichael to plink out some popular tune on our piano.

My parents and their friends seemed happy in their lives, rooted in a way that took much for granted, sharing a faith as well as a hope that they and their offspring would achieve success. They seemed untroubled by the warning that it was easier for a camel to pass through the eye of a needle than for a rich man to enter the kingdom of heaven. Once they'd successfully negotiated their way through the complex thickets of this world—marriage, child rearing, investing, aging—they certainly aspired to enter that other, theirs by right of baptism.

I saw the fullness of their lives but had little wish to duplicate it. I wanted a higher adventure—even if that meant no marriage, no comfortable home, no material comforts—for did not all those nos really constitute a higher yes?

So I believed—and yearned to prove.

I knew you did not merely decide to be a nun. God called you. These women who led me through Cicero and algebra, world history and French—whatever their foibles, they had been called. I longed to be so called and prayed daily, at Mass, that somehow, if God wanted me, He would let me know.

In the meantime I would try to remain open and ready for His call. I had every intention of going off to college. It was understood. Though neither of my parents had had that privilege, they were working hard to give it to their children. Twenty-one would be time enough to enter, should I be called. Certainly not fresh out of high school. Besides, my parents, good Catholics though they were, would never have stood for it. "Too young," they would have said. "Much too young." In my heart I agreed.

I therefore took care to hide my secret. Or so I thought.

On the first Monday of Advent our homeroom teacher, Mother St. David, a red-faced woman with white hair, a beautiful smile, sad blue eyes, and a vicious temper—told us who'd been chosen. I would be Blessed Marguerite.

It was like being singled out to play George Washington in a tableau of the Revolutionary War.

"Why you?" asked Patsy O'Malley in the lunchroom.

We all knew she was going to enter the minute she graduated. She was one of Father Carthy's girls.

"Oh, they've probably got her spotted," said Hattie O'Connor.

Though I knew it might be true, I hoped it wasn't.

"Aw, cut it out," said Helen Dougherty, my closest friend. "It's just that for once, this year, Claire's free of the piano. Anyone can accompany Christmas carols."

Helen knew more than she let on. We shared our dreams. Our parents were close friends. She herself wanted no part of a religious vocation and agreed with me that those who played at being nunny were dumb. Like all of us, though, she believed there was no higher calling for a woman. Less susceptible perhaps to the enticement of heights, she could peacefully settle for that second-best ambition: wife and mother. In any case, she recognized the danger in my selection as Blessed Marguerite and jumped in to protect me. She had been chosen as one of the band of my followers.

It would all have been so much simpler had I been at the piano.

"Did you hear that Mother Magdalena is really bad?" asked Patsy.

My tuna sandwich turned suddenly bitter. No one had talked much about Mother Magdalena since her disappearance. Every morning, first thing, I'd do a quick check on her studio. No sign. It wasn't quite like having one of the nuns upstairs disappear. Mother Magdalena dealt only with her music students, and if you didn't go down to her floor for lessons or Choral Club you might never, in four years, have anything to do with her. The other nuns floated around the halls above, and even if you didn't have them for class, you still knew plenty about them. Mother Beatrice was pretty, young, and understanding; Mother Andrew was picky; Mother Gerard was known to hurl an ink bottle in a fit of temper; Mother Edward had a fabulous sense of humor; Mother Eleanor patrolled the halls to hand out detention slips; Mother St. David played favorites.

Mother Magdalena had only one reputation: strict. She got results.

I wanted her back.

That very afternoon, when I got home from school, a white envelope awaited me in the mail. It contained my invitation to the Revellers, a by-invitation-only Christmas dance held annually at the country club outside town.

I had no hope of going.

I went to a plain Catholic girls' high school. Many of my friends' fathers worked in one of the several town factories. My brother, on the other hand, in his fancy prep school, hobnobbed with sons of men who owned or managed the factories. Only preppies were invited to these subscription dances sponsored by the Four Hundred, as my parents called them.

Once your name was on the list, however, it stayed. Although we'd attended our parish grammar school, our names had been on the list for years—ever since we'd been sent to Miss Graves's dancing school where we learned to waltz and fox-trot, instead of Miss Eppel's, where children of less enlightened parents were taught to tap. Throughout the war years Miss Graves's Friday night dancing lessons offered parents the reassurance that at least some children were still being taught the proper thing to do. Children of the Four Hundred went to Miss Graves's.

For two years I'd thrown my Revellers invitation away—not without a pang. The idea of a formal at the country club—long dress, corsage, live orchestra, to say nothing of a male behind the wheel—was infinitely more appealing than the monthly Catholic Youth dances in the high school auditorium where boys in leather jackets asked you to jitterbug while nuns and priests patrolled the sidelines to keep things "under control." I'd gone to one. That was enough. A boy had tried to feel me up in the locker-room. I was mortified when, in confession the following Saturday, Father Donlon looked straight at me through the grate and said, "He *what?*"

.   .   .

When my mother had found the Revellers invitation in the wastebasket the previous year, she'd said, intending comfort, "Don't worry, Claire. Your time will come." She was always a believer in my great potential. I was sixteen. From her point of view there was still lots of time for boys.

Still, I knew she would have liked me to go to the dance. She herself loved a good party and had a taste for clothes and nice things, but at this stage she could hardly arrange for my social advancement. I was in the wrong school.

The worlds of Revellers and Holy Angels were mutually exclusive. How well I knew that! I felt it every time I walked through our living room where my brother and his school friends sat discussing girls and God-knows-what. They didn't even see me. Catholic high school girls wore blue serge uniforms and stockings and carried armloads of books home on the bus. We looked dull and dutiful, though (as my mother pointed out) some could look "cheap" or "wild." Prep school girls, on the other hand, had shiny hair, good legs, wore real pearls, and often drove their own cars. They worshiped in stone churches, had prosperous fathers unthwarted by Masons, and vacationed in Bermuda. Their mothers were active in the Junior League, and their pictures appeared on the first society page, not the second. Above all, they were untroubled by the idea of Christian perfection. Or if troubled, they kept it well hidden.

So there was my invitation to Revellers. As I skimmed it hopelessly, I noticed it would be the same date as our school pageant. I said nothing, put the invitation under my desk blotter, and started my Latin homework.

That evening the telephone rang for me. Instead of the usual "What's our algebra?" or "Are we really having a quiz in Cicero tomorrow?" it was David, the boy next door. He was two years older, home from college for vacation. Like his older brother and some others in the neighborhood also on the Four Hundred dance list, David had gone to public elementary school, then on to a prep school. He was now at Yale, a freshman.

"Are you booked for Revellers?" he asked.

"Not yet," I managed. *David*—who'd never so much as really looked at me! Our parents were close friends.

"Would you like to go?"

I didn't hesitate an instant. "Yes, I'd love to."

Wait till my brother heard this!

I mentioned to no one the Christmas pageant.

The evening of December twentieth was dry and cold. When you breathed or talked, white puffs formed in front of your face. My mother lent me her fur jacket, and David kept the heat on in his father's Buick.

I had not been to the country club before, although my parents had. It was outside of town, where the wealthy people lived, in Middlebury. For this event it had been handsomely decorated. Wreaths and trees and lights and glitter shone everywhere. In the room with the dance floor, red and green and silver chandeliers cast Yuletide glow upon freshly set hairdos and naked shoulders. Small tables with holly centerpieces had been placed at the edge of the dance floor. The band, twelve mellow men in white dinner jackets, were relaxed and smooth as they played, evidently enjoying this vision of well-dressed teenagers trained in the dance.

At our table sat two other couples. Both girls had been in Miss Graves's eighth-grade dancing class with me. Their dates were seniors at Taft and Choate, competing prep schools in the area.

Ann Wildon, who wore an off-the-shoulder taffeta dress of black and white, looked at me curiously when we arrived. "I remember you. . . . Weren't you—"

"Yes," I said, "in Miss Graves's." I tried to seat myself gracefully without crushing the wristlet David had sent.

"Where are you now?"

I'd dreaded this. What could they know of where I was? They inhabited a totally secular world.

"Holy Angels," I murmured, embarrassed.

"Holy Angels?"

"It's the other side of Waterbury," I said.

"You know," said her date—whom I also remembered from Miss Graves's as a tall boy who did a mean polka and had halitosis. He clearly didn't remember me. "Out near Scovill's."

"Oh."

The other girl, Barbara Newsome, looked at me, smiled vaguely, and turned back to her senior from Choate.

David, it turned out, loved to dance. Too short to be glamorous, he knew, nonetheless, how to move his body. That suited me fine, for within five seconds at that table I knew I had nothing to say to the other couples. They talked about tailgating parties at the Yale-Harvard game that fall, about colleges they hoped to attend, about parties in and around Waterbury I'd never heard of. I had no part in their world. It was the same feeling I'd had walking through my own living room when my brother and his friends were plotting their next excursion to some girl's house. I was invisible. Even here, even in the green velvet dress Mother and I had shopped two days to find, and despite the white carnation, sweet pea, and baby's breath wristlet David had had delivered to me that afternoon.

We had been well taught. David and I did the hesitation waltz, fox-trot, rumba, polka, and tango—whirling about until we grew breathless and silly. He ended every waltz with an exaggerated dip. Then we'd collapse at our table and stir our Cokes, nibbling away at pretzels and other goodies liberally distributed on each table.

"What're you taking in school?" he asked—trying, I felt, to be courteous. But surely bored.

I recited my list of courses.

"Latin, God, how I hated it," he said.

I thought of Mother Ernestine, her grumpy face, her daily Latin quizzes in which I'd learned how to cheat occasionally by writing words I couldn't remember on the palm of my hand in washable ink.

"Any music?" he asked.

David had auditioned for the Yale Glee Club and actually made it. He was a baritone. He also knew I played the piano. Our parents loved to brag.

I told him about Mother Magdalena, everything I could, the songs we'd been learning, what we'd hoped to do for spring concert—Palestrina, Gilbert and Sullivan, Vaughan Williams—everything. He listened, commenting and sipping. It was somehow a relief, there in the glamorous glow of the country club Christmas dance, to be able to talk about my school. Without apologizing or explaining. For even though David was at Yale and had himself gone to a prep school before that, he too had been raised in a Catholic family, was bred to the sense of living in two worlds. We had both knelt at the same altar rail, received the same Eucharist, licked the same weekly envelopes to help the parish liquidate its debt. We shared a faith—a deeper bonding than words or dance could express. We formed our own little pocket of conversation at the candlelit table. When I was eight or nine I'd chased foul balls for him and the neighborhood boys playing baseball in the horse lots. I'd never known he could be so polite.

Halfway through the evening, while the band was taking a break, a photographer from the newspaper approached our table and shot us with a flash. Then he went about the room snapping others.

We girls excused ourselves and headed for the ladies' room. Ann and I occupied the stalls, then stood at the sinks beneath glaring fluorescence, staring at our images. We moved into the plush adjoining room to repair, standing before oval gilt-edged mirrors above marble-topped tables.

Covertly I watched them. Though I regularly wore it outside of school hours, I still felt uneasy about makeup, doubted my ability to apply it to the best advantage. Many times I'd watched my mother, fascinated, as she sat at her vanity table and curled her eyelashes with a fancy metal gadget that turned them up just so.

Mouths seemed to be the thing this year.

"Think we'll make it for tomorrow's paper?" asked Ann, leaning into the mirror to re-outline her wide, full mouth.

"Mmmm," said Barbara, rubbing her lips together, then blotting them with a small Kleenex from the box on the table. "Could be. Hope so."

I was transfixed. It had never occurred to me. There, standing in the ladies' room at the country club, I thought of the event going on at that very moment at Holy Angels. The Christmas pageant.

I'd told no one but Helen. She was to play dumb. I would fake sick. I'd already decided that, for it was far too complicated to try to tell Mother St. David that I'd gone to Revellers. I could have pleaded that my parents wanted me to, but the truth was that my parents knew nothing about my prior obligation. I could have turned down David, of course, but that wasn't a live option. I might never be invited to Revellers again! So I'd decided simply not to appear at school that night, to relinquish my chance of putting on the habit, let someone else stand in my place. Maybe they'd ask Helen. In any case, since no memorizing of lines was involved, anyone could do it. So I thought.

But I knew—and the sense of it dogged me as we returned to the table, the lights went down, and the band returned to play—I knew that if by any chance the picture of our table appeared in the paper next day, by Monday I would be in trouble. And though with one part of my mind I realized this was nothing compared to terminal cancer or unjustifiable homicide, the other side knew well that once you were seen a certain way in a Catholic school, you were labeled. I strove to avoid labels. The nuns, most of them at any rate, did not excel in flexibility of viewpoint. I didn't want to spend my last year and a half at Holy Angels as One Who Didn't Keep Her Word.

The dance ended at one o'clock.

Our drive home through the starlit snowbound night was silent and comfortable. I liked David. I felt he'd had a good time. He'd wanted to dance and that I could do. Perhaps he understood that I felt misplaced. Perhaps he too had trouble integrating worlds. He'd been away at college for months himself.

We wound down the slope of Bunker Hill into Waterbury.

"Like to come to Yale sometime, Claire?" he asked, shifting into low.

"Sure," I said calmly. The tulips nodded toward us as we walked the quadrangles, hand in hand.

"You're a good dancer," he said.

The car glided up Willow Street, past St. Joseph's, my elementary school—so remote now, that brick box of childhood with its recess lines, catechism lessons, and birthday parties with Spin the Bottle. I was traveling with a Yale man.

David rounded the corner at the top of the hill and turned down our street. He pulled into his own driveway, which ran next to ours, switched off the motor, and moved over toward me.

I had necked before, but not like this—my first experience of real gentleness.

I'd tried all the usual things for a well-brought-up, reasonably attractive Catholic girl of that era. The threat of mortal sin kept us from going "too far" and desecrating our bodies, those temples of the Holy Ghost. We had been trained to respect our bodies. Trained as well to fear them. Eight years of daily memorized catechism lessons had imbued us with a sense of the pervasive darkness surrounding the Sixth Commandment, "Thou shalt not commit adultery." As spelled out for us, the implications of those five words reached powerfully into the depths of the psyche. That commandment, we learned, forbade all impurity and immodesty in words, looks, and actions, whether alone or with others. Among the chief dangers to the virtue of chastity were idleness, sinful curiosity, bad companions, drinking, immodest dress, and indecent books, plays, and motion pictures.

The world indeed was fraught with dangers. In fact, so far-reaching was the arm of that commandment that one would have had to be nerveless as well as senseless to escape violating it. A conviction of personal guilt was inevitable as one threaded the perils of adolescent turmoil. Being (like the nuns) only human ourselves, we tried what we could, sustaining the amount of guilt, I suppose, that each could carry. (Of course Catholicism was a forgiving religion. There was always the possibility of confession, though that could entail embarrassment, as I had found out.)

Thus, although we knew that the final intimacies of the flesh were a pleasure reserved for later, inside marriage (when dangers presumably turned safe), other lesser intimacies—kissing, touching—carried their own vibrant pleasure, that of playing on the edge of a taboo.

Until this night, however, the boys who'd taken me out had seemed awkward and clumsy when it came to that play, too young and small, somehow, for their father's big cars. David, kind, gentle, and knowing, was a far cry from the rough young man in the high school locker-room, an even farther cry from the callous friends of my brother. With David I felt safe and valued. For he too knew the limits. And in his arms, behind the steering wheel of his father's car, between our two houses, I felt a sharp urgent stirring within that I identified—contrary to my expectations—not with death, but with life.

Half an hour later I locked our front door, turned out the hall lights, went upstairs, and got ready for bed. To my surprise, my parents had left me a note and were already asleep.

Sunday morning, after Mass, my father stopped at the top of the hill to get the paper. This was a ritual. After breakfast we'd sit around the living room reading, fighting over who got the funnies first.

While Mom fried bacon and I did the eggs, he sat at the kitchen table skimming headlines.

"Well, Claire," he said suddenly. "Wait'll you see this. You made it!"

There it was—the only picture from Revellers on the first

society page. Our table! I actually looked happy, animated, grinning widely at David.

My mother hurried over to look, the long bacon fork still in her hand.

"Did you know it would be in?" she asked.

I didn't answer. I was too busy imagining Mother St. David, her sad blue eyes reading this. The town had only one paper and everyone, even nuns, read it on Sunday. I could see their peaked black heads bending over the picture. "Isn't that Claire Delaney?"

Monday it snowed. By the time I reached school the flakes came thick and wet, making even that ugly factory town briefly beautiful. The inside hall of the school smelled of wet boots, and girls stood around, shaking snow from their hair and brushing it from one another's coats.

Upstairs, Mother St. David was waiting for me outside our classroom, a deep crease between her brows.

"Where were you Saturday night, Claire?" she asked.

I couldn't read the tone, just the face. When she was angry her color changed from red to scarlet. She was scarlet now. Had she seen the paper? I tried to find the answer in the light blue eyes. I could already feel the encroaching pain of being caught in an outright lie. For I would have lied, if it felt safe.

"I had to go to a dance, Mother."

"Did you know that ahead of time?"

"Yes." The back of my neck beneath my starched collar grew hot. As they passed us to enter the classroom, my friends eyed us curiously. No doubt they already knew. They would have seen the paper.

The bell would ring at any moment.

Mother St. David's eyes grew sadder. "Why didn't you let us know?"

Unanswerable. I didn't know myself, except that it had something to do with cowardice. I could have spoken up. Now I was stuck with the consequences. Still, my instinct said this was the easier way.

I stood there like an idiot, longing for the bell. Mother St. David waited, her eyes upon me. I knew she wanted me to wilt, offer an explanation I didn't have. Or apologize. I couldn't. I knew I hadn't seriously disrupted the pageant. All someone had to do was slip into the habit and stand there. It was the principle of the thing. She wanted me to admit I'd done wrong. Her face grew redder and redder.

Inside the room I could hear the girls opening desks, whispering, waiting for class to begin.

"I'm sorry," I murmured finally.

I wished her no personal harm. I was already at Yale, with David.

"And then," she said in a strangled tone as she turned to enter the classroom, "you had the nerve to allow a picture in the paper."

I followed her, feeling red in the face and silly. What could I have done? Run up to the photographer and pleaded, "Please, please, not ours, because then all the nuns will know"?

I could have been in the pageant.

At the end of the period, as we were filing out for Latin, Mother St. David called me off the line.

"You are not to go to Latin this morning, Claire," she said. "Mother Magdalena has asked to see you. She's in Room 332, the west wing of the hospital, and you have my permission to go. Be back by third period."

She turned and swung off down the hall.

As I walked through falling snow toward the hospital, I was almost trembling with anxiety. I hadn't seen Mother Magdalena in about a month. Toward the end of November, just a week before she'd disappeared, we'd had a wonderful long afternoon in the empty auditorium. We'd played the Pastorale arranged for two pianos. In the final movement we had to stop twice, back up, and start all over. Finally we got it right.

What would I see now?

"Yes, third floor," said the woman at the front desk. "Take the elevator down that hall." Pointing.

I pressed the button, waited, then got on and stepped toward the back. A red-haired nurse pushed in an old man in a wheelchair. A light blue blanket covered his lap and legs. His eyes were closed. His trembling head was bent forward, and thin shoulder blades pushed out beneath the back of his hospital gown. Three round sore-looking red patches marked his neck.

Every detail of his withering frame pressed into my consciousness as the elevator rose and I steadied myself for whatever I was about to see. Purple veins lined his hands, and the odor he carried seemed faintly antiseptic.

I sensed Mother Magdalena was dying.

But why had she asked to see me?

Still, I was glad. And flattered.

The elevator stopped at the third floor. I stepped out and approached the desk. The nurse sitting behind it looked up from a sheaf of papers. I felt misplaced in this house of pain. I should be in Cicero. I was in my uniform.

"You came to visit someone?" she asked.

"Mother Magdalena."

"Yes, of course. I had a call that you'd be here this morning. You're—"

"Claire Delaney."

"She asked for you, Claire."

To my surprise, the nurse came out from behind the desk. "She's down at the end of the hall, in 332, and . . ." She started to walk, motioning me to follow, past half-opened doors, carts with small glasses of juice and pills in plastic containers, past a doctor in green hurrying in the other direction, past all the misery I never imagined as I struggled to sight-translate for Mother Ernestine. "She's quite low," said the nurse, stopping before a closed door. "I wouldn't stay here too long."

I pushed the noiseless door and entered the room. The shades were drawn, and the small light on the bedside table shone on a glass of water. Bubbles had formed in the water.

The figure on the bed lay curled, fetus-like, her face toward me . . . a face I might not have known. Gone was the peaked headdress, the white bib, the whole black-and-white identity. Short, fine brown hair showed beneath her small white cotton cap. One arm lay on top of the sheet, a long, thin freckled arm, an arm I'd never seen bare.

But the face . . .

"Claire," it whispered, "I wanted to see you. . . ."

The face was lined and gray, a terrible gray, as though someone had drained it already of life. The glasses were off. I'd never seen her without glasses. The small eyes looked even smaller, and beneath them—pouches of sagging flesh. Something terrible had happened to the face, though it had never been beautiful. But now . . .

I stood by the bed in my blue serge. "How are you, Mother?"

It sounded asinine. But I'd never seen a nun reduced to this— mere pitiful dying humanity. I'd never seen a dying person, period. Seeing the masquerade almost over (for she was beyond the point where costume of any kind could help) made me feel false, somehow. As if death's stripping made my own forms of concealment all the more hideous. I felt embarrassed to be alive, well, standing there about to return to class in ten minutes, fresh from Revellers, dancing, necking, lying, and, above all—unable to say anything. For what was there to say? We'd never talked a lot.

She lifted a hand—dry skin, nails bluish—and pointed weakly to the bedside table.

Behind the water pitcher I saw a small black book. I lifted it and looked toward her. She blinked her eyes as if to say, "Yes."

I tried to give it to her.

"No," she said, her hand lying limp against the sheet. "I want you to have that."

A long pause followed. I didn't say anything, just looked at that face, saw now that cast over the gray was a faint yellow hue, saw that around the neck, just above the hospital gown, there were red dry sores . . . saw the bluish wrists of this emaciated remnant who just a month before had pushed the grand pianos with me and worked through the final movement of the Pastorale.

"It's for you," she whispered. "Look at it sometimes"—she shut her eyes—"and think of . . ." The voice trailed off.

I didn't know if it was time to go. I stood there. I looked at the small black prayerbook, tattered along the edges, the spine disintegrated almost to threads, the whole thing carefully held together with a rubber band. I could barely make out the worn gold words on the cover: *The Imitation of Christ* by Thomas à Kempis.

I knew the book.

From outside the door came muffled sounds of life—trays banging, glasses clinking, nurses talking. Now and then quick rubber footsteps on the hard floor. It had nothing to do with us. Should I just back out and return to class?

She opened her eyes. "Good," she whispered. She moistened her lips. "I wanted to ask you, Claire." Her voice came thread-like, barely audible.

I leaned forward to hear.

"How was the pageant?"

Did she know? *What* did she know? I saw Mother St. David's face of an hour before and tried to gauge. Surely they wouldn't bother a dying woman with news of her favorite pupil's defection? But what if they had? Was Mother Magdalena testing me?

No. I felt certain of that. It was too late to test anyone but herself. And she'd never been given to that kind of indirection.

I'd say as little as possible.

"It was wonderful," I lied. "Really beautiful."

"And the music?" she persisted.

Perhaps she wanted me to express how much she'd been missed. I didn't think so, though. Even at sixteen I could perceive there wasn't that kind of ego operating here. She really wanted

26

to know, disinterestedly, how it had gone. She wanted it to go well. She wanted voices blending, girls standing up straight, not twitching, cues accurate. She wanted it done *right*.

"The singing was good," I lied, "but we missed you."

She closed her eyes. "There will be someone else," she murmured.

That was the last thing I heard her say.

I stood there awhile, holding the book, feeling the raised leather beneath my fingers, watching her breathe. Was she breathing? At moments I thought she'd stopped. I didn't want to watch her die. I backed out of the room and pulled the door behind me.

When I passed the nurse's desk, she looked up. "How is she?"

"Not good," I managed, choking.

As I pushed the elevator button, I saw the nurse leave her desk and head down the hall.

Outside, I was caught in a wind so fierce it tore at my face and hair and burned my cheeks. Only a block to walk, back to class. I was glad to have it. I must ready myself for algebra, press down the bursting need to cry, to scream, to protest something I couldn't have named. I knew there would never be afternoons in the auditorium again.

She'd left me her book. She'd handed it to me over my lie.

I didn't worry about the fact of having lied. I worried only that someone would go tell her the truth and then the duplicity would become her burden as well as mine.

But, I thought, as I arrived at the tall, dark building, opened its doors, left behind wind and falling snow and stepped into the close-smelling, overheated downstairs hallway, that wasn't likely.

There wouldn't be time.

. . . if you have risen with Christ, seek the things that are above, where Christ is seated at the right hand of God. Mind the things that are above, not the things that are on earth. For you have died and your life is hidden with Christ in God.

Epistle of St. Paul to the Colossians 3:1–3

Taking
the Discipline

The August heat, the starched headdress, the smell of shrimp. "The religious should esteem, love, and practice penance according to their strength."

Sister Claire peeled off another shell and held the pale meat on her palm. Soft surface. Yet (she pressed it with her thumb) firm and resilient underneath, like wet rubber. Deceptive. She threw it into the pail. Her blue-and-white-checked apron was soaked with shrimp fluid, and a pile of shells lay on the brown paper beside her stool. Pale clean bodies were piling up for the benefactors.

Esteem. That was the rub.

The one huge elm above them cut the direct glare of the sun, but heat shimmered like meadow haze on a farm. No farmers these, however, but a circle of eight black-habited, white-veiled novices in a Vermont novitiate, hidden away from the world to learn the ways of God, shelling shrimp.

Sister Thomas rose.

"I'll carry these into the kitchen," she whispered, and left with the pail.

Sister Xavier went on reading from Holy Rule. "Although the continual labor of their vocation as teachers does not permit the Constitutions to impose great austerities on them, the religious should nevertheless esteem, love, and practice them according to their strength."

Words of sense. Balance. Appropriate for the mixed life, as it was called: contemplative-active. Already, after twelve months of daily meditations and instruction in the Ignatian method, Claire knew the elation and fatigue of mental prayer. Yet she had always been drawn to prayer and longed to grow in it. She respected the four-century-old tradition of contemplation that the Agnetines so prized. Until she went to college and met nuns who were monastic, she had never heard the Divine Office chanted. There she would kneel in the outer chapel and listen to the nuns chanting the Hours in that high, steady, sweet drone. She discovered that all over the world, at certain hours of day and night, these same songs of praise and need were being chanted by nuns and monks. How glorious a thing! It seemed to her to partake of eternity. And now she herself was learning Gregorian chant, relearning Latin, making her own the great prayer of God's people crying to Him from the desert of time. *"As the hind longs for the running waters, so my soul longs for You, O God."* Despite heat and fatigue, once she was in chapel and lifting her voice with those ancient words, she felt part of something large, significant, something that with or without her would go on and make an incalculable difference in the eternal scheme of things. *"I have waited, waited for the Lord, and He stooped toward me and heard my cry. He drew me out of the pit of destruction, out of the mud of the swamp; He set my feet upon a crag; He made firm my steps. And He put a new song into my mouth, a hymn to our God."*

As for teaching, that part of her vocation, the "continual labor" of it, lay years ahead. It *would* be tiring. She'd seen enough in sixteen years of Catholic education to know that. The college nuns, many of them dedicated scholars, highly intelligent women, must move through a day with rare spirit and efficiency to meet their obligations of study, teaching, prayer, and spiritual mothering. Theirs was not a soft life. But she did not want a soft life. Outstanding women, they had left their mark on her. In her four years with them she'd seen lives given to God, yet integrating the noblest things of this world in a commitment of enlightened worship and service: learning, art, friendship, dedication. They were the finest women she had known.

If you were a Trappist monk, you rose at night after long daytime hours in the field and, conquering pain, nausea, fatigue, chanted Matins and Lauds, your voices merging in one long vowel of pure praise ascending from the darkness of earth. If you were a Carmelite, you lived behind a grille, in silence, uniting your sacrifice with the redemptive sacrifice of the hidden Christ. If . . .

She stopped dreaming and tried to pay attention. Only half an hour to get all these critters done, a mound of them remaining by the large pail of shelled bodies. Each novice reached now and then to replenish her personal pile. Sister Xavier continued to read, seemingly unperturbed by a fly buzzing about her face.

Claire picked at a shell.

Esteem was a problem on one point—despite the satisfaction of at least being in a white veil, no longer a postulant asking to be admitted. And Reception just yesterday, her parents watching from the visitors' gallery, proud but anxious. Afterward her father, tall in his light summer suit, good-natured but strangely shy. "Well, Claire, you always were an idealist. But we're proud of you." He hugged her gingerly, wary of her starch. If he was sorry to lose her, surely he still believed in a vocation. "We're glad you decided to keep the name we gave you," he added. Her mother—resplendent in yellow linen and green shoes, was obviously pleased with her daughter's brief appearance in Harriet Murphy's daughter's wedding gown. They'd borrowed it and sent it to the novitiate weeks before, after Claire wrote: "The Order will supply me with a gown if you can't borrow one." Her mother would want her to look good. Claire did not mention how uncomfortable this part of the ritual made her feel. It was all so literal. To be wholly given to God must one don a wedding gown, then discard it? The phrase "Spouse of Christ" had never touched her deeply. On the other hand, with its prayers and chants, the meaning of the ritual for the consecration of a virgin was truly beautiful and spoke to her deepest desires: *"One thing I have asked of the Lord, this will I seek: that I may dwell in the house of the Lord all the days of my life."*

The early part of the ceremony was over quickly, and then she left chapel in the wedding gown. With the help of a beaming Sister Thomas, she changed into the habit and returned to chapel for Mass. With it came a warm sense of rightness, of peace. At last the feel of the sharp-edged guimpe beneath her chin, the plastic headband against her forehead, at last the ratty postulant's veil gone forever, alleluia! How many years had she prayed for this, that God would find her worthy to serve Him. Now it was beginning. At last her very appearance would signal to the world and to herself the meaning of her life: total dedication to God. A full-fledged novice, she was embarking on two privileged years of learning how to live the vows, how to be a saint. The horizon before her opened to infinity. But there was a scary side, too. Some did not make it. Before final vows, four years from now, the order might decide she did not have a true vocation. She must get through the novitiate, then two more years of formation at a house of studies in Washington. Discernment of spirit was the delicate task of her superiors during those years. For now she must trust, work, and above all . . . pray.

Right now: shrimp.

Sister Thomas was back with the emptied pail. She set it in the center of the circle and returned to her camp stool.

34

Claire pulled gingerly at a sharp shell. Juice ran from her fingers to the plastic plate on her lap. The sole of her foot itched. A small fly landed on the naked shrimp, threadlike legs grazing the pale surface.

"Lest corporal penances, whether fasts, vigils, or other mortifications, should be carried too far and a greater good thereby hindered, no one will practice them without the approbation of the Superior or Confessor. For public penance the Superior's permission is required."

She looked at the black book from which Sister Xavier was reading. Only yesterday it had been put into the hands of the seven new novices to meditate on, memorize, live. That had been thrilling, perhaps more thrilling than receiving the white veil. Initiates now, they could make their own the book containing God's explicit will. Soon, perhaps tomorrow, Our Mother (as they were to call Mother Theodore, their superior during the novitiate) would begin giving them conferences on it. Odd to think of living a book. To become, as she put it, the embodiment of the rule: that was religious perfection.

Sister Thomas dried her fingers on her apron and reached up beneath her guimpe. She pulled out a round pocket watch at the end of a silver chain.

"Five more minutes," she mouthed at them, as Sister Xavier went on reading.

Sister Thomas was in charge of them for the morning. The rest of the senior novices, those in their second year as novices, were in the kitchen and guest dining room preparing for the lunch: salad, shrimp, cake, who knew what else? Once a year it happened. Three decrepit spinsters, all sisters, and their one still vigorous brother drove up to the novitiate from Riverdale and were served a delicious lunch by the novices. During the afternoon these faithful benefactors chatted with Our Mother. In preparation, a box of sterling silver and two boxes of carefully wrapped china were hauled out from under the eaves in the guest bathroom. The table was set in Father's dining room, the small private room between the novices' refectory and the foyer, and Our Mother ordered a special arrangement of flowers for a centerpiece.

Sister Xavier was reading the fast days of rule now.

Claire studied a particularly large shrimp. The final one. Pale and meaty, faint pink ribbed its hills. She threw it into the pail.

" 'They will not forget that prayer is good with fasting and alms more than to lay up treasures of gold,' " read Sister Xavier.

Penance was a mystery. She grasped the principle. She'd lived through years of Lent and Advent, knew the point of "offering it up." They were one in Christ. They were to unite their sufferings, sought and unsought, with His. Our Mother had given them conferences on all the virtues and, most recently, just before retreat, on penance. "It is a mystery, Sisters, how our tiny sufferings, like a pebble cast into a pool, can gather to themselves such meaning, and be joined to the infinite sufferings of Christ. We believe this . . . that as He suffered for us, so we suffer for and with and in Him . . . and that suffering touches the world, heals it."

Claire had sat in the novitiate library that morning and thrilled to her novice mistress's words. They fed her deepest hope, a hope she'd tried once or twice to explain to her parents in the last months before entering: that one's acts, however small, could expand to infinite dimensions. That through living in union with Christ, totally given, one could transcend the limits of this insatiable body, these mortal days. Though they took her decision valiantly, she sensed their disappointment. They had expected her to seek excellence in some more predictable, conventional way. She had been an excellent student, a fine musician. They had sent her off to a good college. But had they not observed, even fostered, her piety all those years, accompanying her to daily Mass every Lent? Encouraging her to respect and honor the sisters? How, then, could they judge such a noble vocation a waste? (Not that they ever said as much.) That one could so expand the possibilities of life, even into eternity, gave mortal life a meaning rich and deep. Her mind was made up.

But when, just four days ago, during retreat days on the Passion, she had to step across the prostrate body of one of her sisters—she nearly vomited. And watching someone kneel for breakfast destroyed her appetite.

How did such acts connect with anything? She understood the meaning of Christ's washing his apostles' feet at the Last Supper. Service. Humility. The last shall be first. *But lying down across a doorway and making your sisters step over you on their way to a meal!* From what could that take meaning? Were these exercises peculiar to the novitiate? A test of resolve? She could not imagine the nuns whom she'd most admired at college submitting to such a thing. . . . At the sight of that black body stretched on the floor two inches from her shoes, she stopped, grew weak, longed for escape. But there was only one entrance to the refectory, and behind her five other postulants waited in line. Sickened, she lifted her foot high and stepped over, then took her place for grace. She could tell by the flush on Sheila's face (Sister Hilary, since yesterday's ceremony) as she stood holding her grace book that she too was disturbed. They'd been together since college, had entered together. Why had they never been prepared for this? What other "voluntary penances" lay ahead? Did some of the finally professed actually wear hair shirts? This was 1955.

She couldn't swallow it. Esteem was impossible.

She knew better than to ask.

Besides, they were deep in retreat, preparing for Reception.

Now, this very morning, at her place in the refectory she'd found a note: *Happy first day as novice! Could you meet me in the laundry today fifteen minutes before noon examen? Important. Your angel.*

Angel. Absurd word. Only now, after twelve months, could Claire say it unself-consciously. What did Sister Thomas want? Surely it would have to do with penances. Claire felt it in her bones. Besides, she had clues. Quite accidentally, just three weeks earlier, she'd stumbled on disturbing evidence that she had not yet discovered everything about religious life.

It was Friday of her first week as bell ringer. At exactly 9:30 P.M. she was to ring the retiring bell by hand in the front foyer by the big grandfather clock thirty-three times in memory of Christ's life and death. Inaccuracy would mean being bell ringer for another week.

She tiptoed down the back stairs. At the bottom, in the hallway outside the guest bathroom, stood three novices in black bathrobes and white night veils, eyes down. What were they doing there? They carried no water basins to dump. Besides, no one except the bell ringer went downstairs at night. The cells were all on the second floor, the sink room as well.

As Claire passed them, Sister Angelica emerged from the guest bathroom and bowed silently to the next in line, who then went into the bathroom. Sister Angelica carried no pitcher or basin. She went back upstairs.

Disturbed, Claire checked the first-floor doors and windows and rang the bell, counting carefully. When she returned, no one was standing outside the bathroom.

That night she lay in her cell unable to sleep. What could have been going on? She'd been here more than eleven months and suspected nothing. What should she have suspected? She knew Our Mother's policy was to introduce postulants to the life gradually. Often the order of logic was reversed: you did something, then learned its rationale. You kept silence, then understood its value; meditated twice daily, then felt its effect on your inner life. Through these months of learning, she'd never felt deceived. Occasionally she'd been puzzled or amused. Through it all, though, ran a thread of belief she could sustain. This was another world. "My ways are not your ways," said the Lord. She'd felt open, ready for the challenge. And now she'd discovered that right downstairs in the guest bathroom something went on every night—no, for she'd rung the bell other nights and met them only on Friday—well, on Fridays, then. What could it be? Why were the postulants not told? It was like discovering a secret room in a house you thought you'd thoroughly explored. Only worse.

Then came the prostrate bodies . . . and novices kneeling for breakfast. With no warning! Father Abraham preached on penance and humility, and she meditated on the Passion of Christ: the scourging, the wounds, the thirst, the humiliation, the sense of abandonment. Still she felt sick. She did not want to step over the body of her sister! Was she coming face-to-face with the stumbling block of her own pride? Was it pride that resisted custom, that drew back before the abasement of others? Was she exalting her own judgment, blocking her own chance to understand?

Sister Xavier had finished the reading. "In the name of the Father, and of the Son, and of the Holy Ghost . . ." She was closing Holy Rule.

The novices stood, a circle of aprons being shaken into the grass, bits of shell falling.

Sister Thomas nodded to Sister David. "Would you take the pail into the kitchen, Sister?" Then she eyed Claire and headed for the laundry.

Claire shook her apron, untied it, and rolled it into a damp ball. It would have to go into the laundry tomorrow. Fortunately, she had another for the afternoon starching session. She turned to follow Sister Thomas and, as she passed Sister Hilary, thought she heard a whisper: "Good luck." Maybe *her* angel was meeting *her* somewhere with an important message.

Sister Thomas was a few yards ahead, almost to the laundry door.

Suddenly, as if from nowhere, a large, striking bird emerged from behind the trash cans and strutted across the back stoop outside the laundry. *What was it?*

Sister Thomas seemed not to notice. She went inside.

Claire stopped.

It was a pheasant, its rich, subtly colored feathers of white and tan shading into orange and green, its long pointed tail sweeping the cement in front of her. It walked like a king, white-ringed neck forward, black-and-red head erect, as if it owned the place. She watched it march to the edge of the woods, then disappear into the shadows. Perspiration was running down the back of her neck.

She stepped inside the laundry. Sister Thomas stood by the two deep tubs. The laundry was deserted, mangle closed, washers whirling. Sister William had put in the morning loads. That afternoon, while benefactors ate shrimp and chatted with Our Mother, the novices would scrub the zinc boards now leaning against the laundry walls and lay them across sawhorses, in the sun. Then would begin the starching ritual: hours of squeezing thick hot starch through white linens and spreading them on the boards to dry.

Sister Thomas faced her.

"Well, Sister, now that you're a novice"—she beamed—"Reverend Mother has asked me to introduce you to the discipline."

Claire looked into the round blue eyes with their yellow centers, the blustery genial face that seemed always to appear when questions arose. Sister Thomas tried, genuinely, to anticipate questions. She explained about weekly baths, the daily order, common good, and all the other intricate rituals that a girl from the world must be introduced to in the first months of novitiate.

Sister Thomas lacked humor.

She held a small metal contraption made of finely linked chain. During the week before retreat, Claire had noticed Sister Elizabeth, official rosary fixer, working on these strange items at evening recreation as they sat in a circle and darned stockings and underwear. Quick and deft, she twisted the small pieces of wire with her pliers, forming something Claire had never seen. The whole affair was about eight inches long. From one end hung small chains of even length, each about four inches. These were attached to a horizontal wire bent into the shape of a miniature clothes hanger to which was attached a smaller oval of wire.

She longed to know what Sister Elizabeth was making. It wouldn't do to ask, especially at general recreation. The unspoken rule of the novitiate was *what and when you need to know, you will be told.*

Now Sister Thomas was holding that very contraption, offering it to Claire, calling it a discipline.

"This is yours to keep." She smiled. "On Fridays we take the discipline in memory of Christ's Passion."

She placed the discipline in Sister Claire's hand. It felt surprisingly light.

"Here, I'll show you."

Oddly, Claire remembered the night her mother told her how to use sanitary napkins. It had been an uncomfortable encounter, for Vivien Delaney was shy about such things. Though she evidently enjoyed many pleasures of the body—good food, comfortable furniture, dancing, stylish clothes—she had never talked to her daughter about the basic facts of life, let alone menstruation. Perhaps she thought the priests in their annual retreats—which always featured one conference on the implications of the Sixth Commandment—covered all the basic information. Then, too, she knew the nuns talked to the girls about respect for the body. In any case, by some genteel osmosis, Claire was evidently to absorb vital information from the atmosphere. She had absorbed it, of course, from her variously informed friends and in particular from Helen, her closest friend, who got her period in the sixth grade. When the crucial event came for Claire, there was a party going on downstairs that night. She could hear her father's laughter, the rattle of ice cubes, someone playing the piano. Finally, able to postpone it no longer, she had called her mother upstairs, away from the party, to ask her help. She had felt embarrassed, stupid even, yet honor bound to act enlightened as Vivien Delaney offered a sketchy explanation, showed her where things were kept, and hurried back to the party. She seemed as flustered as Claire.

But Sister Thomas didn't appear embarrassed. She took the discipline by the oval-shaped end, which Claire now saw to be a small handle.

"Like this." She removed the undersleeve from her left arm and set it on the edge of the mangle. She folded back the wide outer sleeve to reveal a pale forearm sprinkled with light freckles. Then she swung the chain back and forth, striking her bared arm. Small red marks appeared among the freckles. "The object is not to draw blood. It is just to thwack yourself until it stings. A small penance." She handed Claire the discipline and replaced her sleeve.

"Where do you do this?" Claire felt mortified. She'd never heard anyone making such a noise. Surely in their curtained cells she would have overheard a swish and a thwack.

"We take the discipline kneeling, downstairs in the guest bathroom. Just go down there tonight when you're ready for bed and wait in line. Do you know the Miserere by heart?"

"I'm not sure." Though they said it every day going to the refectory, it would be her luck to forget it that night.

"Pick up one of the grace books from the refectory and take it with you."

"Where do you . . . hit?" Idiotic, but she had to know.

"You lift your nightgown and swing the discipline from side to side, like this." Without touching her habit, Sister Thomas swung the small chains from side to side, through the air. "You hit your bottom where it will sting but can't really hurt you."

She handed the discipline back to Sister Claire.

"I've got to go serve guests," she said. "They're to arrive by noon."

Without another word she left the laundry.

There were days that summer when Claire could hold herself in a kind of golden bubble. It started with morning meditation, then Mass. If you made a good meditation, the images might stay with you through the long day of gardening, cleaning, waiting on table, recreation, choir, even to afternoon meditation. The house was silent, chapel was silent, the grounds were silent. You talked only when necessary and grew careful of supposing something necessary. Days of silence helped create the bubble. It expanded when you expanded, contracted when you contracted, a kind of elastic enclosure through which you could see, into which others could see, an enclosure both personal and transparent. Call it the presence of God.

That day the bubble was harder to sustain.

After Vespers she was assigned to cleanup crew while the benefactors had dessert and coffee. She washed. Sister Henry dried. Sister Matthew put away. They worked efficiently, scraping, stacking, washing, drying, with barely a word. She'd never seen these dishes, the special Spode brought out only once a year. And the crystal goblets. The novices washed and dried each piece separately, with care. She liked the austerity of their refectory—bare plank tables, backless stools, knife, fork, spoon at each place. It hadn't taken long to wipe out the memory of other dining room scenes—family meals shared in their large, airy New England dining room, dinner prepared by Callista, who came in by the day. How her mother had loved Irish linen, china, engraved silver. Leaving all that behind was no penance. It was relief, a cleansing that freed one for other concerns. "For where thy treasure is, there also will thy heart be."

Sister Claire washed carefully, scouring bits of shrimp.

The discipline burned in her pocket, a secret. Had the others received theirs? Would they also line up tonight outside the downstairs bathroom? Would Sister Hilary be there? Right now she was outside on the first laundry shift, making starch.

They slid each piece of gleaming silver into its felt sheath and repacked the china. With Sister Matthew, Claire pushed the cartons way back in the closet under the eaves in the guest bathroom. She tried not to think of what would take place later, in this very room. Would she meet Sister Matthew here? They closed the small closet door and locked it. Claire took the key upstairs and dropped it in the box outside Our Mother's door.

Then came the afternoon of starching. Outside the laundry four freshly scrubbed zinc boards shone. Sister Hilary had placed a pile of laundered templets and bands on a stool near each board. Silently the novices divided up. Claire worked at one board with

Sister Eleanor, the novitiate expert at perfectly starched templets. She had a hawk's eye for air bubbles. They squeezed thick hot starch through the linens. Then Claire spread each piece on the zinc, pressing out wrinkles, while Sister Eleanor squatted at eye level with the board to detect imperfections. As they worked, Claire thought she once heard a man's deep laugh from somewhere in front of the novitiate. Perhaps Our Mother was walking the benefactors down to visit Our Lady's garden.

Starching done, the novices moved through meditation, Matins, Lauds, supper, recreation. No one mentioned the discipline.

At recreation Reverend Mother was full of anecdotes about the benefactors: how much they'd enjoyed the shrimp, how Mr. Driscoll loved to see Our Lady's garden, how Minnie Driscoll wanted the recipe for dessert, how the novitiate would have a week of Masses offered for these faithful friends. As they walked toward the orchard and back, the evening air hung heavy and no breeze stirred. An orange halo rimmed the burning circle of sun. Tomorrow would again be hot.

Through it all, the discipline remained a hidden weight in Claire's pocket, a troubling talisman—of what she did not know. Perhaps she alone was being initiated that night. Sister Hilary had given no indication. Perhaps only one new novice would be introduced to the discipline each successive Friday night.

During night prayer she held the strange metal contraption tightly, wondering how she'd manage. The prospect filled her with anxiety.

"Virgin most clement . . . pray for us."

At last night prayer was over. They left chapel and went to their cells.

Something settled over the house after night prayer, part relief after a tiring day, part anticipation of rest and sleep, the delight of at last lying down. If the golden bubble had been ruptured during the day, you might reenter it during Great Silence.

When Claire reached her cell, she put the discipline on the

white washstand and began to undress. She washed quickly. She hoped she'd meet no one tonight in the guest bathroom.

At the sink room Sister Maureen was ahead of her in line. Claire dumped her water, watched it gurgle down the copper-stained sink, then half filled the porcelain pitcher for morning. She left this in her cell and slipped out of the dormitory.

On the back stairs she met no one. At the bottom she turned left and slipped through the pantry where that very afternoon she'd been washing Spode. Evening light through the window side of the refectory made the pine tables glow. She picked up a grace book, nodded toward the alabaster crucifix behind the head table, and headed for the guest bathroom. Still no one around. She was early. It was barely nine o'clock.

The bathroom door was shut. Perhaps someone was in there. She stood a moment in the hall, then put her ear to the door. Nothing.

She knocked lightly. No answer.

She turned the knob and went in.

The bathroom was large, dark, and old-fashioned. Since that afternoon someone had drawn the yellow window shade all the way down. Sister Katherine, perhaps.

She shut the door behind her.

She felt awkward and stupid. Strange that a lofty exercise for a religious end, one required by rule, could make her feel so asinine. How was she to navigate through the whole thing? It would require at least three hands.

Opposite the dark wooden toilet seat was a sink. Beside that, near the window, stood one straight wooden chair. Perhaps she could use that.

Mindful of Great Silence, she lifted the chair and carried it to the center of the room. She knelt on the linoleum, opened the grace book to the Miserere, and laid it flat on the chair. Too dark to read. She got up and turned on the light, then knelt again.

She lifted her nightgown and bathrobe from under her knees. How would this work? It wouldn't. How could she swing the discipline in front of her with the chair there? But the chair was needed because her two hands would be occupied—one to swing the discipline, one to hold up her clothes. It would be better in the future when she'd memorized the Miserere. She could see that.

She felt ridiculous, uncomfortable with the whole thing, as if it were somehow false, some strange make-believe.

It was foolishness. But, she reminded herself, the value of foolishness was not to be discounted. St. Paul said, "We are fools for Christ's sake." To be a fool had its point. Still, it was hard to be a fool in private, in such a setting, in twilight, in an old-fashioned bathroom in Vermont, kneeling to share in Christ's Passion by striking oneself with small metal chains.

"We are fools for Christ's sake." Surely there were fools and fools, distinctions to be made.

She brushed aside the thought and concentrated. Somehow she had to make it work. Other novitiate exercises that had initially seemed strange had come to seem almost normal. Or at least defensible for the sake of a higher goal. Wasn't that the function of the novitiate? How could she judge until she tried it? Sometimes you saw the point of things, or felt the point, if you went ahead and *did* them. So she would do it, and ignore the feeling of absurdity.

But oh—the body, the body. It *was* a problem. It was to be tamed. She grasped that and understood. You kept silence during the day in order to develop a capacity for recollection, attentiveness to the Spirit's quiet whisper within, to the movement of grace in the soul. You avoided looking about curiously for the same reason. You avoided all physical contact with your sisters. She thought that stricture extreme, but trusted she would eventually understand its point. You had one bath a week—but that was simply because the water pressure was so low, the pipes so old. This became a chance to practice poverty. Still . . . the body. You had to tame it, ignore it, mortify it. There was always the struggle. But how, how, did this exercise with a miniature instrument of pseudo-torture really tame anything?

Only later did she realize that in those few moments all loftiness of thought or intention deserted her in the simple act of figuring out how to place herself and how to maneuver the discipline.

She moved the chair to the left. No. That wouldn't do. The chains would strike the chair, not her. She moved the chair back in front but pushed it farther away. Tentatively she swung the discipline and struck her bare behind on the left. Yes. It worked. If she knelt just so—bending forward so she could see the words of the psalm—and swung just so, it would work. She felt the sting. She could see the words.

"Miserere mei, Deus . . ."

She swung. She tried to pray.

"Tibi soli peccavi et, quod malum est coram te, feci . . ."

She continued to swing. Her bathrobe slipped. She stopped, started again. Swung. She forgot her place. Her flesh began to sting. The light thwacking chains did hurt. How much pressure was she to apply? How much was it to hurt? She'd been told not to break the skin, but toughness of skin varies.

"Cor mundum crea mihi, Deus, et spiritum firmum renova in me."

She stopped. She closed her eyes and tried to imagine something lofty, significant, some scene or image that would redeem her feeling of absurdity. Nothing came.

She opened her eyes and stared at the words of the psalm, concentrating, as she swung.

"Domine, labia mea aperies, et os meum annuntiabit laudem tuam . . ."

She was more than halfway through the psalm. She tried not to rush, not to favor herself. Slowly, methodically, she swung the discipline, hitting her bare flesh, pushing against the feeling that this made no sense at all, that she was caught in some miserable charade. Was God Himself laughing?

She stopped.

She did not stop for pain. She did not stop for any clear reason. She could not have told anyone just why—not Sister Hilary or Sister Thomas or even Our Mother.

She knelt there remembering the words of Jesus about going into a closet to pray. She looked at the dark walls, dark woodwork, the streaked yellow shade, the mirror above the sink, the scarred wooden chair. This wasn't exactly a closet, but close.

She prayed.

For forgiveness, if that was needed. For strength. For understanding. For light.

She prayed without words, without thoughts, turning her innermost self toward the God she longed to honor. "A clean heart create for me, O God, and a steadfast spirit renew within me. . . ."

A clean heart. That was the problem.

She couldn't do this yet. Not with a clean heart. Not with a steadfast spirit. Perhaps never. . . .

She stood up, lowered her nightgown and bathrobe, pocketed the discipline, and replaced the chair, careful to make no noise. Outside, the house was still.

She left the light on.

The small, low closet hiding sterling silver and Spode was closed and locked, the shade remained lowered, the cover to the toilet seat was down. Everything was in its place. She took one last glance about the room.

Then she opened the door and went out swiftly.

In the hallway stood Sister Hilary, eyes down, waiting to go in.

Obedience

On a hazy August day when clothing stuck to the body and parched imaginations lusted for ocean surf, Reverend Mother Theodore dropped her passing remark. This was in a time when any remark from such an august source wielded enormous power: it came certified as God's will.

They were walking at noon recreation, a group of fifteen novices sweltering in old-fashioned habits, starched head vises, and heavy veils, luxuriating in a half hour of relief from the labor of housecleaning, gardening, learning Latin, and praying. "Follow Me," said the Lord, and Simon and Andrew left their fishing nets to become fishers of men. These novices, on the other hand, having left all behind, now faced long hours of weeding carrots and string beans beneath scorching sun, polishing floors already slick with wax, praying daily for perseverance in the purgative way, and, for one hour each day, participating in organized inane nonconversation. Nonetheless, the minutes allotted for talk—general inoffensive talk—brought physical relief for bodies aching from more manual labor than most of them had sustained in a lifetime. Recreational words were to refer only to the world in which they now walked, or to that other toward which they were traveling together. The in-between world, the one they'd left with varying degrees of pain and relief only months before, had ceased to exist. For now at least.

It *was* a challenge, leaving the world, but, once left, the pain of its loss dwindled to mere shadow for novices caught up in the exhilaration of beginning. They had put their hands to the plow. Unless a man be born again he cannot enter the kingdom of heaven. A strenuous labor, this passage into religious life. And complex. But there were markers, guides: feast days, vows, the rule, customs, daily order, superiors. And always—the grace of God.

Eventually they would discover how many worlds there are to leave. Too many to number. The journey to leave, to begin, would grow endless, like rings on a tree, waves in the sea.

But for now their task was outwardly simple. They had entered into and were living the mystery of Christ's hidden life. Later would come the trials and temptations of the public life. For these three years their challenge was to find God in the mundane tasks of a day, accomplishing as perfectly as possible each chore. Though she hated housecleaning and liked gardening less, Sister Claire set about her daily tasks with all the fervor she could muster. She had expected more studying in the novitiate, more direct preparation for what would come later. But she knew she was laying the groundwork for her whole religious life here. As Christ had spent thirty years out of sight in Nazareth before he began to go about teaching and preaching, surely she could give herself to humble hidden tasks with an unstinting heart. And in the space of a grueling day there came those oases of special meaning: Divine Office, spiritual reading, meditation on the life of Christ, and Our Mother's conferences. Especially Our Mother's conferences.

Reverend Mother Theodore, a holy woman of few words and palpable prayerfulness, set her novices a powerful example of a life hidden away in God. Gifted with a lucid mind, she composed her conferences on the spiritual life with care, writing her notes on the backs of used envelopes, which she discarded after each conference. An example of poverty. In her one could feel an integration of mind and soul and life all given over to serving God selflessly. For surely, being hidden here, in backwoods Vermont, away from community life, assigned to train eager but ignorant young women in the spiritual life—surely this was not an easy lot. She must be lonely, thought Sister Claire.

"No one, having put his hand to the plow, and looking back, is fit for the kingdom of God." Our Mother gave them a particularly moving conference on that text. Long ago, when she had absorbed those challenging words, they had rung for Claire Delaney with the seductive power of the absolute. She was prepared to welcome them. For years she surveyed the niceties of china, silver, and needlepoint. She watched devoted parents suck whiskied maraschinos as they compared stock options. She took her courses, worked her summer jobs, stymied the over-zealous advances of promising young men, all the while gathering deep within her the certain hope that there was more to life than this. Later, years later and worlds away from this novitiate library, she would hear the soft plaintive wonder in a song by Peggy Lee: "Is that all there is, my friend?" And recognize it.

He who loses his life shall find it.

She had set about finding it.

The novices attended Our Mother's words with the avidity of hungry pups catching crumbs from the master's table. Like super sleuths they strove to decode the hidden meanings of her words, their key to the secrets of God. More than her words, the rule told them, if they could anticipate her wish before she spoke, they were indeed becoming sensitive to the highest ideals of religious obedience. This made for the strange phenomenon of earnest novices jumping up at odd moments to reach for a pencil, open a door, pull out a chair in a kind of mind-reading dance she suffered with benign poise, certain, no doubt, that eventually they would slack off into the more sensible behavior of the experienced religious. They were, after all, only novices, and there was always an element of the extreme in their behavior. For these precious three years they were hers to mold.

She taught them the ideals of obedience.

They learned that, contrary to the assumptions of the outside secular world, it was hard to sin in the matter of obedience. It was easy, though, to fall short of the *ideal* of religious obedience, that cornerstone of the religious life. The highest ideal was to yield oneself "like a dead body"—the very phrase—to the expressed or implied will of those guaranteed to deliver the will of God.

It all sounds marvelously simple now. Even then, it wasn't simple. No exercise of human understanding or denial is simple. What keeps the jogger running in heat and fatigue? What brings on anorexia, or makes the politician lie? Nothing is simple.

On that suffocating August afternoon they walked away from the novitiate and down the dirt road toward the wooden bridge, then swerved their recreating circle and turned back toward the old half-timbered country house where they were learning their new profession.

They were nearing the turn in the road where a large elm shaded the end of the chapel when Our Mother spotted the two little kittens. They crouched by the side of the road, shivering in all that heat.

Sister Edward started for them.

"Don't touch them, Sister," said Our Mother in her calm, low voice. "Just look at them."

The circle of novices stopped and looked. The two pitiful creatures crouching there on the grass were mangy and sickly.

Patches of their fur were matted, and pinkish skin showed through in spots.

"They're diseased," said Our Mother. "Perhaps they'll go away."

Following her, the novices turned toward the house, and Vespers.

"It would be better if they were done away with," she murmured.

Sister Claire didn't know who else heard those words, but with a clarity that attaches to few moments in life, she knew she'd been issued a challenge. Our Mother had spoken. "It would be better if they were done away with."

She looked around at her sisters' faces. None betrayed a thought. Perhaps they hadn't heard. Perhaps no one would beat her to it.

She could hardly keep her mind on Vespers. This was often the case that summer, for heat collected inside the chapel's stone walls and ambushed her efforts to pray. Perspiration would collect beneath her T-shirt and, when she stood, run down her back. Sometimes, as they chanted, it would run out from beneath her headband and streak her face.

That afternoon, however, she glided through psalms and verses and responses and rejoiced that after Vespers and choir rehearsal she would have at least an hour free. It would be enough.

Immediately after Vespers they gathered in the library and sang through the coming Sunday Mass under the direction of Sister Angelica. They practiced the Proper, the Ordinary, the Sunday afternoon Benediction. Then she escaped.

She left by the back door, hoping she could find them. Perhaps they'd died. They hadn't looked too energetic.

Years would pass before she came to understand the intensity of her quest that day. It had to do with a distinctly Catholic notion of equaling things out. In the great scales of heaven she had a failing to atone for that she could explain to no one, least of all Our Mother. It would have made no sense in the confessional.

Trained to the highest ideals of the evangelical counsels—poverty, chastity, and obedience—she wanted to excel. Wasn't that the whole idea behind religious life? Why mount the ladder of perfection unless you intended to climb? "Because thou art lukewarm and neither cold nor hot, I will vomit thee out of my mouth." She had no intention of growing lukewarm. In fact, she feared few things as much as mediocrity. Becoming a half-baked nun getting mired in the letter of the law, not the spirit. She'd seen it. But she'd seen also nuns who seemed to integrate the loftiness of their call with a rare humanity. It *was* possible. Was not Our Mother, Mother Theodore, living proof?

The ideal of poverty went far beyond not owning. The ideal was to reduce one's desires, one's idea of the necessary. You did not own your clothes, your bed, your books, your apron. Monthly, you asked your superior permission for their *use.*

Certain items they'd brought with them (blankets, towels) were immediately put in common storage to be shared by all, as needed. Other, more personal items—underwear, stockings, deodorant—remained in trunks stored a short distance from the house, in the barn. To go "to the trunk," as the trip was called, they must ask permission. In that action, as one knelt before God's representative and requested permission to journey to the trunk for deodorant, the ideals of poverty and obedience met.

Earlier that month Sister Claire had knelt and asked Our Mother for permission to go to the trunk.

"Yes, Sister," she said gravely. "What do you need?"

"I need a pair of stockings, Mother," she said, with a twinge of guilt that she could darn the old ones no longer.

"Be sure to take a companion, Sister," said Our Mother.

The next Saturday afternoon Sister Florence and Sister Claire set out for the trunk. Good friends, they had graduated from college together, along with Sister Hilary.

They climbed the long hill in silence. When they got to the

barn, Sister Florence waited at the door and signaled her friend to take her time inside.

From the top of the hill things looked different. You could see the apple orchard that would supply apple cobbler every night all that fall and yield a seemingly endless supply of applesauce. Beyond that you might spot a cow or two, or even the bull tethered two pastures away which had once gotten loose and frightened Sister Helen and her family on visiting Sunday.

Sister Claire went into the barn. It was large and dark and cool. Rows of black trunks faced her. She spotted hers quickly, row two, near the back. The trunks were left unlocked.

There was something deeply refreshing about being in the barn, as though a cool, moist breath wiped a kind of blur and heaviness from her mind. She was in no hurry to get the stockings.

She opened the trunk. Half empty. Gone were the bright striped towels a college classmate had given her to defy convent white. She'd never seen them again. Gone were the white sheets and pillowcases, the two blankets. Left was a pile of T-shirts, two or three black underskirts, a pile of black stockings, two fresh gingham aprons, and a stack of personal items: deodorant, toothpaste, and—she'd forgotten until this very moment—baby powder.

She took the pair of black stockings. Her own stockings that day felt clammy on her legs. She wore them rolled to avoid the hassle of a garter belt. Nonetheless, she grew hot and sweaty behind the knees, and elsewhere her body harbored a steady grudge against heat. She'd always hated it. Her summers, as a child, were spent nagging to go to the beach and luxuriating in the saltwater of Long Island Sound. The bath schedule here allowed them one half hour in the tub each week. Beyond that, they must make do with the basin of water at night, ablutions taking place in their cells.

As she lifted the stockings, she stared at the Johnson's Baby Powder. She wanted it. She didn't have permission. She should not take it. If she asked, as she could, she'd have to make another trip. But she wanted it *right now.* She would take her bath that very afternoon, Saturday. She wanted to stand naked beside the tub, shake powder all over her body, abandon herself to its cool, clean touch for a few seconds before she slipped back into the layer of black serge.

She took the powder.

And with it came not elation but a kind of despair.

She knew she hadn't really sinned.

Nonetheless, in the mysterious kind of bookkeeping to which they were being introduced, where motive and meaning behind an act were measured to the finest degree, she knew she'd done wrong. She had failed the ideal. She should have mortified herself, waited, asked. She knew also that she might have been denied permission. Already, she had to wash her hair in the tub with yellow bar soap. Why suppose she'd be permitted the hedonism of baby powder?

At the barn door Sister Florence turned and smiled. She glanced at the items in her friend's hands. Did she suspect guilt? Unlikely. One's failings were supremely secret in religious life. The intricate possibilities for failure were proportionate to one's sense of the heights. These are the secrets of the soul.

Sister Claire would use the powder for a year.

She understood that to acknowledge her failure publicly would have been an act of humility, but she kept her secret.

Then came this opportunity: the mangy kittens.

Our Mother had said, "It would be better if they were done away with." Sister Claire had heard her. Did not these words constitute an expressed wish? Was not Our Mother the deliverer of God's will? And did God actually desire those kittens dead? But on the practical level (she still allowed her mind to evaluate God's will) she saw it was true. These were germ-ridden, diseased critters.

Nonetheless, had it not been for her superior's words, Sister Claire could never have summoned the will to commit the act.

.   .   .

After choir she hunted around for a pail. It had come to her during Vespers that there was no other way. She certainly could not use a knife, didn't have a gun, wouldn't have known what to do with it if she did, so what else was there? She would drown them.

Out back, in the laundry, she asked Sister Thomas, who was busy ironing Our Mother's underwear, for a pail.

"Sure. Right over there. Just be sure to bring it back."

Sister Claire took the pail and ran it full from the tub. Then she set it out back, at the foot of the steep mountain where the novitiate building nestled. On break day from thirty-day retreat they'd tried to climb that mountain. A difficult, exhausting task with perilous footing. About halfway up they'd stopped. Looking back down, she'd been struck by how tiny the novitiate was, that building where every minute of their lives was directed and controlled, where life itself was contained. So small. Just part of a landscape.

She would do her deed partway up the mountain.

That way she would perform the most perfect act of obedience she could achieve. For she understood well the danger of secretly wanting to be seen. Self, with its ingenious devices for drawing attention to even the most hidden acts, was always lurking. If she could climb far enough away from the novitiate in the next hour, do her deed, bury the animals, then return and never say a word, no one else would know. Only God would see her. The reward would come later. In that eternal later.

You would have thought they knew her design. There they were, crouching near the withered lilac bush at the edge of the laundry. The small one was brown and white with a large patch, she now saw, of something dark and speckled near its tail. The other one, gray with green eyes that looked slightly mad (if a cat's eyes can look mad) was positively blotchy with disease.

She carried the pail in one hand and scooped them up with the other. "Okay, you guys. It won't be too bad."

Her resolve was aided by the fact that she had never been a

cat lover and was unencumbered by a righteous attitude toward animals. Besides, they *were* disgusting.

Climbing was no easy matter. Even on the day when they'd climbed as a group, they'd struggled to clutch at rocks, alders, bushes, as they made their way up the hill. She couldn't get too far now, balancing a pail of water in one hand and two mangy kittens in the other. And what if they infected her with whatever they had? She'd have to wash later.

Finally she managed to put them inside her wide gingham apron and knot it in such a way that they stayed there. That freed one hand to grab at whatever she could as she climbed.

She got up about a quarter of a mile—no small achievement on a steep hill, through heavy underbrush, in a long skirt and veil. She panted to a stop. She had twenty minutes to do the deed, get back, wash up, and start her afternoon meditation.

Now she had to face it.

She looked inside her apron and thought for an instant that this hardly felt like an act of obedience. That thought flew away, or was put away, for she was trained to distrust spontaneous thought or feeling. She remembered the baby powder, her secret ongoing almost-sin. This, surely, would balance things out. She thought of Our Mother's expressed wish. And the article on obedience in Holy Rule which they were to memorize and meditate on. And the years ahead when she would no doubt have far harder things to do, moments when she would again feel puzzled by the dimensions of God's will.

She set the pail down.

She took the two small bodies and gently set them inside. Water spilled over the top. They did not like it one bit, and quiet as they'd been inside her apron as she'd climbed, they now began to object. They pawed and wiggled, struggling to keep their heads up.

She saw what she would have to do. She did not like it. She must look away.

She was no expert in planning and executing a small murder. From the time she left chapel she had acted as automatically as possible—moving, taking, climbing, trying not to think, knowing that ultimately this was a good act, a virtuous act.

Now she was faced with the fact that she couldn't distance herself from the act. A cover might have done it. Not only could she have avoided seeing them, she wouldn't have had to feel them.

She knelt on the pebbly path she'd found near a bush of wild roses. She took off her undersleeves so her arms would be bare to the elbow. The outer sleeves were already pinned up.

She put her hands into the water, one on each little kitten. She held them.

She feels their bones still. She has never become sentimental over animals. She still does not own a cat.

But holding a small animal under water, feeling it struggle, pushing it down, small bones against your fingers like chicken bones inside thin furry skin holding, holding, until . . .

She stared into the bushes nearby. She could not watch what she was doing or she would have stopped.

So she looked away, down on the novitiate roof gleaming in the midafternoon sun, a bright silver roof sparkling with heat, and she tried to make her mind go blank, not to feel the bones, not to reason (for reason was so limited, so fatal), only to know that at last she was performing, if not the perfect act, at least an act sufficiently difficult, sufficiently secret, sufficiently against herself and her nature that it would weigh in the important balance being even then, at that very instant, measured some-where far above that sparkling hot roof below.

Higher Learning

Scarcely breathing, body tensed, she pushed in the large, flaking door stealthily, lifting the knob slightly to eliminate squeak. Her slippers moved soundlessly across the worn tiled floor. At the first compartment she opened the small door with a practiced movement, slipped inside, gingerly slid the bolt behind her and stood for a second listening. No sound. Then she lifted the single peeling wooden chair and moved it closer to hold her papers. Nimbly, without a rustle, she climbed over the high, rounded rim and settled herself in the large old-fashioned tub, legs crossed Indian style. Faintly gritty porcelain shocked cold against leg flesh as the long white nightgown rode up to her knees. Settled if not comfortable, she reached for the clipboard, balanced it awkwardly on her crossed legs and bent over, pen in hand. At last: sanctuary. Invisibility. Illumination from one light bulb burning all night. She bent over the shadowed half-written sheet thoughtfully. Slowly at first—then more rapidly as moments passed and the bulb-lit bathroom settled again into that eerie half-light and shabby deadness of all institutional bathrooms at night—she began to write.

"You mean no one ever investigated those mysterious scratching sounds at midnight from compartment one on floor four? You mean you weren't sent for after breakfast this morning for the third degree?"

They were walking briskly, just the two of them left outside now at evening recreation. Up and down, up and down the convent drive, fighting late winter rawness by increasing their speed rather than retreating into the stuffy community room where the others had already gone.

"Only one visitor the whole time I was there. Phillipa, I think. Smelled like her. Didn't *do* anything. Just slippered around on her nightly prowl. Last night's chili probably set her off."

They both knew you were apt to meet Sister Phillipa, inveterate night prowler, at any time of night, anywhere. Harmless, the last three superiors had concluded, as well as hopeless. Sacristy wine was under lock and key, the pantry door was bolted. Nothing stopped her. Many an overnight visitor had started in alarm at the lean black figure mushrooming out of darkness and gliding past, flashlight in hand.

"Did she try your compartment?"

"Why would she? Who takes a bath at midnight? I just sat absolutely still and waited till I could hear her fading away down the hall before I started scratching away again. No kidding, it was the perfect place!"

"I'll remember that if I need a cram session before finals. But you're a wonder. I could no more keep myself awake after hitting the bed and then get up later and *think* than I could . . . play a game of basketball after three o'clock dismissal!"

Sister Mark taught seventh grade at St. Bartholomew's, one of St. Gertrude's two offshoot parochial schools. Her rugged, good-natured heartiness could mislead: above the rather coarse-grained features, sharp green eyes took in the world about her and measured it. A strong constitution saw her through long days, years of screaming playgrounds and twelve-year-old intransigence. Her strength and sharpness intimidated the most defiant and equipped her to cope expertly with the range from practiced goody-goody to prepubertal delinquent that navy-and-white uniforms so effectively disguised from the outside eye.

But she had missed coming in under the new educational plan in the Order, initiated in the eastern province of the United States in 1955, just two years before Sister Claire's first profession. Consequently Sister Mark was getting her degree, as they said, "on the side"—which meant she put in a week of teaching seventh grade, supervised the convent kitchen (planned menus, directed help), then went off to class on Saturday mornings while the rest of the house was scrubbing and cleaning, out to the doctor, or seeing Reverend Mother. For eleven years—summers and Saturdays—she had been taking courses, and the end was not in sight. She'd forgotten the beginning. But she was good-natured, even philosophical about it. Sister Claire, still relatively fresh from her own studies, marveled at such self-effacement, such resignation.

For she had timed her own vocation more advantageously. After profession she'd been sent straight to the Order's pride and joy in Washington, D.C.: the recently established house of studies where newly professed young sisters who already had their B.A. would be given two years to complete a master's degree at Catholic University. Their religious formation would be completed here as well, under the enlightened direction of a nun from the college who was not only fervent but also had a Ph.D. Everyone in the Order recognized the opening of the Washington house of studies as a progressive step. It meant they took higher education seriously—in a world where nuns were too often perceived as immature and overwrought oddly garbed guardians of the defenseless young.

Near the end of her novitiate days, Sister Claire had spent

some anxious hours praying for a spirit of obedience. She was being sent to graduate school. The Order was giving her this chance. But what field would they put her in? Science or math would spell disaster, God's will notwithstanding. To her intense relief, in the matter of higher learning His will turned out to coincide with her own: she was assigned to study English literature.

Though that time of formation was behind her now and she was in her third year of teaching, she still yearned to bring to her high school classes some of the excitement she had felt at rediscovering literature.

"So what's your paper going to be on, anyway?" asked Sister Mark as they pumped along together, still chuckling over the last night's adventure.

"Methods of composition." A description tailored to the hearer. Forms of Rhetoric would mean nothing to Sister Mark, but even seventh graders were forced to confront their dangling participles and misplaced modifiers.

"Does it have to be very long? How're you going to find time with *your* schedule to have it all together by this Saturday?"

"I think I'll make it. Give me two more nights in the tub! Wonders, believe me, what that atmosphere does for creativity"—she struck a pose, *Le Penseur*—"drip drip drip, the waters of inspiration are flowing. *Will* our Sister Claire, illustrious invited speaker at the prestigious highbrow oh-so-secular XYZ Conference, finish her paper in time to appear? Prove to the world that nuns can have brains? Stand by . . . drip drip drip!"

"Don't get carried away. We'd better go in."

"You're so right." She curbed herself. "This is my week to keep a low profile."

She was learning this was often the better way at St. Gertrude's. She'd been here barely a year—not long enough to fathom the complex history of this house. But she felt something among the older nuns—not all of them, of course—something like hostility. They were watching the new arrivals, the better-educated young nuns, especially those from Washington, like hawks. As if the identity of the house itself were somehow threatened by these new sisters with their new ideas. Consequently, it took time to sort out where possibilities for real friendship lay.

What a change from Our Redeemer's, the small but flourishing high school in Calais, Maine, to which she'd been sent from Washington. There, the older sisters had seemed genuinely grateful for an influx of energy, of youth. They mopped floors, did menial work, tried in any way possible to relieve the younger nuns so they could give full time to their teaching and preparation. In that atmosphere she had begun her teaching and discovered how much she loved the classroom. Transfer to St. Gertrude's, a surprise as transfers usually were, had meant pain, for she left behind good friends and in two brief years had grown attached to that community.

St. Gertrude's would take some knowing. But a low profile was wise.

Streetlights glimmered on around the hill. The February sky was a cold gray-blue, faint purple streaks shading rapidly into dark. They hurried up the drive and disappeared through the door, heading for the community room and the end of evening recreation.

That was Tuesday.

Late Tuesday night she felt the words coming more freely. How absurd to have to resort to this! Yet something made her persist, kept her from saying quite simply, "No, my days are too full to take on this extra burden." Because it was not only a burden; it was an honor: the first invitation to one of their nuns to address a gathering of secular educators. Not only secular, point one, but *distinguished,* point two. And wasn't this the thrust of their training? To aim for the highest achievement not only in spiritual growth but also in learning? To integrate their spiritual aspirations and human talents into one perfect offering? "There is a variety of gifts but always the same Spirit . . ." From the time she was a child she'd been taught her gifts were to be used. "Do not hide your light under a bushel," her mother would say. Her father, less given to cliché, simply assumed his children would Do Their Best. Here was a chance to use those gifts for the Order, for the house. The Order had given her much: her formation, her higher education. A call was given to the whole person, not only to part. She believed this, deeply. And during her years of formation that belief had been reinforced by all they'd been taught.

Yet this superior, Reverend Mother Rachel, seemed to lack any sense of what was at stake. She'd nodded reservedly as she listened to the explanation and request for permission: "Reverend Mother, this is an honor, really. I am the first nun ever to be invited to their conference. Fortunately, the talk doesn't have to be long, but I do feel it will be hard to explain if I refuse."

"Of course, Sister. We will consider it and let you know soon."

Soon was six weeks later.

Reverend Mother Rachel had spent fifteen years as a principal of a small parochial school in upstate New York where she had distinguished herself by diligent loyalty to the Order. She had, it was said, a way with children. When, in 1958, that school had been closed for financial reasons, Mother Provincial had sought another post in the eastern province for Reverend Mother Rachel. St. Gertrude's was a big operation with its six-hundred-strong girls' high school, its private academy, grades one through eight, and its two offshoot parochial elementary schools, St. Bartholomew's and St. Catherine's. Next to the college it was the most important house in the province for providing vocations as well as income. During the next few years many of the younger, better-educated nuns would no doubt be sent to St. Gertrude's, for the community was topheavy with old nuns. Clearly these younger nuns could profit from living under a superior so dedicated to the Order. Thus had Mother Provincial reasoned with her provincial council over this appointment of what some might call a small mind to a big job.

· · ·

Scratch. Scratch. Sister Claire believed it would come. Fighting fatigue, she forced attention to her own regular script gradually filling the page. A tight line of muscle strain pulled at the back of her neck and crept across each bent shoulder and down her upper arms. Tuesday was a backbreaker: the usual six classes, cafeteria supervision at noon, faculty meeting after school, class preparation sandwiched in here and there before she returned to the convent for meditation and Matins and Lauds at five o'clock. Cramped beneath the clipboard, her legs kept getting pins and needles. No way to stretch them effectively.

Tomorrow night she must finish. She always needed time and a bit of distance to *see* what she'd put on paper. That would come Thursday, the extra free period at noon. Friday afternoon gave her another hour, last period, if Sister Stephen didn't spring a second faculty meeting. She could type it then. That meant a good night's sleep Friday. Good thing. Saturday would be a strain. She didn't know yet who would be her companion.

"How goes the night life?"

This time they met accidentally in the pantry after school dismissal, which was early for Sister Mark on Wednesdays. She came home immediately to help out in the laundry.

Looks tired, noted Sister Claire, studying the ruddy face and sharp eyes opposite as each drained a cup of coffee near the plates of odds and ends set out to sustain the sisters until supper. Every afternoon, between three and four o'clock, they were required to stop by the pantry for this collation.

"I'm bushed. These late hours aren't for me!"

An electric glance silenced her as a lean black shape glided insidiously between them.

"Any doughnuts left, Sisters?"

Sister Mark translated the deceptively innocent question.

"Here, Sister." She picked up the largest and set it on a paper napkin, then poured a cup of coffee for her.

Sister Phillipa's seedlike brown eyes darted about ceaselessly as she was served. A pause in her afternoon route: from here

she would glide into the adjoining refectory, coffee in hand, and
slowly work her way the length of the table on each side, noting
each sister's mail (left at their places after Reverend Mother
checked it in the early afternoon), studying return addresses,
penmanship. She snooped fearlessly, shamelessly, staring back
impenetrably into the eyes of any accuser. Her skill at reading
the outsides of other people's lives went unremarked now: she
enjoyed the immunity of a high-ranking incurable.

"Whew!" breathed Sister Mark as Sister Phillipa left them and
began moving through the refectory. Silence for a moment; then,
when the black back was safely out of earshot: "You'd better
watch it! All you need now is to have her on your trail. Hear
her last night?"

"Not a sound but the old drip drip and my spouting pen."
Sister Claire gulped cool coffee apprehensively, alert to the humorous possibilities, but more alert to the unpleasant consequences of being discovered in her midnight den by the night
prowler. It would mean being reported for disobedience (she
was to be in bed at that time in the large sleeping dormitory),
facing Reverend Mother's blend of incomprehension and in-
flexible virtue, having to explain there was literally no time in
her packed day to do this extra thing, then meeting the obvious
response that first things come first: renounce this vanity.

"Well, watch it." Tiny lines radiating from the corners of Sister
Mark's eyes deepened, though her face remained serious. "I
don't fancy a squaring off between you, her, and Reverend
Mother. No way you'd win."

They parted hastily, Sister Mark off to the laundry, Sister
Claire back to piles of papers and a session with a recalcitrant
student. She felt warmed by her friend's concern. Sister Mark
was a brick, her friendship, like others she was slowly discovering here, a gift.

This was the meaning of "Ecce Quam Bonum"—the final
beautiful chant at the conclusion of her profession ceremony.
"Ecce quam bonum et quam jucundum, habitare fratres in unum . . ."
One felt it in precious moments, when the community gathered

to praise God at solemn feasts, in the quiet, unspoken look of comprehension from a sister when one was embarrassed or troubled, in the concern of someone like Sister Mark whose day, whose life, surely bore less excitement than Claire's. They warmed her, these moments when she felt so supported, so unselfishly understood. They offset other moments when Claire felt herself on the brink of a darkness she could not fathom. Such as when Mother Hildegarde, the aging, crotchety choir mistress and organist, reluctantly allowed Sister Claire to help her, since Reverend Mother had decreed she should. "Don't expect to take over just because you're musical," she said in that first encounter. "I've lived in this house for forty-five years. You've just arrived. You've a lot to learn."

Claire felt the truth of that statement. Nothing was simple about navigating the waters of community life.

Wednesday night she finished, as planned. It took longer than she'd expected, but she saw it through, and it was two-thirty when she finally slipped papers and clipboard under her bathrobe, silently slid back the bolt of her compartment, and glided across the tiles, relieved to be leaving behind the dull light of the deserted bathroom. She stepped gingerly into the hall, looking each way down the long, narrow tube of darkness. Nothing could give her away now. She hugged her hidden achievement to her ribs with warm satisfaction: *wise as serpents . . . guileless as doves*. The fruits of her wisdom held close, she could spend the next two days passing as guileless. She moved quietly forward, alert yet distracted, the concluding words of her speech trailing in her mind.

Suddenly, just at the entrance to the dormitory, she struck a form—a tall, lean wedge mushrooming silently out of the dark.

"Oops, sorry!"

Clatter . . . the clipboard hit the floor with an apocalyptic bang. Papers scattered—not too far, fortunately. Tensing herself to explain, she looked up, confused and apprehensive. Sister Phillipa's tiny eyes gleamed inscrutably. Then, wordlessly, she glided away down the corridor, leaving Sister Claire to scramble and retrieve in confused panic.

No other bodies rose.

"You mean she didn't say *anything?*"

"Not a word."

They were at recreation again, this time inside. Cold, steady rain all day Thursday had layered dampness throughout the house, and spirits grayed and sagged like the snow-turned-mush outside. It was one of those general recreations at which nothing came easily. Attempts at conversation bunched up like knots on a string: an eruption of words, then a long, awkward pause as the more earnest struggled to think of something to say that would include all the sisters. That was the rule governing their recreation: no particular interests to be aired, no exclusions, no depressing anecdotes. *Re-creation:* all needed it, they were told.

Some sewed, darned stockings, veils, or linens; a few of the older ones knitted or crocheted. Some sat silent, hands spread on laps, waiting for recreation to happen. They formed the usual circle in the inadequately lit community room–library, and Sister Mark and Sister Claire, in the second row of the circle—near the books on Mystical Prayer—were whispering under cover of a conversation originating from the corner near Canon Law.

"Think she caught on?"

"How could she not?"

"But Reverend Mother hasn't said anything to the community yet."

"She's seen the mail at my place"—the invitations had come through the mail—"and she hogs portress duty." There had also been a few phone calls about the conference.

"Well, play dumb is my advice. If you're forced to it, tell the truth."

Sister Mark turned her face back toward the rim of recreation. Sister Claire bent her head and began darning her good veil, trying to quell the worm of uneasiness that had tormented her since the night before. She knew Sister Mark was right, and once again she was grateful for her friend's concern.

The sound of her name jarred her, and she looked up. Between the black heads directly in front of her she met Reverend Mother's eyes bearing down on her, commanding her across knitting fingers and impassive shapes—to recreate them.

"Perhaps you could tell the sisters, Sister Claire, of your plans for this Saturday."

Needles paused. Heads lifted. Eyes focused. Something *new*.

"Sister Claire has been invited to give a speech at Columbia."

She felt the stir of interested recognition: not St. Mary's, St. Xavier's, Our Lady of Hope, but Columbia. A secular establishment. Beyond the pale. What was their Sister Claire doing going *there?* Daring to be a Daniel? Tell us about the lion's den, Sister Claire.

"Can you tell the sisters something about it, Sister?"

Desperation. No escape. A wicked urge struck. *Certainly, my dear sisters in Christ. I'm perpetrating the higher wisdom of the bathtub on the unsuspecting secular groves of academe.* Clairvoyant Sister Mark sent her a warning glance.

"Well, I was invited as part of the follow-up program of the course I took last summer." Surely they would remember furnishing her with a different companion every day for six weeks! Every able body in the community was asked to sign up at least once. Each day she found her companion an obscure seat in the library—for knitting, crocheting, reading, or staring—then picked her up after class and drove home. Senseless, that was obvious, but the price one apparently paid for an excursion into those courts of higher learning.

Silence.

Faces were turned toward her, vaguely expectant. Reverend Mother was looking her encouraging look. Beside her, in front of Hagiography, Sister Phillipa stared at her.

"It's really quite a short speech. Just a report on what I've done with teaching twelfth-grade composition this year as a result of that course."

"How interesting, Sister." Sister Eunice specialized in the kind of universal interest that made pointed conversation with her impossible. "Perhaps you could give us a preview?" She resumed knitting.

Dear God, save me. Puny Euny.

"Well, I think it's marvelous that she can find time to do this—we keep all our young teachers so busy," chirped Sister Cletus from the Asceticism section. Aged, benevolently unsuspicious, she spent long hours praying her beads for the younger sisters and begging the Lord that the work of the house might prosper.

"Will there be many there, Sister?" asked Sister St. Aedan, unfailingly practical.

"About a hundred and fifty, I think." She hazarded a guess based on the number of first-rate colleges within easy driving distance. Two representatives from each, as well as two representatives from certain prep schools in southern Connecticut and New York.

She spotted the bell ringer nodding to Reverend Mother. Saved, thank God.

"Well, I know you all wish Sister Claire well on Saturday, Sisters. I'm certain she will be a credit to the Order." Reverend Mother looked around pointedly, then stood to declare recreation ended. They all stood silently and followed her to chapel.

After night prayer was over, Claire stayed a few minutes in the darkened chapel. She felt the need to pray. She knelt in her stall, closed her eyes, let her surroundings fall away. She wanted to find that secret spot within, the deepest center, the place where in moments of quiet prayer she could sometimes enter and feel herself in communion with God. The place where she had answered His call. In that quietness now she prayed that she would not be deceived. She prayed for clarity of mind, for the ability to know when, indeed, she was acting from personal vanity. For that she did not want. She longed to be delivered from the blindness of self, that darkness she was striving to leave through a life of dedication. One left the darkness of self by

72

living for something, someone larger. She had found that. What had drawn her in particular to the Agnetines had been their vision, their commitment to learning and teaching. Although she'd long been drawn to the nuns, it was not until college that she at last met women who read serious books, who gave lectures, who conducted classes on a level that commanded respect even from their secular peers. From men. To this she had responded—and longed, finally, to be one of them.

Now she was to carry forth that vision, represent them to the outer world, the very world she had left almost eight years before. She wanted to do it well, to be a credit to the Order. She longed to show the world what wholeness there could be in a life given over to God through prayer, study, and the teaching of others. *Dear Lord,* she prayed, *help me. Let me be a success.*

Surely this was His will.

Friday afternoon Reverend Mother sent for Sister Claire. She was in the high school typing room, checking the freshly typed manuscript, when Sister Stephen poked her head in.

"I think that's your bell in the convent."

All day she had been expecting it. Details for tomorrow still had to be settled: companion, transportation. As she moved through Friday classes, she felt herself growing nervous: her stomach was knotting, she had the runs. Except for last summer's six-week course, it was almost three full years since she'd been in an academic setting—and even then she'd felt herself an outsider. Three years away from that atmosphere of leisured articulateness and easy sophistication she had noted with fascination among her graduate professors as she scurried about in diligent silence like some kind of strangely costumed mole eating her way through Anglo-Saxon conjugations, the Canterbury pilgrimage, the Renaissance world view, masticating the Miltonic sublime, then chewing assiduously through the Great Chain of Being, only to gag on the dilemma of Narcissus and the bifurcated self. On paper the list of courses was impressive; acute indigestion didn't show. She was, the Order said, educated.

Then the sting of that first day at Our Redeemer: thirty strange faces, glazed eyes faintly interested, measuring her, opaque presences daring her to awaken them. She soon confirmed what she'd already suspected: Chaucerian subtlety, Wordsworthian ecstasy, the charm of antithesis and balance, the naughtiness of Belinda or even Don Juan, had little to do with those smoldering lives. Or at least the burden of proof was on her to show that it did.

She threw herself into it. She loved it: closing the door mornings on her very own classroom, discussing stories with her English students, arguing about the meaning of a poem. She was new to them, young by convent standards. She carried the glamour of the unknown. How could they guess the pleasure it gave her to be in charge, at last, of her own class? She longed to deepen their faith. Yet the hardest subject to teach was religion. Their book was a purple hardback, *Our Quest for Happiness.* She opened to shiny pages of diagrams, charts, exhortations, classifications of virtue, and knew it was hopeless. This had nothing to do with deepening faith. It was like trying to teach a mystery from graph paper.

So she replaced the opening prayer of the morning with a Gelineau psalm. Beginning the day by singing together conveyed what a book could not. "The heavens proclaim the glory of God, and the firmament shows forth the work of His hands . . ." The students loved it.

Then, after two short years, had come the transfer—God's will delivered on a typed slip to be read in chapel, before the Blessed Sacrament. To St. Gertrude's which was known to have its share of problems—a rather simpleminded superior, difficult older nuns, and a long history about which she knew nothing. Several of the sisters who went through the novitiate with her had come from St. Gertrude's. She'd been struck by their intense loyalty to the school. She felt little of that toward Holy Angels, her old high school in Connecticut. For her, it was college that had made all the difference.

Summer had brought her an unexpected boon, a help over

the bridge to St. Gertrude's: a six-week course with a stimulating professor in something called Forms of Rhetoric. Suddenly she discovered that what she struggled to do with her students had a name, a history. She could create a voice to meet a situation or re-create the situation with a voice and a tone: the course fascinated her. Her papers were called brilliant by the detached, respectful, trim-bearded professor who wrote careful annotations in the margins but avoided more personal contact. Throughout the course they corresponded through the margins: little else. It became clear that even there one could communicate effectively. She had saved all her papers, reread the margins before she set about creating her short bathtub masterpiece.

But today her prose looked depressingly flat, high-schoolish. Daily battles with mind rot and chalk dust dimmed her memory of the living exchange that had carried her so buoyantly through last summer. It all seemed so remote. How would she ever carry off tomorrow with any aplomb? Why had she pushed so hard to go, anyway? Moles belonged underground.

She hurried now to answer her bell.

Reverend Mother was waiting for her where high school and convent joined. With her, Sister Phillipa.

"I have to go out this afternoon, Sister." She was pulling on black cotton gloves, working one button at the base of her left palm. "I wanted to settle our plans for tomorrow."

Our.

"Yes, Reverend Mother."

"I think we should take one of the cars. See Sister William to arrange that, if you would. As far as I know there is only one doctor's appointment tomorrow; that should leave the station wagon free."

"Yes, Reverend Mother." Courage. "Are you planning to come with me then, Reverend Mother?"

"I think it would be a good idea, Sister." She buttoned the second glove. "Be sure you get a good night's sleep."

Inscrutable seed-eyes watching.

"Oh, and Sister." Reverend Mother turned back hastily.

"Would you be good enough to ask Sister Francis to get ready my good habit and veil for tomorrow?" Fastidious and discreet, Sister Francis took care of Reverend Mother from the underwear out.

With that, both figures disappeared down the convent corridor, and Sister Claire hurried back to finish proofing.

Over dishes that night, between scraping, stacking, and feeding huge loaded trays to the belching monster that dinned in the pantry for an hour after supper, she passed the word to Sister Mark.

"Reverend Mother *herself?* Whatever for, do you suppose?"

"Don't ask me! That's all she said."

"But didn't you expect it would be another English teacher, someone who might at least tread water in such distinguished company?"

Sister Claire slammed in a tray, appreciating her friend's grasp. Then, through the whoosh of spray and clouds of steam, "I gave up trying to imagine who'd come. Maybe she's just plain curious."

"Could be. Or starved for adventure." Perspiration oozed from beneath the plastic band that cut into Sister Mark's forehead. "You'd better behave!"

"Whatever that means!"

From the moment they left the convent next morning, Sister Claire had a sense of Reverend Mother's deep disorientation. When they were delayed by heavy traffic on Riverside Drive, she tried not to listen to her superior's nervous prattle. "Move left, Sister. Oh, dear, is that van too close in our rear? Did you have the oil checked, Sister?"

Reverend Mother didn't drive.

Despite this irritation and her own anxieties about the traffic, Claire felt oddly calm. Her superior could never have guessed the picture opening full-blown in her driver's head . . . a memory whose sudden, sharp poignance caught her by surprise. Why

now, on Riverside Drive, as she steered the convent station
wagon between nudging limos and trucks? Was it the dynamic
thrust of Manhattan beneath a cold February sky? She thought
she'd forgotten. . . . Unsought, she saw the whole scene, suddenly present—her father, her mother, her older brother (he
would have been about fourteen) at the table. A round, white-
covered table in, of all places, the Waldorf-Astoria.

She must have been eleven or twelve, grade seven or so . . .
yes, she remembered, it was her brother's first year away at prep
school. For March break their parents had decided to take them
to New York City. It was not their first trip by any means.
They'd been there for the Fair in '39 (just beyond the edge of
her memory, but she'd seen pictures and the specially printed
newspaper with the headline: *PAUL AND CLAIRE DELANEY
VISIT WORLD'S FAIR*) and every couple of years after that to
see, as her father said, the sights. He loved Manhattan—eating
out, seeing Broadway plays, showing them off. On one memorable trip he'd danced with her on the Starlight Roof. In any
case, for this trip they were staying in a modest hotel called the
New Yorker. One morning business friends of her father's, a
childless couple, had met them in the lobby. And when Mr.
What-was-his-name?—she could see him now with his flourishing white moustache, his dark suit and polished shoes—when
he asked the children where they'd like to go to eat (probably
expecting they'd say the Automat) she'd piped up, "I'd like to
eat at the Waldorf."

Later her mother explained in no uncertain terms that she'd
been too forward.

But she'd heard of the Waldorf, knew it as a place where
movie stars went. She collected their pictures. Who knew what
she might see there? Here was her chance. And with gallant
good humor Mr. X smiled and said, "By all means, Claire. A
perfect choice. Let's go."

So they found themselves in the main dining room at the
Waldorf, seated around a table, about to be served lunch. Not
too many people there, she recalled, maybe ten filled tables in

the room. Perhaps her parents had urged early lunch hoping the children would behave.

She had heard of Oscar of the Waldorf. So she asked her father, "Dad, will we get to meet Oscar?" Amused, he arranged for a chef to come from out back and talk to them at the table. And when, in the course of things, it came out that she played the piano, this Oscar asked, "Would you like to play something for us?"

Ah, what a moment! She felt the double pressure from her parents, different pressures. Her mother, instantly anxious, nervous that she'd fail, burst out, "Oh, Burt, she'd be too nervous"—or something to that effect. But Burt, calm, seemingly certain of her capacity to carry this off, simply said, "Well, Claire, what do you say? Want to try?" She knew it would make him very proud.

So she did.

Terrified, she left them all behind, walked alone with kindly Oscar in his tall white chef's hat across the room and up the few stairs to the platform where the piano stood. Her hands had begun to perspire already. It was a beautiful piano, shining black, its white keys gleaming, its top raised as if waiting for her. She was in a yellow jumper that day with red, brown, and green felt pieces inserted around the neck. She could see it now as clearly as she saw her hand with its gold ring on the wheel of the convent car.

She sat on the piano bench a moment, looked out across the room to her parents at the table on the other side. No one else in the dining room seemed to have noticed her. Her mother's head was down. She couldn't watch; she was probably praying. Her father, though, looking at her with his friends, already proud of her accomplishment. She said a quick prayer: "Help me remember, dear God. Please don't let me forget." For that could happen to anyone, even Horowitz. Then she began.

Debussy. "Clair de lune." She loved it . . . the muted opening thirds, then the wonderful gradual downward movement, that quiet approach to home, the tonic chord. As she struck that, crossing her hands for the satisfying D-flat-major chord, she knew it would be all right. She would remember. She gave it her heart.

"Look out, Sister!" said Reverend Mother. "He almost clipped you."

"It's all right," she said, returning from the Waldorf. "It's okay. We'll make it, Reverend Mother. We're almost there."

The first thing that assailed her in the large room on the third floor of the Goddard Building was *smells*. Suddenly she was a surge of confused emotion, limp with anxiety. She clutched the manila folder tightly under her arm and reminded herself how little was expected: just a brief explanation of one high school class's adaptation of college material. Manageable. She had to survive only the morning part of the meeting. Reverend Mother had other business that afternoon.

Stepping into the large, comfortable room, she felt distressingly inept. How would she survive this morning? Did they see her panic?

"Yes, yes, come in, Sister." Obviously waiting for them, fingering the finely linked gold chain of his large pocket watch— Professor Zanzibar, now as always impeccably groomed in subtly blended mocha tones with gleaming white shirt.

"We're very glad to see you at last." He beamed welcomingly at Reverend Mother. "And this must be your companion." Sounding just as if he also traveled by twos. "Do come in. We're just about to begin, I'm afraid, so we'll get you both settled and then perhaps afterward you'll have some time for introductions." He smiled pointedly at Sister Claire, careful to include Reverend Mother in the compass of his graciousness.

With marvelous efficiency he steered Reverend Mother to a seat, near the back as she modestly requested, though they had saved her one up front. Sister Claire found herself with four others on the other side of a long table, each behind a microphone, all facing out at the audience, all strangers except her old instructor and Reverend Mother.

Still—the smells. Even now, when pipes and cigars had been extinguished as requested, there lingered an unmistakably male smell in the room. Ladies were sprinkled here and there, most in suits, several looking like trim grandmothers, but somehow they made little dent. Acrid, pungent smells she identified as male invaded her senses, seemed to float into her head and inflate it. And textures—like the arm of the jacket on the table beside her, lovely soft blue and gray (*herringbone*—from some buried jar of memory she extracted the term), a slight nap that invited her fingers, hidden now in the extra fold of long black sleeve designed to render nuns armless, handless, in public. Somewhere out there Reverend Mother was buried. Invisible.

Professor Zanzibar had been introduced. He was talking about Plato's *Phaedrus.* She remembered vaguely, but its meaning had shrunk for her since last summer, and she half-listened with a sense of strangeness to the voice that had reawakened her delight at the subtleties of literature in his class just six months before. She studied the shapes of legs in the first row, stocking colors—deep brown, navy blue, gray, one black. She felt herself growing giddy, light-headed. She was representing the Order. No sister had ever before spoken to this group. She longed to do well. . . . The man opposite her had a marvelous beard, exquisitely trimmed. *How does he do it?* she wondered. *His wife? Are there special beard trimmers now? What does it feel like?*

"And now we are very pleased to have with us as a guest this morning Sister Claire from St. Gertrude's High School. She participated in my course on rhetoric last summer and has been doing some interesting things with her twelfth-grade honor students this year. We are indeed very honored to have her with us this morning."

She moved forward to the central microphone, suddenly feeling strangely confident, ready. In a flash her nerves seemed to recompose themselves. The faces before her looked warm, friendly, accepting. *Dear God, help me,* she prayed. And began.

"It is a pleasure to be with you this morning." Her voice

sounded higher, thinner than she had expected. Young, very young, a trifle breathless and hurried.

"My experiments this year have been modest." Suddenly she caught sight of Reverend Mother leaning forward attentively. Flanked by two men.

She'll like that, she registered, as her voice went on describing the weekly exercises she'd worked out.

It was soon over. She was back at the table next to blue-gray tweed. Ready for questions if there were any during the discussion period.

After the inevitable pause, a dribble of questions, but none directed to her. She grew eager. Still none came. The dialogue around her grew more intense. She felt cut off from the smooth articulateness. A mole again. They all knew each other, it seemed, had taught together perhaps in years gone by. Had read the same books: Aristotle, Plato, Burke, Frye . . . a battery of names tossed back and forth. They breathed the same air: books, wine, tobacco. Blue-gray tweed was smoking now. Wisps of smoke trailed toward her, coated her throat, seemed to fill her lungs. Her head began to ache faintly, and a small longing started to grow deep within: to be done with this.

Finally—a question.

"Mr. Chairman, I would like to direct a question to the charming lady in black and white who graces our platform this morning."

She leaned forward to the table microphone.

"First of all, I would like to say how very pleased we are to have you with us, a beginning, I hope, of a broader embrace by this Institute. And indeed I rather envy Professor Zanzibar's good fortune in having had such an alert student for a summer. Many of us have heard of your outstanding participation in his classes, and we are pleased to meet you at last."

Patting my head. Means well. Oh, Lord, he won't be answerable, she thought. *What does he—dark suit, horn-rimmed spectacles, so elegantly patronizing—what does he know about mind rot and chalk dust? Bathtub composition?*

"I wonder, Sister Claire, if—since we have you here"—(*like a lion,* she thought, *caged?*)—"if you might tell us whether you find, as a twelfth-grade teacher of some distinction, the same problems with illiteracy and creeping slovenliness in the art and discipline of composition that I am sure my fellow professors here all meet in the first and, yes, even in the second year and later on the university campus?"

Waiting. Poised. *My words of wisdom,* she thought. *Illiteracy.*

"Yes," she replied tentatively. "We're certainly in no way exempt from what seems to be the general human condition." Professor Zanzibar had turned sideways to watch her. She caught a gleam from his eye. Blue-gray tweed was sending smoke her way. "I think problems in composition—rhetoric as you might prefer to call it—*are* universal, aren't they?"

"Ah, yes, well, I suppose you might say that"—he was stroking his chin thoughtfully—"but then there is the long-standing opinion, prejudice, you might call it"—he smiled deferentially—"certainly a *happy* prejudice, that students in parochial schools . . ." He seemed to be stumbling, a bit embarrassed.

"You mean that if nothing else we teach them grammar?"

She grinned at the appreciative ripple throughout the room. The bearded man in front of her exchanged an approving look with the lady on his right.

"Well, now, certainly not only that. . . . I have admired the disciplined control of many students from your schools, which no doubt is intrinsically connected with your overall program and with your"—he bowed respectfully—"disciplined way of life. But do you feel, Sister, that the disintegration of various forms of discourse, the inability of our university students to express themselves in plain English, to communicate effectively, is partly the consequence of earlier training? In other words, are we too late?" He caressed his chin.

You were too late before you ever began, she thought. Drip drip drip. *Let me tell you of my bathtub orgy. Discipline with a new twist. Could* you *comprehend, much less communicate with, a convent spook?*

Professor Zanzibar shot her a glance. She knew that eye. Although they had never openly acknowledged as much, it said what he had conveyed through the margins months before: come on, Sister, *show him.* As before, he buoyed her failing confidence.

"I am afraid I'm not really competent to answer further since I haven't taught in college. I do think, of course, that there's a connection between earlier training and later performance." The beard before her was blowing smoke rings. She felt a certain appraising curiosity in his look. Zanzibar's gleam continued. "I'm only experimenting in a modest way, of course. But I have found that the most basic incentive to actually writing well and, for that matter, speaking well, is to have some sense of your audience."

"Ah . . . indeed so."

Her questioner paused. She could feel him winding up, storing breath to *go on.*

"And my sense of the audience at this moment," she dared, taking courage from the eyes about her, "is that they would like to stretch and have coffee."

Laughter outright.

Professor Zanzibar was on his feet in a moment. Vindicated.

"Perhaps we could defer any further questions until over coffee. I am sure Sister Claire will be glad to visit with any of you then."

The one thing she hadn't anticipated. How could the real horror of the lion's den turn out to be refusing a cup of coffee, denying those eager hands?

"No coffee? Would you prefer tea, Sister?" Solicitude. Graciousness.

How to explain you weren't allowed to eat with *seculars?* That it had always been this way since the novitiate? That you couldn't eat with your own mother if she came to visit you? The students absorbed such absurdities and took them for granted: the way things were. Every world has its own absurdities. But this was different. No way to explain to people who met you only this once. Tone failed. No form of rhetoric explained this elusive distinction between sharing a thought and sharing a teacup. The fact remained it was forbidden.

She found herself marooned in polite conversation with the few around her, hiding her hands in her loose sleeves in lieu of holding a coffee cup. Professor Zanzibar, denied the comfort of serving her coffee or annotating her margins, puttered about her nervously. Conversation focused briefly on her remarks, then eased off into exchange about problems in university, changing student attitudes, alumni contributions, the state budget, tax breaks.

Where is Reverend Mother? she thought hopelessly. Then, as bodies parted briefly, she spotted her superior two clumps of people away.

Coffee in hand. Still flanked by her two men. Flushed. Animated. Nibbling.

"Thank you. Excuse me, but I think we really do have to leave. It was very kind of you to invite me."

She smiled at smiles, met hands briefly, then followed the path cut by Professor Zanzibar, who was relieved to have found the function of plough.

"Yes, we are very proud of our younger sisters," Reverend Mother was mouthing to two sets of half-glazed eyes. Sister Claire saw it in an instant. Innocent. "Sister Claire, we were proud of you!" Reverend Mother smiled encouragingly, wiping tiny crumbs from the corner of her mouth. "And I must say I'm certainly glad you brought me down here with you . . ." She smiled at her court, then at the larger crush of bodies about them, drinking, smoking.

"Reverend Mother, if you want to make your afternoon appointment, I think we'd better go now. No telling what the traffic will be on the highway."

"Indeed," chimed in one of Reverend Mother's charmers. "And do you drive, Sister?" Half interest, concealed curiosity.

"Yes, I've always kept my license." Continuities: there are such things.

"Reverend Mother, I do think we should go."

It was done quickly. Professor Zanzibar saw them to the door of the room, bowed them out chivalrously.

"It has been our pleasure."

Dense traffic. Chirpy Reverend Mother. Sister Claire's knees felt like water. But Reverend Mother's obvious pleasure in having been introduced to the world of higher learning insulated them both from the kinds of strain that might have followed the meeting. Claire felt too tired to be furious, too empty to be actively disappointed. One moment she had enjoyed: her puncture of the windbag. Another she had hated, still writhed under the memory of—refusing coffee out of scruple. Not even scruple, really. The sense that it wouldn't do to break a rule with Reverend Mother there. Cowardice. And then—betrayed.

As the large station wagon slowed to a stop in front of the convent, Reverend Mother turned to her, chirpiness abated. Her face had recomposed itself into lines that fit the keeper of eternal verities. The set of jaw was resolute.

"Sister, now that we're home I would like to say something to you that I did not want to bring up before your speech today. . . ."

Sister Claire suppressed the impulse to turn off the ignition, and kept her foot lightly on the pedal, idling cautiously. *Now* it would come. She had been reported. Old seed-eyes had done her duty.

"You have looked extremely tired this week, and I am concerned about you. I have reason to believe you haven't been getting enough sleep. . . ."

"I have been a bit tired, Reverend Mother, but now that this is over I can relax a bit. I would have liked a good strong cup of coffee after the talk, but"—a long, steady look passed between them—"perhaps there's some left in the pantry."

Reverend Mother was suddenly very busy collecting her skirt and purse. She hesitated slightly, then pushed down the car door handle.

"There are times, Sister, when we must make certain adjustments to meet the world. I know you are mature enough to understand that." She slammed the door behind her with a set smile.

Nosing carefully into the garage, Sister Claire considered the unspoken equation of midnight disobedience and a forbidden cup of coffee. Surely the lost delights of Eden hardly weighed in such a balance. She felt dull with fatigue.

Carefully she let down the heavy garage door and turned the handle until it caught. Then, heading up the hill beneath the bleak February sky, suddenly and urgently she longed to hear what Sister Mark had been doing all day.

Cloister

She hated going for permissions. One would have thought that, like most repeated exercises in any life, she would have gotten used to this one. She, too, had originally thought that, over the years, kneeling in front of superior after superior. Reciting her needs, receiving her permissions, giving an account of her regularity of observance, she would have gotten used to it—like other rituals that originally had been a hurdle in religious life: chanting a lesson at Matins, being first chorister, preparing for chapter, reading in the refectory. But none of these, absolutely none, made her stomach churn like this monthly exercise. She was happy when the superior was sick—though she knew she shouldn't be and felt a bit guilty about it. She was happy when the superior was away. She was happy, in fact, when any turn of Providence interfered with her obligation to summarize her inner life verbally to her superior and await her response.

As she sat in line outside Reverend Mother's office—any Reverend Mother, though there were better and worse—she sometimes felt she might vomit. Every three years superiors could be shifted to other houses in the province or have their term renewed in the same house. Reverend Mother Rachel, superior at St. Gertrude's since Claire's arrival there, was suddenly, abruptly gone, transferred to St. Martin's in New Jersey, a flourishing private girls' high school. Their new superior, Reverend Mother Dolores, seemed reserved and cautious. She had been with them just six months. Perhaps having Mother Provincial, the head of the whole province, living in the same house made Reverend Mother Dolores nervous.

Mother Provincial, a woman of slight education, easy enthusiasms, and impulsive kindness, was caught these days in her own web of complexities. After Vatican II there were bound to be changes. A circular had already come from Mother General in Rome advising each province to solicit suggestions in all the houses for a change in the habit. There would be a general chapter in 1966 in Rome. Several college nuns were becoming more outspoken, particularly since reading Cardinal Suenens's *The Nun in the World.* Nothing in Mother Provincial's makeup or training had prepared her for quite these developments. She was keeping a careful watch on her province. And although they saw little of her, since she and her secretary lived in a separate wing of the house when they were not away making visitations, even a fleeting glimpse revealed that their provincial was looking tired these days.

For her part, as she sat outside her new superior's office door, Sister Claire had one strong desire: to get through this. She had developed a range of strategies for coping with permissions. She must not think of the encounter about to occur; she must not try to read. She saw others making their spiritual reading as they waited, and she wondered at her own inability. The haunted dark eyes of Teilhard de Chardin looked at her from the back of Sister Andrew's book. Didn't she mind this task? Were others really as placid as they appeared when they emerged from the office, nodded, and headed into chapel to say the penance imposed for this month's faults? Was she the only one whose insides contracted, who felt dampness gather along her spine? She must be lacking something.

The door opened. Sister Anne limped out, a trifle flushed, nodded toward her, and passed by into the chapel.

Sister Claire stared a moment at the closed office door, grasped her notebook firmly, and got up to knock.

"Yes, Sister?"

The voice from within.

Acting quickly as she had learned was wisest, she opened the door and then shut it tightly behind her. She knelt beside the superior's desk.

"Reverend Mother, may I please have your blessing?"

Reverend Mother leaned forward to press the sign of the cross on the crown of her subject's head.

"I humbly beg you to renew my permissions for the following. . . ." Claire moved rapidly through her list of requests for things needed: toothpaste, deodorant, an extra supply of notecards and a file, a new winter nightgown, aspirin. This part was easiest: simple material needs. The answer was yes or no. Invariably it was yes.

"Yes, Sister." Reverend Mother sat quietly, hands folded loosely in her ample black lap. Long, tapering fingers with perfectly groomed nails, hands that seemed unacquainted with manual labor.

"And, Reverend Mother"—looking up from her notebook— "I have felt especially fortunate this month. My prayer life has been peaceful. I'm meditating on the gospel text for each day, as that seems most fruitful." She hated the sound of her voice. Sometimes when she got to this section of the renewal formula, she reported no graces. But she had learned it was wisest to have a few now and then; declaring one's desolation of soul had proved more nuisance than it was worth. In her curious moments she wondered what personal graces the worst community characters noted and reported; more often she regretted a prevailing sense of irony within herself that undercut her own attempts at simplicity.

"I'm glad, Sister. Meditating on the gospel always brings us closer to Our Lord. And if you are experiencing a period of consolation, thank God. But remember, God sometimes allows dryness in those who are His favorite souls. We must be prepared to accept all from His hand with gratitude."

The pale elegant hands resting before her magnetized her attention momentarily until she looked upward, directly into the small, deep-set eyes behind Reverend Mother's thick glasses. How could she admit that it was absolutely impossible for her to stay awake for the hour from six to seven these cold mornings, that the most dramatic New Testament texts left her dull of mind and heavy with sleepiness, longing for Father to arrive for Mass so she could move about legitimately, leave her place, go to the choir loft, turn on the organ, and prepare the hymns. It brought relief to put her hands on the keys, to wake herself up with music. Two days a week she was permitted to play for Mass.

"I would like to ask your permission to see Father Purcell, Reverend Mother. It's been quite a few months, and I do feel the need."

She did not elaborate that need. Superiors differed, and she did not yet know this one. With most it was wiser to leave needs acknowledged but undetailed.

"Well, Sister . . . You have been out quite a bit lately. And we must never become careless about our rule of cloister, difficult as that may be in today's world." She looked at the kneeling nun significantly, as if they both understood that magic measure of time out and time in that constituted a well-balanced religious life in the year of Our Lord 1963. Rules were becoming shaky. Bishops were fighting it out in Rome. "Would you wish to go this week? Holy Week is a particularly busy time for everyone.

As you know, Father will be saying Mass here on Holy Thursday."

Her heart sank. She did not want to see him here. She knew well the difficulties of maintaining any kind of private life within the cloister. Not that anyone would comment openly. But inevitably there was curiosity. Beneath its palpable silence and discretion, the house breathed a lively alertness to sounds and voices from the guest parlor. The kitchen would be notified. Ginger ale and cookies for Father. A paper doily on the plate. Reverend Mother would stop by to greet him.

"Yes, I know, Reverend Mother. But there will be so much commotion here on Holy Thursday. The procession, reposition, the special dinner. He'll have enough to think of then without my adding to it." A motive of charity—that should do it.

"True. How would you get over to see him at the university then? Can you find a companion?"

"There is a car going over tomorrow." She had checked it all out and knew that technically there was little Reverend Mother could object to in her request. Other nuns would be in the car; they would qualify as companions. Her right to a spiritual director was guaranteed by the Constitutions—a right that the Order did not, in fact, encourage her to exercise.

Not that she actually claimed Father Purcell as a spiritual director. Nothing that grandiose. He was simply an intelligent priest, one of the best-educated and most understanding people she knew. He seemed to embody a freedom of spirit; at least she felt that must be what made him so attractive to many in the Order, old and young. And he served them with astonishing fidelity: early Mass every morning, confessions before Mass, sermons—memorable ones—on Sunday. He had been doing it for years and was by now a familiar figure to most of the nuns in the province. Over the past two or three years he had done the retreat circuit from Vermont to Washington, D.C., and somehow he could make even the Exercises come to life for those eight days. When he interpreted them, the Ignatian metaphors of warfare made sense—no small feat.

"Well, if you feel that for the good of your soul this is the time you should go, Sister, then see if there is room for you in the car. You can let me know tomorrow after breakfast, or just drop a note in my box."

Reverend Mother sat very still, hands resting quietly. She peered through her glasses, waiting. Sister Claire was familiar with that pause, and she steadied herself to resist. It was the invitation to confide. She was not obliged, strictly speaking, but she was encouraged. Her inner life was her own personal affair—the Order recognized that—but then again, they had been trained since the earliest novitiate days to see all superiors as God's representatives and more—spiritual mothers whose care it was to guide their subjects toward sanctity. How could that be done without mutual trust? The question often troubled her.

She wanted to be a good religious; she detested hypocrisy. Yet, when it came right down to it, ever since leaving the novitiate, she had resisted revealing her interior life, such as it was, to each successive superior. Superiors varied. Counting Mother Theodore, the novice mistress, Sister Claire was now facing her fifth. She had learned that what one Reverend Mother saw as freedom of spirit another might judge a lapse in obedience. Caution was therefore in order. Claire regretted that necessity. She craved light. This watchfulness cast a shadow. This was not living in the wide-eyed trust as a child of God. This was living another way, darker, more obscure.

She scanned her notes on regularity of observance, notes that fatigued her with their cumulative innocuousness. They were allowed to report only external faults. Sin was reserved for the confessional.

"Reverend Mother, I have failed in several ways this month in observing the rule and constitutions. I feel I've given in to my curiosity and disedified my sisters by carelessness in religious modesty. Especially during Office I have looked around a good bit."

"Yes, Sister. A few of your sisters have mentioned this to me." Reverend Mother leaned forward slightly, raising one hand to touch the wooden crucifix in her cincture. "It is very easy to become careless about mortification of the senses. Yet Our Lord rewards those who curb their curiosity about the outer world by speaking to them within. Unless we quiet worldly curiosity and mortify the tendency to look about, we shall never hear Him when He speaks."

Sister Claire held her expression steady. The inner voice. She thought of Saint Bernard looking the other way as he passed the beauties of Lake Desanzano, Saint Somebody spitting out his tongue at the temptress. She remembered Keats's nightingale and Stevens's Ursula. God was about, that she believed. Where should she look to find Him? Yet, Reverend Mother was right. God spoke to the soul in silence, not noise. There had come that final crucial moment when, kneeling in the college chapel during her senior year, praying that she would know, she felt in the depths of her soul a stirring . . . a sense. That stirring—call it a voice—touched the subtle thread of her own most deeply felt freedom. "I want you," He said. And on her free response in that moment hung her future, her life. Perhaps her eternity. She was prepared. She had responded *"in toto corde."* That had been the moment of her true profession.

But this was not something you revealed to any old superior. Why should you? It was between God and you in the sacred spaces of the soul. Some secrets resist the claim of any outer power—be it religious or secular. In moments of pain and confusion she returned in spirit to that one moment. She trusted its truth—as if in the ineluctable onward movement of days, of life, that one sacred anchor of her spirit would secure her fast to her God, her vocation.

"Is there anything else, Sister?" asked Reverend Mother, glancing at the clock.

The line outside was long. That might help her cause.

"I've been wondering if you and Reverend Mother Provincial have decided whether I may accept the invitation to the Eastern Linguistics Conference this June?"

Once more she resisted the urge to elaborate her request.

The invitation had come weeks ago. She was one of three religious invited, the only Agnetine. The others were secular scholars from name universities in the East. This might mean nothing to Reverend Mother Dolores. It was too early to tell how she would evaluate some opportunities. She had a reputation in the province as a woman of prayer and of caution. Beyond that, Claire knew little except that she did encourage them to follow everything that was happening at the Vatican Council. In the real order of things, of course, that might count for little.

"I noticed last Monday, Sister, that you received a request in the mail for final acceptance or rejection. It's June when, did you say?" She picked up the small desk calendar from her blotter and carefully turned over the pages to June.

"June fifteenth to twentieth, Reverend Mother." Her right knee had begun to tingle. She had given all this information to Reverend Mother weeks ago. Shifting her weight slightly, Sister Claire fought a rising sense of irritation.

"Right during retreat. Father McDonald arrives on the fourteenth."

She fought a surge of anger. She had suspected right along that the answer would ultimately be no. This summer it would be someone else's turn to take a university course. She had planned to study a bit on her own, practice the organ, devote herself to the community. She would learn a Bach fugue.

Then—with no warning—had come this invitation. After asking permission and waiting a couple of weeks, she had written one courteous note to the chairman apologizing for her delay and implying a conflict of plans yet to be settled. How could she say that Mother Provincial was a chronic procrastinator, that perhaps this new Reverend Mother distrusted her motives and saw her desire as self-seeking? All outgoing mail was put in Reverend Mother's box unsealed. Improprieties of tone never passed. So her letter had been brief and noncommittal. Then she had waited. Bided her time and bitten her tongue. She was beginning to feel acutely embarrassed about the whole affair. *How would it make the Order look?*

"Should I notify them no, Reverend Mother?" In a way it would be a relief to be done with it all, though she wanted to attend. She'd been experimenting all year with Roberts's *English Sentences* in her ninth-grade class. That very subject would be dealt with at the conference.

"Mother Provincial will be back from her visitation in New Jersey on Sunday, Sister. We should surely have a definite decision for you by then. Is there anything else?" She began to finger her crucifix.

"No, I don't think so, Reverend Mother. I humbly beg you to give me a penance."

"Say three Hail Marys, Sister."

Again the light pressure on her head.

Sister Claire opened the door and nodded to the next in line; she headed for chapel to say the penance immediately.

The next afternoon, waiting outside Father Purcell's office, she sat quietly on the straight chair and watched the secretary. Obviously an expert in mediating between Father and both his worlds, academic and religious, she typed efficiently, ignoring Sister Claire. The telephone rang.

"No, I'm sorry, Father Purcell is busy all afternoon. Would you care to try again in the morning? He should be in after his nine o'clock class. Thank you."

Laconic replies, thought Sister Claire, so no one waiting could glean whether Father, in the inside office, was dealing with matters of soul or modern languages.

As chairman of the university's modern-language department, he was highly regarded. His active professional life gave him access to a variety of thresholds, and he crossed these with enviable ease. Sister Claire respected that, as did his colleagues. Several of his books were in the convent library signed with his distinctive flourish. He was being consulted by *periti* at the Council. Yet, considerable professional acclaim did not seem to have affected his religious commitment. His sermons—brief, explicit, based on the Gospel—always contained some kernel of human meaning that reached her. She thought of their many laughs over breakfast, his breakfast, during the months she had been charged with serving him after he finished saying morning Mass.

The first time had been a nightmare. She had never had that charge before and although she was not particularly shy, contact with priests had been strictly limited to confessional, retreats, or Mass. She had never been sacristan.

The day before she was to take over the charge, she left Mass early and followed her predecessor through the routine. They put coffee on immediately in the tiny pantry outside the priests' dining room.

"Father likes it *hot,*" emphasized Sister Marion as she carried a small pitcher of cream from the little refrigerator into the dining room and set it by his cereal bowl. "He'll drink three cups, the last with his cigarette after breakfast. He likes to be left alone for that. If he wants company, he'll make it clear."

They hurried downstairs to the kitchen for eggs. The cook was primed to have them ready for seven-forty, two over easy, yokes unbroken. She never failed. At Christmas and Easter Father sent for her to congratulate her in person, and she loved it.

"He likes them soft but not runny," whispered Sister Marion as they panted back up the stairs and down the long empty corridor to the priests' dining room. "I try to make it back up here before the nuns leave chapel. Otherwise you'll get stuck on the stairs waiting for the line to pass, and the eggs get cold."

Back in the pantry she plugged in the toaster with one practiced hand, took the cover off the eggs with the other, then hurried in to Father. He was halfway through his cereal. Sister Claire heard guffaws of laughter as she waited outside in the pantry, buttering his toast, preparing his coffee, and mentally rehearsing her debut the following morning.

That morning had been a disaster. She had somehow gotten herself trapped on the staircase. As she stood there waiting for the silent black line to pass, she could almost feel the heat leaving the carefully prepared eggs. Back then to the pantry. He was already in the dining room. She knocked lightly on the door frame and hurried in, carrying the pitcher of cream she had forgotten to put on the table after she started the coffee. Obviously, he had been waiting; the cereal was untouched.

"Good morning, Father." Not really looking at him.

"Well!" He set down his cigarette, exhaling slowly. "So you're the new one." Looking her up and down attentively, he laughed shortly. "I'm difficult, you know. But you'll grow to like me."

The cream pitcher clattered against the saucer as she set it near his right hand. A large hand, she couldn't help noticing, with blunt clean nails and blond hairs covering its back. It expertly tapped the accumulated ash from the cigarette it held.

"I'll get your eggs, Father. My name is Sister Claire."

"Yes, I know," he replied. "Don't worry. Marion primed me about you."

She hurried back to the pantry and grabbed the eggs and coffee in confused haste. Toast would have to wait. "Marion." For that she had not been prepared. *Marion!* Would he call her Claire? How should she respond? It irritated her not to know. The good-humored masculine sound of his voice in the confessional before morning Mass had always pleased her with its subtle blend of intimacy and respect. This was somehow different. It touched a nerve, awakened a response she had thought dead.

Men—the big taboo.

Returning to graduate study after the novitiate had brought her back to the world of men. On campus at the university and in class the junior nuns must meet them, be with them. Learn from them, even. No longer were the only men in their lives priests on the altar. Mother Jerome, the superior at the house of studies, scrupulously careful of their formation, was, as Claire even then perceived, warped on the subject of men. She warned her nuns, cautioned them. No talking to men. No casual exchanges. As little contact as possible. If there was a verbal exchange, report it to her.

Yet, when Sister Claire had found herself in Romantic Poetry class with a humorous jean-clad fellow who joked with her and reminded her of her older brother, she liked it. And laughed with him. Ignoring the twinge of guilt, for she judged it inane. And when her Modern Literature professor stopped her to comment on her work, it warmed her. In teaching, she had always gotten along well with her students' fathers. She liked their banter. Her own father had indulged in practical jokes, loved a witty turn of phrase.

And now . . . in this strangely half-domestic setting, she was offering no stole and chasuble to a priest, but cereal and coffee to a man. That's what he made her feel.

He was challenging her.

Why?

She had bungled through that morning—burnt toast, cold eggs, embarrassed inexperience—and had escaped as fast as she could, angry at herself and him. Bristling. She couldn't stand him. She had not been prepared to feel anything in executing her charge except the usual nervousness at beginning something new. Instead, he bothered her. He teased her, making her feel awkward and embarrassed. His tone struck her as annoyingly familiar, and she left the dining room feeling hot, confused, vaguely troubled or exhilarated, relieved to be done with it for the morning. Then the pressures of the school day would claim her consciousness—until the next morning came and she knelt through Mass with half her mind anticipating what was to come afterward.

Yet, as days passed and she got beyond the toast-burning stage, he grew strangely deferential. He asked her opinion. He refused to let her be overly serious, but when they discovered a common interest in linguistics, he talked about it with her. They discussed new approaches to language. He seemed to respect her mind. Gradually she concluded that his initial aggressiveness had been a maneuver to shake her preconceptions so that he might talk to her simply as a person, regardless of her habit. Or perhaps her own judgment of what constituted aggressiveness was not to be trusted. She was inexperienced in such areas; she distrusted her responses, for she was aware of her own highly conditioned outlook. Even so, there was something oddly seductive about it all.

His approach flattered her. He made her feel like a woman. She began, gradually, to look forward to those brief daily encounters, planning ahead what she might talk to him about the next day. Then, after eight months, her charge had been changed. Now no longer the easy casualness of assigned task and daily meeting: she had to ask permission and make appointments. *That* she hated.

"Father will see you now, Sister Claire." The secretary nodded toward the closed door and resumed her typing.

When she entered, he was leaning way back in his chair, feet on the desk. It was a small office, rather dark, lined with crammed bookcases and filing cabinets. A faint smell—the mixture of newsprint, tobacco, and other, indefinable odors—met her. Next to his feet, the desk was littered with loosely stacked papers, batches of mail, unemptied ashtrays, a telephone. On the floor beside the desk lay a newspaper folded carelessly, as if just dropped there.

"Come on in, Claire." He waved her toward the straight chair near the desk. "Make yourself comfortable." Then he surveyed her closely through the smoke he was calmly exhaling. "Want a cigarette?"

It was a joke between them. Everything was changing these days. Daily bulletins from Rome meant anything could happen. She laughed and quickly sat down, remembering that, yes, she had shut the door behind her. Surely the secretary knew how offhand Father could be. Still, it was habit with Claire to remember which doors she had shut and which were still open.

"Mmmm." He drew deeply on the cigarette with exaggerated pleasure. "Few satisfactions like it, Claire. You women don't know what you're missing. It helps one love one's neighbor to see him through a cloud of smoke!" Three perfectly symmetrical rings glided softly upward. She understood that if she said yes he would simply give her one and light it gallantly for her. This knowledge alone freed her of any such desire. Besides, she had never been a smoker.

"Well, Claire, you're looking a bit piqued. How's life treating you?"

His way of asking disarmed her momentarily and made her want to talk.

"Really, Father, you know just about how it goes. I'm still waiting for the answer about the Conference."

He slammed down both feet and stood up abruptly. "That's part of it, is it? By God, I wish they'd wake up!" Moving out from behind the desk and rustling the newspaper as he brushed by it, he stalked about the small office. "Do you mean to say that Provincial of yours still hasn't made up her mind about such a simple request? Why on earth is there any problem? This is 1963—not the Middle Ages!"

She felt again the ridiculous explosion of hopelessness and anger. She had thought it well under control—had, in fact, prayed hard to be spared showing how strongly she felt about this. Why had she brought it up immediately? It was stupid to get so upset. Yet, the fact was that she could not reconcile herself just to writing off the whole matter as God's will. That very phrase puzzled her—as if His will were some frozen block of meaning that could be invoked by authority at their will. How on earth did one know God's will? She had *known* it only once, in the college chapel, in the depths of her soul.

What galled her especially about the present issue was the Order's apparent blindness to its own best interests. "Make unto yourselves friends of the mammon of iniquity . . ." Not that this was the mammon of iniquity. Used wisely, however, the Conference could be a great help to the Order in planning future programs for its own schools as well as developing contacts with the larger professional world outside. It was important, even for high school teachers, to keep abreast of what was going on in their fields. She knew that probably Father Purcell had put in a good word for her. Surely it was ultimately due to him that she had been invited. He was well known in those circles. Of course he never told her this outright; he was delicate about such matters. But she surmised.

"You know how it is with us, Father. You've been around the province. The official line in the Order is commitment to learning. And they've made it good in many ways. All the nuns in this province have at least a B.A. and many of them have a master's before even stepping into a first-grade classroom. That's a real achievement. . . . But there are problems. Mother Provincial is so easily threatened. She never got through college herself, though that's never said out loud. And she's appointed a Council that won't threaten her, four superiors from small communities who themselves have never even taught high school and have been out of any classroom for years. She's been moving them around from house to house for the past six or seven years. On top of all that, now she's got a new superior at St. Gertrude's, and that's never been the easiest community to govern. Add to this a general chapter to prepare for. And at the college rumor has it some of the younger nuns are giving trouble. You can't escape the feeling that things are going to change after Vatican Two is over." She smiled briefly. "We've lots of discussion in community about 'issues'—largely about the hemline of the new habit!"

She rested one elbow on the desk and succumbed to a sudden rush of weariness. Within the past month they'd had four community discussions on "Christian Maturity"—time stolen from class preparation. The question of papal enclosure was a vexed one . . . and traveling with companions . . . and not eating with seculars . . . customs that had gone unquestioned in community for generations, centuries even. Discussions were going on in all the houses—controlled discussions, of course. Reverend Mother Dolores had asked them all to meditate on the chapter of Holy Rule that dealt with obedience. They must prepare themselves, she said, to respond to the directives from the Council Fathers, to follow Saint Ignatius's rules for thinking with the mind of the Church. A mind which, she did not add, seemed deeply divided on so many crucial issues.

Sister Claire's fatigue was out of proportion to the question at hand, and she knew it. *Permission to attend one measly linguistics conference!* There were larger issues, to be sure. But somehow, she felt it instinctively, this small question connected with them. How exactly did you compartmentalize a life intended to be lived as a whole?

Father Purcell stopped moving about the office and stood squarely in front of her. "Look, Claire," he said, "it isn't a case of a religious principle being at stake. It's just a question of common sense. You'll learn something at this conference. And you've got something to give." He made her feel warm inside. "Are they afraid they'll lose you if they let you out?"

She did not answer. The question did not really seem to touch her. She had vowed her fidelity forever. "*In toto corde.*" It seemed to her that in a world of change it was a marvelous grace to have one fixed point of reference—one center. His question did not engage her mind. It touched her *feelings* . . . the overpowering sense of hollowness that yawned inside her—like the hunger that came after long Lenten fast, or the strange silent blank that opened within her at the end of the school year when she went back to clean her classroom. Empty desks, empty closets, nameless, faceless room. Cherished identities vanished, personal challenge dead. It was too suddenly quiet, too totally empty. Later on in the summer that emptiness would turn a different way and begin to feel familiar and deeply peaceful to her. Then even the tiny particles of dust suspended lazily in slats of afternoon sun across empty varnished desks would become warm, silent friends of her summer solitude. But that came later. Before that stage there was this kind of emptiness . . . the intimacies of the classroom gone—the open summer to face.

Deep inside she could feel now the beginning of tears. She prayed for composure. His understanding touched her; blindness was easier to handle.

"Well, anyway . . ." She stopped, swallowing. The lump in her throat grew monstrous. There must be another topic, some way to turn their attention from her. She felt him looking at her and longed for instant invisibility. He was a big man, squarely built. Early middle age seemed only to have intensified the impression of solid strength his body conveyed. She felt the power of that body. *Body*—the problem of life. *Body*—that she had sought to tame, to rule. Not because she despised its powers, but because she wanted with her whole being, body included, to serve. She felt now the urgent compelling power of his body near her. "There's not a thing more I can do, so we might as well forget about it. How are things over here? Have you settled your plans for the European trip this summer?" Gulping desperately, she wrenched her mind to another focus. It infuriated her to be held in such a vise of emotion. Had she expected it, she never would have come.

He glanced at her quickly, then started moving about the office again as he lit another cigarette. "It's pretty well set. First, the conference in Lucerne. That looks promising. Spatz will be there to elaborate his new theory of vowel development. And after that I'm on my own. I plan to spend a lot of time in Spain this trip."

She saw herself kneeling before Reverend Mother, wondering if she would get permission to travel four miles for this official visit with a friend (was he a friend?). Beneath clanging emotions lay the other dull, familiar ache of consciousness—the consciousness of irony.

"Do you have friends there?"

"One or two. One especially interesting one . . ." He paused in front of her, blew out smoke, and grinned again broadly. "Met her during my last sabbatical. I never dreamed she'd be in Spain six years later. But there she is! So we'll hook up at some point. Then there are several friends from the scholasticate. We'll find out what we've all turned into, God help us!"

Claire thought of friends from novitiate days, Sister Hilary, Sister Florence, others. She'd give a lot for an unsupervised hour with Sister Hilary, now at the college teaching, of all things, Greek. She hadn't seen her for almost two years—since they'd left Our Redeemer's. Sister Florence was still in Calais. Other friends from the novitiate were sprinkled about the province.

"That's what you need, Claire." He turned away again, musing. "A European trip. Fat chance!" He snorted and stepped behind her.

It was too much. The lump in her throat grew large and heavier—first a wad of cotton she could manage with care, then a marble, then an orange, then a rock that would neither melt nor budge. It would all be over shortly. Bending her head forward, she rested it on her clenched fist and closed her eyes. The tears came—burning, rapid. Hot all over with embarrassment and the effort to control, she sensed his silent form behind her and couldn't bear to look. Just to breathe was a struggle.

"I'm—I'm sorry." Hearing her own ugly choking sound, she gave up.

The silence in the room, heavy and smothering, was broken only by her gasping movements. The hard wood of the desk's surface pressed against her elbow, while from outside came the faint *rat-a-tat-tat* of the secretary's typing. Tears ran down her plastic guimpe, and she thought briefly of what a mess she would be when it was over. Then, through thick emotions, the lump sticking in her throat, the gulps for breath, through her perspiring sense of disintegrating order and clumsy discomfort, she felt a prop. Gently, it held her fast. Closing over her fist so that it grazed her cheek, she felt the rougher texture of a firm, comforting hand, a hand whose male tobacco smell penetrated even her clogged consciousness. She remembered that hand. The arm was tight around her from behind.

Two swings of response vibrated wildly through her tautness—spiraling, subsiding, rising again, fading in a confused blur of contradiction and longing: comfort, panic, comfort. First, a welcome relenting of strained will. Then a stiffening again beneath the wakeful eye of consciousness that warned: be careful, be careful. She felt his strength holding her, and she tried to relent or resist. Impossible either way. Above all, though she couldn't name it then, she felt what she would later recognize as tenderness.

"Now, Claire." The voice was gentle, understanding. She remembered the early morning confessional. It had something of that intimacy, but more. She felt herself a cumbersome confusion of starch and veil. Beneath that—real panic. She could not answer. Nothing was clear. Stilling the urge to react openly, she waited to see.

"Claire." He came around in front of her, bending down, looking close at her messy face. On the breath, tobacco. She could feel it, faintly warm. And some other smell, vaguely sweet and very clean. "You're too tense."

She barely grasped the words; her panic was too deep. Then, on her back, she felt the slightest pressure. He had slipped his other hand under her veil and it pressed beneath her shoulder blades, large and steady. Through the thickness of serge, its power and warmth seemed to press reassurance into her.

As if some secret spot had been touched, some unsuspected reserve spot of her own, resistance rushed through her body, just enough to act. She pushed him back urgently and tried to stand up. Only one thought drummed now at her pounding temples and made her powerful. He did not resist; in fact, after a swift glance at her, he stood back and waited for her to move.

It was embarrassing. There was little to say. Was he merely offering comfort? That question she could not ask. *It was not comfort.* She took out her white handkerchief and silently mopped, straightening her headdress as she did so.

He had turned away and was walking toward the window, lighting another cigarette. It was over. She sensed his reading of her profound rejection. It was over.

"Anyhow . . ." Somehow the burden was on her to pick up the thread. She stood up and grasped the edge of the desk, trying to feel and look in command. Perspiration trickled down her back, and her stomach churned. "I do hope you have a good trip." It sounded lame. Stupid. Silly. She heard it. What did it matter?

He stood, back to her, rhythmically exhaling, and giving her time to compose herself. She glanced at the black breadth of

shoulders and briefly felt their enigma. She knew she had to go.
Quickly.

"Okay, Claire." He turned. His face was serious, quiet, slightly
flushed. He came toward her, one hand in his pocket, the other
holding the cigarette. She was already at the door. Opening it
deftly for her, he nodded toward the secretary outside as she
glanced up inquiringly.

"I'll send you a card from Spain." His voice was steady and
kind.

Why did she feel so angry?

"Thank you, Father." She was aware of the secretary's listening
presence. "Have a good trip." Her voice—she could hear it—
was barely under control. Thin and light, it was the sound of
a stranger from far off, echoing through the opposite end of
a tube.

As she turned and walked past the secretary's desk, she missed
hearing the closing click of his office door, and she registered
vaguely that he must have business in the outside office.

Then she glanced at her watch. In fifteen minutes the car
would be leaving. There was just time to find a ladies' room and
clear away the outer traces of turmoil, lest she feel the pressure
of her companions' discretion as they carefully looked away from
her red eyes and smudges.

Tightening her cincture as she went, she moved purposefully
down the long corridor. Her steps grew quicker and quicker.
Near the end, she paused before a door marked by the silhouette
of a female. Then, grasping its handle, she pushed open the door
and went in.

The
Golden Thread

"Well, it seems to me that K is caught in a treadmill. He can't even remember what it was like before his arrest. We never get a clue. His whole world consists in never getting anywhere."

It was Joellen, the student most eager to jump into any class discussion. She was erratic. She could be brilliant; she could be so far off the track that Sister Claire despaired of ever steering the class back. Today seemed one of her better days.

"You would say, then, that a treadmill is the same as a labyrinth?" Sister phrased her question carefully, holding her tone of voice as neutral as she could.

"I don't know about that. The labyrinth business is more complicated. I mean there *was* a way out of that, right?"

"Ariadne brings the golden thread, remember?" Carla Williams threw the slightly patronizing reminder over her shoulder toward Joellen, who was sitting several rows behind her.

Carla Williams was a neat, mousy girl who usually sat in row one and always did her homework to the last dot. Beneath her pale complexion and limp blond hair she was highly competitive, and she liked nothing better in Sister Claire's class than the chance to expose the limits of Joellen's flashy imagination.

"Exactly. Ariadne brings the thread," she cut in briskly, suppressing the urge to retell the story. They were supposed to know it, and, besides, the test would be on Monday.

"Then what would we identify as the golden thread here? Everyone who offers K help turns out to be on the other side." Joellen threw the question back to Carla, ignoring Sister Claire.

"That, Miss Lynch, is an excellent question. You think about it over the weekend when you review for the examination."

"Now what about *Absalom, Absalom?* Would you say that Faulkner there dramatizes a labyrinth for us?"

They had found the book hard. But they were, after all, a special class, Senior Honors, and should be able to handle first-year college work. She pushed them.

Joellen's hand shot up. Sister Claire looked around for other prospects, then relented.

"Yes, Joellen."

"Isn't the real labyrinth here *time?* I mean not just present time but the past, too. Seems to me that everybody in the whole book is hung up on the problem of time. They're all trapped somehow by their own idea of the past. And how that connects with their present. When you put the whole thing together and try to figure out what Faulkner's getting at . . . he seems to be saying there's just no way you can escape the past. Even at the end Charles Bon comes off as a reincarnation of his grandfather. It's weird. There's just no real progress at all."

"What might *you* mean by real progress, Joellen?" That should hold her for a moment.

"Well, you know. Getting ahead. Understanding where you are and moving on from there."

The class was fidgety. She sensed she might lose them.

"Is there no design in the book then?" She glanced around quickly and saw Leona Smalley in the back row smirking at Ellen Smith. They were bored. Five minutes more of class. "There has to be some kind of design in a labyrinth, though of course it's invisible to the one in it."

"Yea, but Faulkner doesn't give old Sutpen any wings, that's for sure."

A slight titter. The class was tired. It had been a busy week in school, full of activities that had to be over before the examination period, which would begin Monday. She was ready for a break. So were they. She would let them out a few minutes early.

"Very well, girls." She moved to collect her books and papers from the desk. "The examination on Monday will be two hours, as you know."

Groan.

"Will it be objective, Sister?" Joellen again. Always Joellen.

"I told you at the beginning of this course that we would proceed on a college level. It will consist of one essay question which allows room for some subjective interpretation."

"You mean one essay will count the whole thing?" Carla was already calculating.

"One question will count the whole thing."

Leona Smalley looked vacant. The thought of writing one essay for two hours overwhelmed her little mind.

"No identification? No true or false? No multiple choice?"

Sister Claire smiled, savoring a ripple of pleasure in her moment of power. The girls thrived on objective tests and memory work. She prided herself on seeing around that system and giving them a broader experience.

"Good afternoon, girls."

They filed out.

A deadly hour for class, as she had seen from the beginning: Friday afternoon at two o'clock. Sister Claire slowly gathered her books, erased a few scribbles from the board, and left the room.

The late afternoon sun outside was filtering to a thin, frosty glow by the time she picked her way through the catacombs. It was always cold and dark in the winding underground passage that joined school and convent. As far back as anyone could remember, they had called this place the catacombs. Only the nuns used it, since it was part of the cloister. A door off the high school gym read: CLOISTER: DO NOT ENTER—threshold of mystery that spawned a string of tired student jokes over the years.

From there the catacombs led to the basement of the large stone convent. The passage was long and narrow, with even narrower steps winding here and there to accommodate the contours of the slope on which the whole institution had been built. You had to be careful as you moved through. At the other end a door opened into the nuns' laundry room.

The convent building itself was very old, much older than the new high school, and its original plan had placed the kitchen in the basement on the same level with the laundry. This was in the old days when everything, school and convent, fit under one roof. After morning Mass a nun could get breakfast quickly in the kitchen, wash her own dishes, finish laundry chores, run up one flight of stairs for a visit to chapel, and be at her class in no time.

Things had changed: now you had to plan where you would be when. Over the years the convent building itself had expanded—first out, then up. Before long, the nuns outgrew their days of crowding together into the kitchen at mealtime, and food had to be sent by dumbwaiter from the kitchen to the new refectory on the floor above. The jump from ten to twenty-five, then gradually to ninety nuns in one community had made the once-simple tasks of housekeeping formidable. When the last prioress finally consented to automatic dishwashers so the nuns scheduled for dishes could stop being late for night prayer, she had them installed in the small pantry adjoining the long monastic refectory.

The final addition to the convent building had been completed twenty years ago: a fourth floor with two dormitories for the younger nuns, two large bathrooms, and a few single cells for the elderly. At this time a realistic prioress had installed a small elevator for the older nuns, whose numbers were steadily increasing. It was understood to be their strict preserve, and any nun under sixty who entered the creaking vehicle armed herself with an apologetic look. Even then she was liable to hear a sour "Hrumph" as the elevator started.

Sister Claire had learned this the hard way on her first day at St. Gertrude's. She was hurrying from the fourth-floor dormitory to meet her new principal, Sister Stephen. Innocently, she pressed the elevator button and waited. The old metal cage jerked to a stop. She pulled open the heavy outside door, slid back the rickety gate, and stepped in.

"And just where, may I ask, do you think you're going?" rasped a voice from the back corner.

The face might have been chiseled in stone—hollow cheeks and heavy lids etched on the high frontal of some stark medieval cathedral. Deep-set eyes burned out at the offender.

"I—I have an appointment with Sister Stephen." She tried to sound calm. Someone was buzzing for the elevator from below.

"Sister Stephen can wait," declared the wraith. "This elevator is reserved for the older sisters. Sister Stephen herself doesn't take it."

They began to descend. Claire flattened her back against one side of the cubicle. *Who was she?*

"You're one of the new ones," said the nun. "Well, just remember, Sister Claire, we were here before you were born. Don't think you can run this house just because you're fresh from the new house of studies and have your M.A." As she spoke, she pressed a cylinder of nasal decongestant into one nostril and inhaled with a snort.

Slam! The elevator thudded to a stop at the first floor.

"Wait! Don't open it!"

Sister Claire took her hand from the grate.

"You're in music, Sister?"

"No, English. At least I think so. Sister Stephen is going to give me my schedule."

"Do you know who I am, Sister?"

"No, I don't," she had to admit.

"I, Sister Claire, am Sister Hildegarde. I have studied at the Sorbonne." She sniffed from the cylinder again. "I am on the faculty of the high school. I teach French. And I am in charge of all the music in this house." She pushed back the grate and held it, her long black arm stretched across the opening. Her knuckles grew blue, and veins bulged on the back of her thin hand. "Remember, Sister Claire. When one of us needs this elevator, we expect to find it available."

With that, she sailed out.

From rising at 4:55 A.M. to the retiring bell at 9:30 P.M., the rumbling elevator punctuated conventual silence carrying its aging passengers from refectory to chapel to library to Reverend Mother's office to infirmary rooms as they moved through the unchanging rhythm of the daily order and waited for the final ride. Up, down, up, down. Vertical ticktock of passing years, lives measured out in a calculated siege of eternity.

Meanwhile, below, the catacombs—dark, chilly, spidery— continued to be the most popular route to and from school. Quickly and invisibly the younger teaching nuns moved back and forth several times daily for lunch, dinner, examination of conscience, divine office, or simply to answer their convent bells, which could be heard faintly in the high school, if you listened.

By using the catacombs, you could save time in several ways. You seldom got stopped on your way through. Anyone hurrying, as Sister Claire was this minute, obviously wanted to keep moving. Here you were safe from the older nuns, who often relieved their burden of time by whispered monologues that went nowhere and used up precious minutes. Besides, this was not a tempting place to pause, even for the most gregarious who wouldn't hesitate to break silence in warmer spots. In mid-January, when winter had thoroughly penetrated the narrow stone passageway with damp chill, your hands went numb if you delayed. All you wanted to do was to keep moving in whatever direction you were heading. Sister Claire was heading for the refectory for a quick cup of coffee.

She poured herself a cup from the pot that sat all afternoon on the little hotplate in the refectory pantry. Then she headed into the refectory to stand at her place and face the crucifix, as was customary for collation.

The next thing to be gotten through was the weekend. They would all be arriving after supper tonight. She had been given charge of two of the guests, Sister Lucy and Sister Carol from Massachusetts. They would be staying in the fourth-floor dormitory in the two cells next to hers. She had to make their beds, check their cells for essentials, then meet them after supper and make them feel at home. She was not in the mood. She had not even made out her exams yet, and she knew what next week would be with correcting and recording grades. Sister Stephen was a beast about records. But there was no way out. They would be here in about three hours.

One unexpected boon—she might get to see Sister Hilary. Mother Provincial *never* called a provincial meeting in the middle of the school year. In fact, Sister Claire had never before attended a full meeting of representatives from all over the province. Everyone knew it must be important. Several nuns from the college were coming, and Claire had heard that Sister Hilary would be among them. At last—a chance to compare notes on the past two years. They'd not seen each other since good-byes at Our Redeemer's in Calais, where both of them had been sent after the house of studies. They'd started their teaching careers together. From Maine Sister Hilary had been sent to the college where she was teaching Greek. She would have lots to tell . . . if they could just manage time together alone.

Upstairs she paused momentarily at the entrance to the dormitory. Silence absolute. Ten small cells faced each other in two rows like mirror images, their white curtains drawn back on the horizontal iron bars that defined each cubicle. Each cell contained a small metal bed, a washstand, a small wooden chair. On the top of each washstand rested a white enamel basin holding a white enamel pitcher. The hardwood floor, polished to a dull glow, yielded faint warmth to one band of early sunset slanting gently across the cell in the far corner. The rest of the large empty room—implacably sterile, repetitive—offered no clue to the lives it held by night when the single fluorescent light flickered this blankness into a great spook world—darkly silhouetting movements of each silent shape as it poured water into its basin (sound muted by a washcloth spread on the bottom), washed discreetly, slippered to the bathroom in self-contained black, knelt briefly by the bed, then creaked gently in it until the body found the best position for sleep.

Even in Great Silence one felt here the rub of eccentricity, difference. When she reached her cell, Sister James, never one for patience, whipped the curtains shut, clinking the small hooks over the rod with a loud metallic *zing,* to the intense annoyance of her neighbor Sister Mary, who set great store by maintaining recollection during Great Silence and lifted her hooks one by one, noiselessly, as they had been taught in the novitiate. Frequently Sister Cornelius slopped her water just as the retiring bell was ringing. During the night a small cold trickle would reach Sister Suzanne's cell and greet her bare foot next morning as she struggled through smothering folds of sleep to answer the first sound of the rising bell. Over the past few years Sister George had developed the habit of talking to herself in a hoarse whisper. Every morning the whole dormitory could hear her muttering the prayers that went with each item of dress as she put it on: habit, cincture, beads, crucifix, headdress. Once the new simplified habit was decided upon at the general chapter in '66, she would have to change her ritual. So would they all.

The sisters kept their headdresses assembled for a full week, fresh linens being distributed only on Saturday—except for first-class feast days. At night when curtains were drawn and the light was out, a lone wanderer through this cubicled plot would have rustled against rows of hanging religious identities hooked by two wire hangers to the rod of each cell: one for the habit, a long dark heaviness bulging behind the curtains; one strategically bent to hold the assembled headdress, its face opening now vacant, waiting to enclose its wearer's features the next morning. Within each cell the ritual of divestment was similarly arranged: on the chair back the cincture, over the washstand the long heavy rosary, under the pillow the crucifix. A silent night world of curtains, darkness, empty habits, and symmetrically spaced sleeping forms.

None of this showed now in the late afternoon paleness. Only the immaculate facelessness of a vacant dormitory.

Sister Claire spotted the guest cells easily by the towels and bedding piled at the bottom of each bed. Systematically she checked through the things that had been left: small white washcloth and white hand towel, Ivory soap, small notebook and pencil. Then she rapidly set to work.

As she tucked hospital corners, she thought of one morning conference in the novitiate—nine years ago now, but unforgettable. Right after spiritual reading that golden October morning the novices gathered for their usual conference with Mother Theodore, the novice mistress. As they filled in and took their places on the straight chairs lined up in the library, they found that in place of Reverend Mother's desk an unmade cot had been set up. In those days one didn't comment by even a surreptitious whisper about such things. Their observance of silence was scrupulous and, equally fastidious about modesty of the eyes, they studiedly avoided the exchange of quizzical glances such a break in routine would normally evoke.

Then Mother Theodore came in—a stern woman in her early sixties, straight, silent, awesomely detached from the things of this world. Secretly afraid of her uncompromising otherworldliness, in moments of deepest spiritual aspiration they longed to achieve just such detached clarity of vision and practice.

"Sisters," she said after the opening prayer, "I want to impress on you this morning a lesson for your entire religious life." She paused and looked around at their attentive faces. "There is no task too small to do well for the sake of Our Lord." They knew what was coming. "You will read in Rodriguez many examples of the saints taking care in the minutiae of their daily lives to imitate the patience and humility of Our Lord. It is not given to many of us to carry a great cross. But it is in the humble, day-to-day tasks of our religious lives that we must strive to be conformed to Jesus." She paused again, gravely. "Starting with the senior in rank, Sister Jonas, I want each of you to come forward and make and unmake this cot for us this morning."

How stupid and clumsy Sister Claire had felt as she smoothed and tucked, stripped and folded, wanting only to be done. Here they were, in their twenties, getting instructions in bed making! A microcosm of the whole novitiate experience: the painful discovery that all one's ways had to be unlearned, that putting on Christ extended to trivia, was in fact lodged in trivia, that in the willing embrace of such details for His sake lay their hope of one day attaining the third degree of humility. But her father had already insisted on it years before: whatever is worth doing is worth doing well. She was accustomed to striving.

When each sister had finished, they watched in fascinated silence as Mother Theodore, step by step, demonstrated the way to have absolutely *no* wrinkles, *no* raw edges, how and where to tuck in sheets and blankets and, best of all, how to get that infernal white bedspread as smooth as the underneath sheet.

Now Sister Claire automatically reenacted each of the steps blazed into her memory that early October morning in the novitiate library. With a quick expert tuck she pulled the white cotton spread in under the pillow. Not a wrinkle. Then she stood back a moment for one last check. Everything in order. Time for Office.

"But no warning!" said Sister Lucy as she stirred her coffee in its Styrofoam cup. It was the next morning and the opening conference was over. She and Sister Claire were standing in the back of the high school auditorium where a table had been set up for coffee break. "Never a word that this might be coming!"

She pushed the wooden stirrer around and around and stared at it, mesmerized. "How shall we ever explain to the students?"

"There's no easy way it can be explained at all," replied Sister Claire, stifling her impatience at this somewhat silly nun who was her responsibility for the weekend. Sister Lucy had a simpering personality; that had been clear the moment they met the evening before. She had ooh-ed and ah-ed her way through the old convent and new high school with that predictable kind of enthusiasm that suggests congenital blindness rather than a discerning eye.

She was younger than Sister Claire, perhaps twenty-four or twenty-five, and taught third grade at Holy Family Academy in Wilbraham, Massachusetts. One could imagine her waxing enthusiastic over Red Rover. Her thick, round glasses gave the light eyes behind them a kind of blank solemnity, and in shape she was something of a dumpling. Since last night Sister Claire had conscientiously shepherded her about. Her second charge, Sister Carol, a much more experienced and independent type, had wasted no time in finding old friends from around the province who were also there for the weekend. Sister Claire was left with this pliant lump of meaningless sociability.

"I thought when we were chosen to come to this meeting as delegates from our communities we would learn something about a new school opening up," said Sister Lucy. "Or a new educational program, maybe, maybe a new novitiate even. Why, just last week I told our parents—I'm in charge of our Parents Club in Wilbraham, you know—I told our parents at our monthly meeting something about the distinguished history of our Order, how it had famous schools in Europe in the seventeenth and eighteenth centuries, and all sorts of things like that. *You* know." She poured another bit of cream from the pitcher next to the coffee urn. "I just wonder how they'll take it." Stirring again, she peered curiously at Sister Claire. "You don't seem too upset. Did you have some warning?" Sister Claire concentrated on pouring her coffee. She was glad her inner turmoil didn't show, for she felt vulnerable to such bumbling intrusions.

She did not want to be standing here stirring coffee and making conversation with this person. She wanted to be off with Sister Hilary, discussing the meeting, hearing what she was thinking— what she was feeling. Their one chance, and here she was, stuck with this dumpling. There was no way out. The others had wandered off from the now-empty auditorium where they had all gathered an hour before for Reverend Mother Provincial's opening remarks.

"We've had no warning," she replied laconically, then roused herself to try harder. "In fact our enrollment went up slightly in the high school this year. We have an excellent academic program here." She tried to remember no more; Joellen Lynch's bright face slid before her mind's eye.

"I'm sure that's true," said Sister Lucy, sipping. "Well, in Wilbraham, of course, our school is new. But there's so much adventure connected with a new school! And the parents are so grateful and enthusiastic to have a parochial school in the area at last. . . ." Her voice trailed off vaguely.

Sister Claire tried to relish the slightly bitter and too-cool coffee she swished in her mouth.

"But it has all seemed so promising." Sister Lucy went on. "I had my parents up recently. They stayed in a nearby motel and Reverend Mother even let them visit my classes." She smiled, unaware that her companion had stopped listening. "Then we all did a little program for them. The children were very sweet."

This can't go on, thought Sister Claire desperately. *Just a few moments before the next meeting.*

"I hate to do this, Sister, but I'm afraid I'll have to leave you alone for a few minutes. Reverend Mother asked me to tend to something before the next conference begins." She pulled out her watch. "And I see now I have only ten minutes. I hadn't realized it was so late."

"Oh, that's all right. I'll just sit here and save your seat. I'll get in a little spiritual reading while I wait." She patted her copy of the history of the Order she had brought with her.

Sister Claire left the auditorium rapidly. She tried several classrooms before finding an empty one. In most, clusters of nuns were sitting or standing about, chattering excitedly. Finally she found a deserted room and collapsed at a desk in the rear, away from the door, to collect herself. Hilary could be anywhere. And they had only a few moments left.

Into their world of ordered living Reverend Mother Provincial had dropped a bombshell that morning. With no warning.

After breakfast Claire had led Sister Carol and Sister Lucy through the catacombs to the high school auditorium where all the conferences would be held. The rule of silence lifted for the day, the nuns were clustered about in small whispering groups, friends hailing friends from other houses and gradually settling themselves in the front rows to await Mother Provincial. Sister Claire spotted Sister Hilary with a group of college nuns on the far side of the auditorium. Curiosity vibrated through the ranks. What was this meeting for?

Finally Mother Provincial arrived and took her place at the small table on the stage. After the prayer she began immediately to read from the sheaf of papers before her.

"My dear Sisters. I know that you must wonder what has brought you all together here this morning at my bidding. I have news that for many of you will be disturbing and saddening. But I know I can count on you all to receive it in the spirit of faith. We must remember that God tries those He loves. . . .

"Due to many considerations, which I shall outline, we have decided we must close two of our schools this June. We have come to this decision after much prayer and consultation and are convinced it is God's will for us at this time. We will therefore be closing St. Bartholomew's parochial school and also St. James's Academy in Red Bank. We will also be phasing out St. Gertrude's private school here, grades one to eight, over the next two years. I have instructed all these principals to work out a way of notifying parents. As you know, Sisters, many of our schools in this province continue to flourish. We have, however, a heavy financial burden in our Washington house of studies. We must cut somewhere to maintain the effectiveness of our other schools. And . . ." Here she looked up over her half glasses at the assembled nuns. "Mother General has indicated that for now St. Gertrude's High School will continue as it is. It is the oldest high school in this province. However, at the time of the general chapter in 1966, we must be open to total reorganization of the eastern province. By then, the mind of the Church as determined by the fathers at the Council will be clearer to us all."

She looked back down at her papers and read on. But Sister Claire had stopped listening. All around her she seemed to feel one deep spasm of disbelief. St. Bartholomew's would close. And the Academy elementary school. Where would Sister Mark go? What would happen to her studies after all these years? Would she be stuck way up in Maine or some similar place, far from any opportunity to finish her degree? Where would the others go—Sister Mary Ann, Sister David? And Sister Florence, who'd been with her in college, and through the novitiate? Even St. Gertrude's was threatened in two years. Surely Reverend Mother had been warning them. That meant the house itself might eventually close. What would happen to the old nuns?

Reverend Mother Provincial's voice thinned into the distance.

Suddenly Sister Claire felt deeply one with the other figures sitting silently near her in a sea of black, figures she sometimes saw as separate from herself, more simpleminded, bothersome, officious, or lovable . . . figures whose stoop and walk and smell and tone she was growing to read with sure familiarity. St. Gertrude's was becoming, had become, *her* community. This was her third school year here. She had grown to feel understanding for many of the more difficult characters, women whose whole sense of identity and purpose was bound up with continuing St. Gertrude's in the way it had always been . . . who looked with suspicion on any innovation. Who understandably might feel cheated (though they never said that) by the greater opportunities given now to the young. Above all, she loved old Sister Gertrude, her true friend, with whom she had spent the occasional golden hour at the piano playing four-hand, redeeming the quiet of a Sunday afternoon by an excursion to this very auditorium where they would play together from the stack of ancient pieces Sister Gertrude had kept from her days as a music teacher. Sister Gertrude was seventy-three and ill. Once, in her inimitable way, Hildegarde had looked into the auditorium and seen them. She departed, slamming the door, but made no comment. For old Sister Gertrude was almost bent in half now, and in a year or two would no longer be able to reach the keys.

"One thing I have asked of the Lord, this will I seek: that I may dwell in the house of the Lord all the days of my life." This Sister Claire Delaney had sung at Reception with a full heart. And now . . . why was she so shaken? The Lord had many houses, many mansions. Her vocation was intact.

But . . . it was as if she had lived long years in a house of the most durable stone whose every corner she knew—a house guaranteed to outlast her, a house she had learned to move about in comfortably, sometimes relishing its warmth, sometimes numbed by its coldness, but basically habituated to the inconvenience of its varying temperatures and inner arrangements. Then one fine day, a bright winter morning when the sky gleamed extraordinarily blue, as she moved about that house—quickly, for it was large and kept her busy—she put a hand to one wall and its flimsy thinness yielded slightly to the pressure of her touch. Frightened, she let go. It was not stone at all. It was cardboard.

Hurrying into the central hall into which the other rooms opened, hoping to reconfirm her sense of solidity, she found herself standing in the center, not of one hall but of a hundred different halls branching in a hundred different directions. Dizzying.

". . . insofar as we can, we shall try to meet each sister's needs individually and with consideration."

She wrenched part of her attention back to Mother Provincial's words.

"But in such a time as this you will understand, I know, when I say quite frankly that you will all be asked to make sacrifices.

Within the next two months each of you will have the opportunity to speak either with your own superior or with me. I
would ask you to be candid and also open to suggestion. We
shall have to be willing to compromise on all sides. Some will
be asked to do things for which they do not feel prepared or
which do not appeal to them at all. Let us rise to this golden
opportunity, this challenge of obedience. The care of our older
nuns is paramount, and we must bend every effort to meet their
needs first of all. This may mean building a residence for them
in the near future."

Reverend Mother set down her papers and looked at them.
It was clear that she herself was moved by what she was doing.
She had a florid face, with kindly blue eyes unenlightened, one
soon learned, by subtlety of mind. She tended to be impulsive
and emotional, but in this moment a certain warmth commu-
nicated itself effectively.

"I would ask you, Sisters, as you speak with one another
during the rest of the day, to try to develop as constructive and
hopeful an attitude as possible. Faith is all. 'I have come not to
do my will, but the will of Him Who sent me.' After our coffee
break this morning we shall have a panel presentation on the
traditions of the Order."

Their break was over.

Sister Claire managed a small smile as she nodded to Sister
Lucy and settled back into the seat saved for her. Her notebook
rested closed on her lap. What point in taking notes? From the
corner of her eye she noticed how pudgy Sister Lucy's hands
looked as they managed notebook and pen: small hills of flesh
rising to enclose the gold band on her right hand. Where was
Sister Hilary?

Her attention was diffused as she heard the familiar recapit-
ulation of the Order's glorious history and tradition. She was
thinking of others, the particular lives that surrounded her in
this house, that would share the question of a future with her.
Her memory played over vaguely associated images, images so

familiar through daily contact that they usually went unnoticed, like furniture in a room. From time to time she lifted herself out of her reverie to hear the speakers, old pros all of them, three nuns Mother Provincial had obviously chosen to bolster any loss of confidence in the Order her announcement might have caused.

She thought of Sister Emily. Strange her mind should move to Sister Emily—who could never know what was going on, who was immune from any shock. Sister Emily lay in a crib on the third floor, a case of extreme senility. She had lain there for years, cared for by the community. When Sister Claire first came to St. Gertrude's, she occasionally heard of Sister Emily in vaguely mysterious contexts that tantalized her imagination. Unlike the others, the door to that cell was always shut. Sister Emily was prayed for annually on her feast day but otherwise was seldom mentioned. During the day Sister Mary, the infirmarian, went in and out of that room periodically, efficiently, and silently.

One day in her first year here, she had met Sister Mary closing the door to Sister Emily's room and was swept by the impulse to say, "Can I see her?" Curiosity, plain and simple. An absurd impulse with a touch of indecency. She recognized that and suppressed it instantly. Pretending not even to notice the infirmarian, she went her way.

Then came her turn. Last year she had been given the charge of carrying trays on weekends. That took her to the rooms of all the sick, including Sister Emily. Her instructions were to leave the tray on the chair in Sister Emily's room; Sister Mary would get it on her rounds.

There she lay. At first Sister Claire had felt almost sinful in her desire to stare. She had seen age in many of its forms—crabbed, vague, repetitive, domineering, crafty—but never this: a shrunken, wizened-up old lady lying in a crib. Unable to see. Unable to hear. Drooling.

Was she aware of anything? Did she sense Sister Claire's face, flushed from carrying the tray up three long flights of stairs, staring over the side of the crib with fascinated loathing? Listening to the periodic babble-gurgle that issued from the toothless mouth? Little grooves ran from the outer edges of her eyes, worn there by tears that fell heedlessly. She was dressed in a white hospital gown. The arms protruding from the short sleeves seemed all bone, scaly with flaking skin. Her hands were wrapped in white cotton mittens tied at the wrist. Beneath the transparent nightcap thin white hair lay in separated strands across an almost bare skull. Rutted with wrinkles, her face was punctured by two large gray eyes that stared back at her younger sister unseeing.

Later on Sister Claire had conscientiously made herself meditate on Christ's special love for the poor, the lame, the blind. "Whatsoever you do unto one of these, the least of My brethren, you do unto Me." But this—this was grotesque. Something to be forgotten, suppressed. Eventually she trained herself not to look toward the crib where she left the tray on Saturdays. It grew easier and easier to forget that wrinkled dwarf, for in the course of a normal day she moved through a world of pressures far removed from such vacancy. Why did the image of it surface so vividly now?

"During the twentieth century our Order has seen an astounding growth, particularly in the United States. Vocations rose dramatically in the forties and early fifties, with the result that we opened several new schools in this province. We all know that whereas this house once had only a small private elementary school attached to it, it now carries the apostolate of a large high school and two outside parochial schools. This is perhaps the most dramatic example of our growth in the last thirty years."

Sister Esmerelda's tone waxed glossy with enthusiasm. Glancing at her absentmindedly, Sister Claire noted again the curiously automatic precision of that voice. Sister Esmerelda was fond of numbers, statistics, columns of figures, calculations of any kind. Both Reverend Mother and Sister Stephen had absolute confidence in her.

Sister Stephen. How would she cope with this blow if in fact

St. Gertrude's was closed? All those explanations to parents! Would she send out a formal notice with a semester's tuition bill? Sister Stephen was difficult, a small mind untroubled by self-doubt. Careful at each staff meeting to see that everyone had freshly sharpened pencils that she distributed, she could never hope to hold the whole curriculum in her head. On precise points of order she was a stickler, but one could almost feel her mind falter and recede into vagueness when faced with abstraction or called upon to generalize.

"Let's see, Sister," she would say, a slightly vacant look settling over her pale features. Then, reaching for a sharpened pencil and a fresh sheet of paper, she would begin to figure laboriously. Or, if the moment was public and there was an agenda to get through, she would turn to Sister Esmerelda and say quietly, "Would you figure that one, Sister, so we can proceed to the next point of business?" A few minutes later would come forth Sister Esmerelda's flawless columns—clear, accurate, stunning: so many credit hours, so many students, so many anything. No wonder Sister Stephen counted on her.

Sister Claire felt the slight rhythmic pressure of her neighbor's elbow as she wrote busily, listing the numbers of students, numbers of sisters in each house in the province. The wedge of gold moved regularly back and forth across Sister Lucy's notebook page.

"And so a long look at our history shows that there have always been cycles," went on Sister Esmerelda. Her voice thickened with resolute cheer as she churned out her statistics. "Periods of upswing and downswing, times of prosperity, and then, of course, lean years."

She was winding up. Sister Claire tightened her grip on her notebook and prepared to bolt. She would escape Sister Lucy, find her way to some quiet spot for a few moments before she had to serve the superiors their collation. That was her charge today, and she dreaded it. After that—Hilary.

The nuns rose as the members of the panel and Mother Provincial left the stage. Joined by the superior of the house, they all disappeared quickly out the back door of the auditorium. Then the others moved about, rustling notebooks, stretching, whispering, gradually straggling out. Sister Claire did not pause to look back for Sister Lucy. She escaped.

"Thank you, Sister, just set it here."

Mother Provincial was sitting in the priests' dining room with the superior of the house, Reverend Mother Dolores. She moved some papers from the table between them to make room for the tray Sister Claire carried. On it were two tall glasses of ginger ale and a small plate of tea biscuits. She set them in the place indicated.

". . . but then again perhaps Sister Esmerelda should be given a chance as superior. She has a talent for administering, I believe, and has not yet had the opportunity. Sister Stephen, now . . ."

As she spoke, Mother Provincial rustled some papers. Passing behind her, Sister Claire saw that it was a list of community members. Reverend Mother Dolores was apparently unaware of Sister Claire—so caught up was she in the affairs of the day. At that moment, though, Mother Provincial was more alert, and she made a move to include their server and curb the superior's indiscretion.

"Well, Sister"—she looked at the nun who was about to leave the room—"how did you take this morning's news?"

Typical of the kind of question Mother Provincial asked. What was there to say? Worlds crashed. Words evaporated. Sister Claire paused, the image of a gold ring encased in flesh whisking through her distracted mind.

"It was a great surprise, Reverend Mother." What else was there to say? And when you get to my name on the list, please be good to me? We have not here a lasting city.

"Don't worry, Sister," said the Provincial in her well-meaning, flustered way. "We'll do our best by all our subjects. God will take care of us." She turned back to her papers and reached for a glass of ginger ale.

.   .   .

"I don't know," declared Sister Cornelius as she passed the potatoes at dinner that night. "It really seems unlikely that we'll stay much in education at all. It's clear that's not the most promising direction for the future."

Sister Cornelius should have been Pope, thought Sister Claire, surveying the impassive pallor of the older nun.

"But we've always maintained that apostolate," she responded aloud. She could not let this pass. "Do you really think we could throw out teaching, just like that? Most of us entered with that in mind."

She thought of the college nuns, her own excitement at discovering their way of life . . . her hope that she could one day duplicate it.

"Speak for yourself," said Sister Cornelius. "But don't forget the Order's beginnings. We didn't run schools in the beginning."

Sister Cornelius had never liked the classroom. For that, Sister Claire pitied her. When she crossed the classroom threshold each morning, nausea all but overcame her. The convent doctor blamed the intestinal spasms on the strain of teaching. Reverend Mother Dolores had admonished her to watch her diet and work on her attitudes. Though Sister Claire did not like her, she felt for Sister Cornelius's dilemma. Imagine having that struggle every day of your life!

"Centuries ago our sisters did work in homes," said Sister Cornelius. "In the parish. *They* weren't cloistered. Remember who cloistered us: holy bishops. The early nuns did what we'd call social work today. You know that as well as I do. We've all heard that chapter in our classes on history of the Order. It's just never been stressed. It's seen as past—for obvious reasons, when you've got umpteen schools to maintain in this country. Now the holy bishops are pushing into the modern world. Just wait. Things will change. . . . But for now the superiors are confused. Too much pride and money bound up in education to bail out. Pass the pickles, please." Today she was unworried about spasms.

Sister Claire could see Sister Hilary's back at the next table.

Ann Copeland

Their places for dinner had been assigned. There seemed a conspiracy against their ever getting together! And here was Sister Lucy, ever-present, assigned to this table, about to utter another platitude.

"Well, I'm sure our superiors will work out the solution that's called for," said Sister Lucy, her emphasis slightly muffled by a mouthful of mashed potatoes. "Reverend Mother Provincial is discerning. She's sure to feel the movement of the Spirit."

Sister Mark eyed Sister Claire from diagonally across the table. They hadn't yet had a chance to talk. *What was she feeling?*

Sister Claire chewed on her roast beef. Dry. Her stomach had not felt right since last night.

"Yes, but you can't close five schools and turn able-bodied nuns loose to do social work without retraining them. That takes time and money. Consider the investment they've already put into our educations. And this is happening so fast." The image of Reverend Mother holding the list flicked through her mind. Destinies arranged over ginger ale.

"Don't worry," came from the opposite side of the table as Sister James heaped her plate with turnips. "They won't get around to disposing of us till the last moment. There's just too much paperwork to be done. Complicated business, closing houses. Wonder if they'll keep all the cars?"

Sister James's experienced cynicism would obviously tide her over any change with no drastic loss of faith. In the Order twenty-seven years, she had celebrated her silver jubilee two years before, a big affair with lots of former students back. It was the only time Sister Claire could recall seeing her visibly moved. But there was something in her that appealed, a kind of bedrock common sense. Unexciting in the classroom, she ran the bookstore with unfaltering competence, and they all depended on her to order uniforms, class rings, yearbooks, take care of the convent cars and see to the myriad details of daily living. A born manager, her steady no-nonsense reliability offset Sister Stephen's ineffectiveness and kept more wheels running smoothly than most suspected.

128

Back and forth they swapped opinions about the Order's future as they ate, full stomachs and the distraction of guests begetting a certain public optimism. Amid the clatter of dishes and silver, the squeaking serving carts, the muted thump of servers' rubber heels tapping efficiently back and forth across the linoleum to serve one hundred thirty women, the general tone, to an outside listener, would have sounded positively celebrative. Festiveness always filled the house when guests were there to break the usual round of faces and conversations, bringing firsthand news of what was going on in other houses about the province.

Sister Claire felt herself disturbingly at odds with the prevailing mood. Her public face seemed poised on the verge of disintegration; she felt an invisible tic in her cheek. She kept wanting to withdraw from meaningless speculations, to find a spot where she could think and sort out her conflicting responses. But evening time was rigidly apportioned: after supper the nuns visited chapel briefly, then went to recreation together. No easy escape. And she had music to plan for tomorrow's Benediction.

After dinner a few headed outside to brave the cold, but she followed the others into the community room. In a far corner she spotted Sister Gertrude, already established with her sewing, and headed toward her. Because of her age and infirmity, Sister Gertrude was permitted to go directly from the refectory to the community room, omitting chapel.

"How're you surviving?" With one shaking hand the elderly nun lifted her needle high toward the central light in the room and tried with the other faltering hand to thread it. She would not welcome help. She was darning an unstarched linen from the stack piled next to her on the table. "Seems to me you've been pretty well glued to your companion for the weekend, so far."

"She's gone outside now."

"Did you get to see your friend from the college?"

"Not yet."

"Have you had any contact with Reverend Mother or Mother Provincial yet?"

"Only to bring their collation. What do you mean, contact?"

"I don't know for sure, but I have the impression that between the morning and afternoon sessions today, as well as after this afternoon's talk, Reverend Mother sent for a few in the community. Starting with the teachers from the Academy and St. Bartholomew's. But I could be wrong." Sister Gertrude spoke tonelessly as she studied a tiny hole in the linen, then attacked it.

"That probably won't affect me," said Sister Claire—wondering if, in fact, it would. How did you judge what would affect you in this business, anyhow? "Did you expect this news? I think people are pretty upset."

"Expect, expect." Sister Gertrude carefully laid the linen on her lap and looked at her companion. "I'm past that, really. Live long in religious life and you stop *expecting.* Remember, I knew this place when we were ten subjects and one small struggling school. . . . But I can't say I'm totally surprised. Mother Provincial's been looking peaked for months. There's lots of talk about change—as you well know." Every evening the refectory reading brought the latest information from the Vatican Council, including the mysterious Xavier Rynne's running report in *The New Yorker.* "What surprises me is that *three* schools, counting our academy here, are being closed—and two of them immediately. Seems to me it'll take some arranging, with students in the midst of their programs. Of course this Provincial isn't noted for her prudence!"

"But what do you think will happen to *us?*" Sister Claire put the question that was beginning to gnaw at her.

"You mean younger nuns like yourself?"

"I mean this community. I'm not that young."

Convent age was a joke and they knew it. You were young until fifty, enjoyed a brief middle age, then were classed as "one of the older sisters" to whom all owed a certain deference. Faults in the young and middle-aged merited attentive correction;

among the older nuns they were generally overlooked or silently tolerated.

"Ah," said Sister Gertrude, darning with concentration, bending over to study her stitches. "Eventually we'll be split up. They'll close this house. That was what she was warning us about today. The subject is just too touchy to come right out and announce. But wait and see. The Order will build us a home. There we'll be—praying, doing such work as we're able, waiting . . . waiting."

Sister Claire thought of the older nuns she'd known in Calais, their sense of selfless devotedness to the school, their willingness to help the younger nuns. Here, too, one could find that in some quarters. "But the Order's always made a point of keeping older nuns right in the community that's theirs, where they taught."

"That's right." Sister Gertrude pushed the needle in and out. Her hand trembled relentlessly. "Times change. The old and sick far outnumber the young ones now."

"That gives me the chills, just to think of you and others like you sitting around in a kind of senior citizens' home. No school around, no younger sisters."

"You never know." Sister Gertrude stopped sewing, her needle poised in midair. "Maybe they'll use this house for us. They talk about building, but in many ways this house would be suitable for the elderly, sick, and dying. There are good infirmary facilities, the elevator works, there is a lovely view from the cells. It's not been made clear that this house is being closed, just the elementary school. Who knows . . ." She bent over her sewing again.

"Our second grade is doing a program for the parents next week that should be interesting, Reverend Mother."

Sister Lucy had come in and joined the circle near Mother Provincial. Her high voice, carrying above the other muted sounds in the room, shattered them into tinkling bits—rainbow-colored fragments from the world of toy whistles and floating balloons. Then the broken murmur of voices recomposed its brightness around hers. Pieces of conversation floated quietly around Sister Claire and her friend as they ignored the rule of general recreation that one not discuss topics disturbing to the serenity of community life. They inhabited a bubble, a fragile membrane protecting them from the swish of sound all around, sound that swirled about one certain subject never discussed.

After night prayer Sister Claire went to the choir loft to select hymns for tomorrow's Benediction. Sister Hildegarde was gradually being relieved of her duties as choir mistress and organist, not without a struggle. But Reverend Mother Dolores, to her credit, had held firm. Sister Claire needed time to practice, for before long Sister Hildegarde would simply not be able. Besides, she resisted the directives from the Council concerning liturgy. Every feast day became a struggle. For some feasts, therefore—only some—she grudgingly handed the organ keys to Sister Claire. This weekend was one such time. Hildy wanted to be free to float about the meeting, gathering provincial gossip from her old friends.

Choosing tomorrow's hymns was important. How well Sister Claire knew the difference that music, especially music in a liturgical setting, could make to one's spirit. She would choose something particularly beautiful. Not polyphony. Gregorian would be more appropriate—simple hymns that would remind them of their monastic tradition, their history. She loved Gregorian chant, the pure arsis and thesis of melody ancient and timeless. Like the psalms themselves. She found the sheets for the *Ubi caritas,* the antiphon from Maundy Thursday. "Where there's charity divine and holy love, surely God abides . . ." Appropriate. Then the solemn *Salve Regina,* a hymn they all knew by heart after singing it nightly to close Compline. Then the familiar *Tantum ergo* and doxology from Trinity Sunday. These she had known as far back as she could remember, from her childhood. A simple Benediction. It would speak.

She set the appropriate sheets of music in piles at the back of chapel for distribution tomorrow.

Then she climbed the stairs to the dormitory. Tomorrow she

would see Sister Hilary. A note exchanged between recreation and night prayer had established time and place: the priests' dining room, after the morning conference, before examen, about eleven-thirty.

She pulled the white curtains around her cell . . . muting the sound of the water she poured in her basin, slippering quietly out to the bathroom past other silent black shapes, kneeling briefly by the bed, then finally settling into it with relief. Solitude at last. A chance to examine questions and anxieties she had suppressed since morning in an effort of charity toward Sister Lucy or discretion toward others. Yet before she fashioned a thought, exhaustion claimed her and she slept.

Deadly chill pervaded her dreams. She discovered herself enclosed in a hollow place strangely dark and cold, heavy with the smell of death and filled with mounding dust as in a vault that has stood shut and airless for aeons. No object touched her except a fine gauze of darkness. She gasped for air, relief from dryness that coated her throat and thickened her breath threatening to choke her. As she gagged, a sudden whiff of heavy sweetness like the blended odor of burning candles and incense opened her throat, filling her lungs with saving oxygen.

Then, ever so gradually, her body felt penetrated by this heavy sweetness pressing in upon her senses. From somewhere far outside, thin voicelike sounds filtered into her chamber. Blurred and indistinguishable, they were nonetheless compelling. As moments passed, her house of darkness whispered into light. Shadows fell and danced and played against the moldering stone, a whorl of shapes woven by flickering torches flaming points in the air about her. The leaping fire licked each subtle crack of the rugged walls into light, waving a ballet of monstrous shadows across the jagged surface. Immobilized, she beheld walls of stone no longer but a trembling kaleidoscope of brilliant icons, the flaming torches merging now into tall burning candles quivering symmetrically on all sides, heavy rich robes of gold-embroidered damask and brocade—dalmatics, chasubles, humeral veils, a jewel-encrusted baldachino glittering and swaying heavily overhead—all fused in a glowing light of rich solemnity and grandeur that quickened a response in her parched soul. The dance of light and form magnetized her, held and warmed her.

Gradually a new darkness gripped her, falling heavily upon her, threatening to crush her as it pushed her downward with powerful blocks of dark weight. Heavy and cold, one by one these blocks of darkness struck and held her. Behind them, now even farther away, she heard the other voices. One was Joellen Lynch. Then from nearer, above her, she recognized a familiar droning of bloodless precision counting the stones as they fell into place on her form, recording their precise weight and shape:

Stone one, five pounds; angular Stone two, twenty-two pounds; square Stone three, twenty pounds; square Stone four, fifty pounds; oblong Stone five, seventy pounds. . . .

Rhythmically the voice chanted above her, arsis and thesis, shaping its monotonous litany as, miraculously uncrushed, she continued to breathe and listen from her bed of stone beneath the falling darkness.

Voices faded. Stones dissolved. She found herself held once more by the empty vault. Blowing toward her from thin air, mysteriously luminous, was a perfectly round golden circle. It hung, single and free, in the vacuum above her head. Straining, she reached for it, grasping it lightly while it lifted her. Yet even as she was pulled upright she felt the ring change at her touch. Its hardness expanded to pass over her hand, wrist, elbow, accommodating its shape to each contour of her body. Then the touch of its cold, smooth metal surprised her ankles and began to ascend, pausing momentarily at her waist, then continuing upward self-propelled—a cool sleek finger chilling nerves beneath her skin, raising bumps along her flesh.

Upright she was clamped in a vise as unyielding as the stones that held her prone. It rose above her shoulders, then *slip, click, clamp* about her neck. Inexorably it tightened, slowly cutting off her gasping breath. The flesh of her neck rose quickly on either side of the gold ring, half burying it. She strained to move her head. Impossible. To breathe. More and more difficult. Gasping—

"Are you all right?" A whisper—urgent, persistent—reached her through the heavy curtain of her cell. "Are you all right?"

She struggled to focus. Darkness everywhere. Silence. Then the familiar objects—washstand, basin, chair—began to isolate themselves from the dark. She saw the heavy form of the hanging habit dimly visible against the curtains and recognized the whisper of Sister Suzanne.

"Are you okay in there? You've been gasping and moaning in your sleep for ages." Sister Suzanne whispered quietly, mindful of forms sleeping all around them.

"It's okay. Just a dream. Thanks."

She rolled over quickly to shake off the strangling grip of fear and confusion. Bumps in the thin mattress pushed against her. The rasping metronome of Sister James's snores thickened through the sleeping dark. Somewhere far off the lingering vibrato of a train whistle mourned through the night. She lay there, nose into mattress, willing muscles along her spine loose, giving herself over to the sleep that came quietly, dreamlessly.

After breakfast next morning she heard her bell: five-one. She was upstairs finishing her cell. The first conference would begin in an hour. One more in the afternoon, followed by Benediction. Then the guests would leave, the ranks close in, the world return to normal. Almost.

Five-one. She quickly tucked the spread under the pillow, glanced around the cell, and hurried out. Better use the stairs. The elevator worked constantly these days.

On the first floor she hurried to the portress's booth near the front door where the bells were rung.

"Reverend Mother wants to see you, Sister." Sister Josephine's fat freckled hands held the crochet hook loosely in the loop of baby-blue yarn she was working as she looked curiously at Sister Claire. Bells on Sunday morning were unusual; Sister Josephine loved to *know*.

Turning quickly away from the pressure of that curiosity, Sister Claire hurried past chapel down the hall toward Reverend Mother's office, trying to quiet her stomach. Sister Gertrude's remarks the night before flew through her mind. Her dream. The sense of suffocation. Through morning meditation, Mass, and breakfast those forms had held her senses like a fine web.

"Come in, Sister." Reverend Mother responded immediately to her knock on the closed door.

"Sit down." She did away with the usual blessing. The occasion was obviously special.

"How are you, Sister Claire?"

A strange question. Although she saw her subjects every day in refectory, chapel, and at recreation, unlike some superiors Reverend Mother Dolores remained on exceedingly formal terms with most of them. She believed unwaveringly in the values of faith and obedience; at times her counsel could be staggering in its simplicity. By that very fact some called her saintly; others secretly thought her obtuse.

"Fine, thank you, Reverend Mother." She tried not to notice too obviously a familiar sheaf of papers on the desk.

"I know that many of the nuns must be deeply concerned over the news from Reverend Mother Provincial, Sister . . ." Reverend Mother's pause gave Sister Claire time to respond, but the nun simply waited. Such indirection made her nervous.

"Now you must be wondering why I have sent for you, Sister." Another pause.

"Well, I thought you would be quite busy this weekend, Reverend Mother." The most innocuous reply she could manage.

Sunday. . . . somewhere outside, a carillon sang faintly of grace and Sabbath peace.

"True. But we are, of course, all caught up in a special time of grace for our Order. It is a time when God is showing His

particular love, for He is making a demand on our faith. I am
sure you understand it that way, Sister."

Sister Claire willed her face to be inscrutable but not hostile.
She felt a pulse beginning in her cheek, tried to arrest it. What
did Reverend Mother *want?*

"I hope, Sister, that should you have the opportunity, you
will encourage your sisters to respond to this test in a true spirit
of faith."

"I don't know just what you're referring to, Reverend
Mother." A slat of sun through the Venetian blinds caught her
in the eyes, and she shifted her position slightly.

"Only to the fact that decisions will be forthcoming that may
be hard on many of our subjects. We have to rely on you all to
help one another. Criticism of authority is always the devil's
work."

From what knowledge did her superior speak?

Did she guess Sister Claire's appointment with Sister Hilary?
Had she noticed Sister Claire and Sister Gertrude talking quietly
during last night's recreation? A warning flicked through
Claire—troubling, unidentifiable. Already this superior had
warned her that she must be more discreet in her relationships,
that she had been seen too often talking to Sister Mark and
others in places reserved for silence. That she was too friendly
with the students. That she must be more reserved, less direct,
in her dealings with people. Now this . . . Perhaps Reverend
Mother feared, somehow, that Sister Mark would be too emotional about all this—though that was hardly likely. Sister Mark
was a trouper. She'd weathered many a storm. Or maybe—yes,
that was probably it—the real concern was that Sister Hilary
would tell her friend what was going on at the college. News
from the college was always limited. The nuns there had con-
siderably more freedom. Their responsibility toward higher education meant managing their own prayer lives, organizing their
time schedules, with more flexibility than any other house in
the province.

Reverend Mother's grayish eyes were opaque, yielding from their centers only a pinpoint black-and-white reflection of herself. This self-portrait faded in an instant, and the glasses became transparent, their faintly tinted lenses circling two large gray eyes.

"I will do the best I can, Reverend Mother." She suppressed irritation.

"I would hope that, should you hear of any response less than what would serve the honor of the Order, Sister, you would have the confidence in your superiors to inform them. For only through the golden chain of obedience can we truly come close to God, our Center. A time like this teaches us the cost of our vow of obedience. We must be an example to the outside world in our unity."

"I doubt, Reverend Mother, that anyone would speak to me."

No more could be said. Reverend Mother's movements suggested an exit. The interview was over.

"Very well, Sister. It is nearly time for the morning conference. Reverend Mother Provincial will speak to us this morning on the meaning of our vows."

As Sister Claire knelt by the desk, her superior leaned forward and traced the sign of the cross on the crown of the inclined head.

After the morning conference, about ten minutes before the noon examination of conscience, she heard her bell ring again. This time she was on her way through the catacombs with Sister Lucy when she heard the far-off five-one, five-one.

"Excuse me, Sister. That's my bell."

Leaving her companion behind, she hurried forward through the narrow passage toward deliverance. At the portress booth stood Sister Hilary.

"This was the only way I could figure out to get you away from your companion. Who is she?"

"Sister Lucy, from Wilbraham. Holy Family. You know, the new parochial school up there."

"She certainly has you in her clutch." Sister Hilary grinned.

"Come on into the priest's dining room. No one will bother us there. Father left long ago."

It was the room where the priest had his breakfast after Mass each morning, the room in which Sister Claire had served the superiors collation yesterday. The place had been cleared and set back in order after Father Purcell's breakfast, heavy carved chairs symmetrically arranged about the trestle table. It was not customary for the nuns to use the public rooms. In a sense, this guaranteed the privacy of their conversation. Most of the others were already in chapel. They sat down out of sight from the hall.

Sister Hilary wasted no time. "Well, what do you think?"

"What do you mean, what do I think? It's hard to tell anything. You probably have more information than I do. All I know is three schools are closing, and maybe even St. Gertrude's High School after a couple of years. The oldest high school in the province. Every conference is a kind of gobbledygook designed to retain our great confidence in the Order. 'The lady doth protest too much, methinks.' What do *you* think?"

"I think that what have been proclaimed as timeless principles will soon be perceived, at least by some"—she smiled—"like maybe you and me, as less than principles. As just expedient ways of organizing us, or maybe habits maintained for no real reason."

"Like what?" Sister Claire felt suddenly refreshed.

"Oh, you know . . . like traveling with companions. They're already easing up on that at the college."

"And eating with seculars?" It had always galled her. Had not Christ broken bread with his friends? Though she'd held herself to the letter of the law, on several occasions Claire had felt embarrassed not to share a cup with a friend, not to respond to a simple gesture. As if eating with a secular somehow contaminated you.

"Probably. But there are bigger things at stake. . . . That's what I feel behind this. The whole Church is rumbling. Poor John the Twenty-third. Little did he guess . . ."

"Maybe he did."

"You've heard about what's going on at the college?"

"Don't be ridiculous. You know we never hear what's going on over there." How far away the college world felt now. Twenty miles away . . . worlds away.

"The campus is seething. No wonder Mother Provincial seems worn out. It's been one thing after another. The faculty's up in arms over a tenure issue. No one you'd know. . . . And the students want open discussion on birth control, the new I.U.D., all that. Everyone seems to have read Rock's book."

Sister Claire felt ignorant. What was "Rock's book"? What was the I.U.D. issue? The biggest argument she'd had in school was over including *Catcher in the Rye* in the Senior Honors reading list!

"Who's Rock?"

"The book is on birth control. . . . Anyhow, it's just that *everything* seems to be an issue right now. Students, some of them, are involved in civil rights, want a public declaration from the college on its admissions policy. . . . And now—this. The province feels a bit shaky! No one is prepared to deal with open discussion and criticism."

"But they'll never close the college."

"No. Probably not. Were you out at last night's recreation?"

"Stayed inside. I've been so glued to Sister Lucy that I haven't heard much. Besides, they've given me the guest collation job, and you know what that is. My life is measured in doilies and ginger ale this weekend." She smiled ruefully, thinking of old Sister Gertrude.

"Apparently one group that walked outside at recreation got quite heated in its discussion. Two or three spoke of breaking away into small splinter groups, living out of community in apartments or something like that. I've never heard anyone speak openly that way before, have you?"

Sister Claire thought of the occasional disappearances with no explanation, the cloak of secrecy that surrounded any exits from the Order. There had been only three since she'd been professed. Each time—absolute silence about it. No explanation given. It was as if someone died, was buried. Gone. Nothing was discussed openly. That made it all the scarier.

"Never."

"What really gets me is everyone seems convinced the thing we should be doing is social work. You know . . . the nun in the modern world kind of thing—rehabilitation centers, teaching catechism in the ghettos, working with drug addicts, clothing the poor, feeding the hungry."

Claire thought of Mother Theodore's conferences in the novitiate on those very words. "Remember Mother Theodore? According to her, teachers *are* feeding the hungry. I believe it. 'Not by bread alone' . . ."

"Exactly. But morale about teaching, its value, is very low. It's hard—even at the college, believe it or not—to find nuns really committed to the belief that *teaching* is a worthy apostolate. That it really matters. And from what I've heard around here this weekend, morale isn't likely to pick up. Worst of all, the superiors seem out of it. Nervous, but out of it. . . ."

"Reverend Mother sent for me this morning," said Sister Claire. They were due at examen any minute. "I couldn't figure out what she wanted. Maybe she's heard the talk and is just nervous. Maybe she thought I knew more than I do."

"Look, Claire." Her friend grew quietly serious. The bell for examen was ringing. "I really am disturbed, somehow. I haven't talked about this with anybody. I don't know what lies ahead for me . . . not that anyone does, of course." She smiled briefly. "But we started together. . . . That matters." She looked her friend in the eye. "If I make any big decisions, I'll try to get in touch with you. Okay?" They left the dining room, started toward chapel, their voices lowered. "Just don't believe everything you hear, okay?"

Sister Claire knew better than that. Rumors flew in the province. "Agreed. You could always get word to me through one of your students."

She held the chapel door open for her friend. "Keep the faith," she whispered.

"And remember Shadowbrook," whispered Sister Hilary. She winked and entered chapel.

Remember Shadowbrook . . . ah, Shadowbrook. The thought, the imagery, followed Sister Claire to her choir stall, where she knelt to examine her conscience. But she examined nothing as she knelt quietly in the row of praying nuns. She was seeing Shadowbrook again, feeling the golden days there . . . days neither she nor Sister Hilary had supposed life in religion would ever hold. It was their first summer in Calais, their first summer with a real community. They'd survived their first year of teaching. Sister Claire had propelled reluctant sophomores through *The Mill on the Floss,* prodded freshmen through *amo amas amat* and other alien felicities of Latin I. Then, in July, she and Sister Hilary had discovered the boon of a *vacation.* Nuns in community, it turned out, actually had a week or two of vacation. Our Redeemer School had a summer cottage at a small lake in northern Maine, in the midst of dense pine woods. It wasn't ocean, but it was *water!*

Here, deep in the woods, far from the world of students, a unique and wonderful atmosphere prevailed. Except for meals in common (they took turns cooking) and prayers of rule, the sisters were free to do as they pleased. Some fished. Some knit. Some read. Sister Peter played her harmonica in the woods. Sister Catherine built a tree house. Some walked and prayed.

Sister Hilary, who'd been teaching Greek as an extra class to interested seniors that year, had brought to the lake a translation of the *Oresteia.* Sister Claire readily agreed to read it with her. For a couple of hours each day, reveling in the coolness of the students' blue gym suits which they wore except for meals and prayer times, they set chairs by the lake and mused on the rashness of Orestes, the fate of Agamemnon. They explored the mystery of *hubris*. It was fun.

A golden week. Never before had Sister Claire felt such an atmosphere of tolerance and openness in religious life. Nor would she afterward, though she would enjoy other vacations. But the first one—so unexpected, so free—coming after six years of regimentation, would linger long in her memory with the radiance of a blessed time.

Not least was the shivery touch of the water into which she forced herself every day, cold or not, willing its numbing finger against her toes, her feet, her shins, her thighs, nerving herself up for the shock against her stomach, her breasts. There came the memorable afternoon when she dared, alone, on the other side of the raft, to ease from her shoulders the top of the blue gym suit and swim about with cold water icing her breasts, her nipples, her back. Strange and wonderful, that alien embrace. She would have shed the whole gym suit if she could—remembering nights years before at a cottage on Long Island Sound when she and childhood friends had skinny-dipped beneath a full moon. . . .

All this Sister Hilary asked her to remember.

She would.

Later that day Sister Claire entered the chapel behind Sister Lucy for the final Benediction. It was all over, the last conference, the last panel discussion. Sister Esmerelda had carried the day. Asked to review in more detail the developments in the recent history of the Order in the United States, she had charts, tables, statistics galore arranged to best advantage.

As she listened, the pudgy hand next to her writing busily, Sister Claire felt deeply depressed. No one had publicly put direct questions about the future. She found the statistical approach tiresome, the optimism clinical.

Now it was over.

Reverend Mother had closed the meeting by saying, "Now, Sisters, let us, in the Benediction that follows, renew our com-

mitment to Our Lord and to the Order. Let us all pray together
for a deepening of that unity of spirit that has blessed us from
the beginning. Let us ask God to deepen our charity and faith
so we may respond obediently to whatever He asks of us through
our superiors during the next few months."

The chapel was crowded with nuns.

Father Purcell entered the stone sanctuary, and they rose in
a body, then knelt as he opened the tabernacle.

Sister Claire, at the organ, felt the subtle relief that always
filled her when she was about to play. She intoned the opening
phrase, then quietly moved hands and feet in the beautifully
simple chant she had chosen the night before:

Ubi caritas et amor, Deus ibi est.
Congregavit nos in unum Christi amor.
Exsultemus, et in ipso jucundemur.
Timeamus, et amemus Deum vivum.
Et ex corde diligamus nos sincero.

She loved the words of this hymn. There was something ineffably pure in the curving melody that rose heavenward as Father
incensed the Blessed Sacrament. The sacristans had clothed both
sanctuary and priest in gold for the occasion—golden cope,
golden humeral veil, even golden pom-poms in the stately vases
of gold on either side of the gold-veiled tabernacle. A richness
of color and odor flooded her as she sang with her sisters the
second verse:

Ubi caritas et amor, Deus ibi est.
Simul ergo cum in unum congregamur:
Ne nos mente dividamur caveamus.
Cessent jurgia maligna, cessent lites.
Et in medio nostri sit Christus Deus.

Although their breviaries had been translated into the vernacular and they now chanted the psalms in English, at times
Latin did express what nothing else could. She was glad she'd
chosen a Latin hymn. She felt herself one with the song. She
knew old Sister Gertrude would be down in the front pew, bent
over, shaking, singing from her awkwardly held liber. What was
she feeling? She sat there in a pew for seculars since she could
no longer manage the position required for the choir stalls. Of
course the pews today were filled with nuns, for not all could
fit in the stalls.

Their voices rose in the simple melodic line of mode one for
the *Tantum ergo*:

> *Tantum ergo sacramentum*
> *veneremur cernui:*
> *et antiquum documentum*
> *novo cedat ritui:*
> *praestet fides supplementum*
> *sensuum defectui.*

After the second verse, the simple amen. Father emptied the
gold monstrance and closed the tabernacle. Then, in chorus,
their voices recited the Divine Praises:

> Blessed be God.
> Blessed be His Holy Name.
> Blessed be Jesus Christ, true God and true man. . . .

It was over.

Father left the altar. She turned off the organ. Clouds of
incense hung in the sanctuary. Sister Claire breathed deeply of
the heavy sweetness as she settled back to make evening meditation. The chapel was still, a residue of quiet harmony hovering
there as softly colored streams of late afternoon sun filtered

through the windows across the still black-and-white forms lost in prayer.

Next morning she hurried through the catacombs toward school, trying desperately to collect her thoughts. Fortunately there would be only one essay question for the exam. So distracting had her weekend been that she had not turned one thought toward making out that exam. This was unusual. She took her teaching seriously. Larger questions had absorbed her. Now she was pressed.

The catacombs felt chillier than usual, and she shivered slightly as she moved rapidly down the three steps where convent and high school joined, then rounded a narrow curve. No one else was about; the week of exams shifted everyone's schedule. Usually at this hour of the morning the catacombs were busy.

Her mind clicked through the books they had read during the semester, and she reviewed vaguely the myth of the labyrinth. Crete. Theseus. The Minotaur. Ariadne. The golden thread. That was it. The golden thread.

As she rounded another bend, she brushed against the aging wall and felt it snag her veil. The seven Athenian youths. Not relevant.

Almost at the door of the gym. Here the three steps leading up to that door were worn in the center. Her foot felt automatically for the groove in each step. Then she was at the door, through it, and moving rapidly across the polished gym floor. They were trained not to run, but she walked very quickly, a half run. She had wanted to have the question on the board before the students arrived. This much, at least, even if she couldn't hand out mimeographed copies. Obviously impossible now. She was too late.

Up the stairs to the second floor. Down the long corridor. Room 213. She went in.

There, waiting in the front row, was Joellen Lynch. A few seats away, Carla Williams. They were ready, carefully spaced competitors for Senior Honors. Behind them the rest—nervous, expectant, whispering quietly or just sitting.

They rose.

"Good morning, girls."

She struggled for composure. No point in their guessing she carried only half-formulated questions in her head.

"Be seated. Miss Williams, you may pass out the blue books."

Carla came forward to the desk, picked them up, and began distributing. The class sat in nervous silence. Sister Claire turned toward the board, then waited a moment. Dear God, let it come out a whole question.

She began to write.

1. *The Minotaur at the center of the labyrinth in this story could be identified as . . .*

2. *The golden thread that leads us through the labyrinth in this story enabling us to find its unity and design is . . .*

She turned to the class as they tried to stifle a groan.

"Choose any five books we have studied this semester. Using these books as a basis for your essay, answer either of the above questions. Please be specific in your discussions, girls. You may remember that at the beginning of the term I told you that I, too, would take the examination. We have studied these books together. Therefore I intend to keep my word."

She sat down at her desk as they bent over their papers and began writing or doodling. Pushing the piled blue books aside, she took one, opened it, and reached for her pen. The room was quiet, a trifle stuffy. The chilly glare of early morning winter sun just touched the last row of girls.

She thought for a moment, trying to choose. The questions had come as she had trusted they would. They were adequate. The Minotaur . . . the golden thread.

Then, bending her head, she too began to answer the question of her choice.

The Nature of Love

Isn't it absurd that with a drugstore on every corner, we have to worry?

That was the line that struck her.

She was sitting in the emptied classroom, four o'clock September sun touching the globe at the end of the stuffed bookcase, motes of dust lazing in the slanting beam that cut right across the row of desks in the middle of the room. Above her, on the third floor, the hum-whirr of the floor polisher. Charlie wouldn't get down here until later. A good hour alone now.

What did the sentence suppose? That she would grasp it instantly, see the situation, appreciate his bitter humor.

That she would be worldly somehow, or if not that . . . understanding.

The plain bond on which he'd typed had a light circle of dried coffee in the upper right-hand corner. Had he typed it late at night, working on his latest book in the bright poster-lined office where she'd sat a few memorable times last summer, self-conscious but exhilarated, feeling herself so oddly free?

She had been lucky. Now that St. Bartholomew's was closed, the community was short on young able-bodied nuns. Ten of them had been sent off to other communities about the province. So there was really no one available to accompany her every day to Columbia for her course in Modern Poetry. Two nuns, Sister David and Sister Andrew, were going to Hofstra for a course, so they could bring her as far as Columbia and pick her up at four o'clock each afternoon. Reverend Mother had hesitated to give the permission. But already a few nuns about the province had been allowed to travel alone. Things were loosening up gradually, thanks to Vatican II. So she finally had allowed Sister Claire to spend the day in class and on campus alone, fortified by the usual caution: do not talk except when necessary, above all with men. Sister Claire did not remind her rather preoccupied superior that her professor for this course was a man, and that there would be men in the class—including, as it turned out, Ted Johnson, the math professor and friend of Professor Goldsmith, auditing the course just to expand his horizons, as he told her, and have a break from the stratosphere of theoretical math.

As the summer proceeded and she grew to know the class, Professor Goldsmith, and Ted (whose seat was beside hers), she felt more and more herself, a self she hadn't realized she'd lost, or disguised, or maybe simply shelved in some quiet way for a future chance. And here was a future chance.

So he wrote to her. And the letter got through unslit.

Reverend Mother must have been busy. Meetings with the Provincial all this week. The superiors were already preparing for the general chapter in Rome.

She took up the letter again, reread carefully.

*And now my right cheek has begun to twitch, an old malady
I haven't had for years. And I'm writing to you because somehow
I feel you'll understand. You're trained to understand love. You
live it.*

His words troubled her. They touched a nerve. For love was
the core of her vocation. What *was* love? Once, she'd thought
she knew. *Greater love no man hath than this, that a man lay
down his life for his friends.* Love was sacrifice. Love seeketh not
its own. Above all, they'd been taught, their vowed life as nuns
in community was a witness to love. A symbol the world could
read. *Could it?* Sometimes she wondered. In so many ways the
simplicities of the Gospel seemed obscured by their way of life.
Cloister. Habit. Caution. Suspicion. Of course, some of that
would change now—though it would take time for fresh winds
from Vatican II to blow through a worldwide Order with four
centuries of tradition.

What was love?

Christ met a woman who'd sinned, and He welcomed her.
He ate with sinners. He offered food to the hungry. He broke
time-honored rules in the name of practical charity. His gestures
were free, straightforward, uncluttered, compassionate.

He was love incarnate.

"You're trained to understand love. You live it."

What then was love?

Was it the chance he was taking? Falling in love (so he said)
with someone younger—a student, perhaps?—but still not wanting to leave, suspicious enough of himself that the thought of
breaking up a home was too terrible, and yet . . .

His letter hinted at satisfactions she had never known. He
was direct, a quality that appealed to her.

They'd become friends, though never had he confided like
this. Their conversations had often centered on poetry, the
meaning of an obscure line or metaphor. Ted Johnson, free for
once of his summer teaching obligations, drew obvious refresh-
ment from his explorations of a new universe of discourse.

Ann Copeland

Though long ago, in high school, he told her (not *so* long, she thought, deducing he was about five years her senior), he'd loved English literature.

In any case, now, months later, somehow he'd found heart to put pen to paper, actually send her word of his distress, never dreaming all letters were slit if not read, a violation she had from the first deeply resented.

By now she knew ways around that, but how could he? Periodically, she and Sister Hilary, her friend at the college, exchanged notes through trustworthy students. But how could he imagine there was so little privacy in religious life? Wouldn't he think just the opposite? Her own father had been outraged that, after eleven years in religion, she must still submit to having her letters opened.

Isn't it absurd? the letter asked.

Yes. He meant birth control. What were those things they used? She felt her ignorance. She'd been born too early, entered too innocent—no, not innocent, just inexperienced—fending off her dates from going too far as every good Catholic girl did in those days. Mortal sin was an effective deterrent, feared pregnancy even more so. And now, young (according to convent standards) and appealing (she knew she was appealing), she held his confidence. It flattered her. Confirmed her. To hold a man's confidence was a compliment. This was not the first time. But it was dangerous.

Not for the reasons Reverend Mother would have said. Complexity of any kind spelled danger to Reverend Mother. "Do not meddle," she would say. "The Lord will take care of it." Ted Johnson might become an anonymous request for prayers on the community room bulletin board.

But prayer did matter. Sister Claire would start immediately.

His words were graphic. She saw the two of them—where? On a bed in an apartment, perhaps. Sister Claire couldn't mentally furnish the apartment. She'd never had one herself. But she could furnish the bed. She had a body, a brother, a father. So she could furnish the bed and see them upon it, naked and

152

loving. *I have never known anything like this before,* his letter said, charmingly direct. That was how he was.

And sitting in his office last summer (one floor up from Professor Goldsmith's) she'd half fallen in love with him herself, though that of course was impossible. He'd never known a nun. He was fascinated to discover (so to speak) flesh and blood beneath the black. He was funny, witty, disarming in his thoroughly Protestant ignorance. She played on it, made jokes, let them all see that really she was human. Could understand their misconceptions, forgive their ignorance. Could sympathize with their anguishes and dilemma, could catch their ironies. She was good at projecting human understanding. It worked. They came to accept her almost as if she were not the only one there in black and white, delivered intact from her cloister each morning, each afternoon snatched incorrupt from impious Manhattan, her daytime cloister. What could be more absurd?

Bag ladies poked through rubbish, half naked children played in the fountain, ragged old men shuffled by, tossing bread crumbs to bloated pigeons. Students in ragged jeans and T-shirts played Frisbee on the quadrangle, lunging and laughing in the sun. She watched them as she ate her sandwich out-of-doors on a bench or a cement step. Others in the class went off to the cafeteria together at noon. She'd been instructed not to join them. So she didn't. The rule about not eating with seculars was still in effect. As she came to know her classmates, the stricture felt more and more inane. She ducked their invitations to join them, laughing about how this was her one chance to eat alone in the fresh air. But she longed, sometimes, to go off with them. Occasionally, after his lunch, he'd find her on the quad and they'd chat before classes resumed.

And here she was now, hostage to a letter that paid her the ultimate compliment, gave her his confidence, his trust. In terms that spoke to her deepest hope. *You're trained to understand love. You live it.*

Had she asked for this, invited it? That he should write to her not for advice, clearly, but for—

What? He wanted her to meet him somewhere. How could that be? The deeper current stirred. Here was someone speaking to her as an adult, a woman, trusting her comprehension if not her experience. Was it possible to understand without identical experience? Keats, she recalled, had posed that very question.

"So how are you going to do it?" asked Sister Mark that night, as they walked up and down the driveway out front, skillfully avoiding involvement with the others until they all went inside for the round circle finale of evening recreation. "How will you ever manage it?"

Sister Claire smiled as they passed Reverend Mother. There were six or seven gathered around her. Always cheerful, Reverend Mother smiled and nodded at the two of them, went by.

How would she manage it? Impossible to know. For the moment, though, she cringed at one thought: the possibility of another letter. It must not happen. He must be warned. How would she let him know? And what would she let him know?

"Somehow I've got to talk to him," she said.

"Why?"

Ah—*the* question. She seemed to hear a reservation in her friend's voice.

"I'm not sure," she replied. Was it simply because she *wanted to?* That in her heart she looked forward to the pleasure of another meeting with him? She did not know.

"Well, be careful. That's all I'll say."

It wasn't the first time she'd felt Sister Mark's more experienced caution. Yet she knew she could count absolutely on her friend's discretion.

"Somehow I've got to manage it," she said.

"Good luck," said Sister Mark with a sigh.

Reverend Mother was nodding toward them. The others were climbing the steep steps toward the front entrance to the convent. They would go in now to the community room, swap harmless anecdotes for the next few minutes, then the bell would ring. Compline. Night prayer. The final *Salve Regina*, which she loved.

"Put a prayer on it," Sister Claire whispered.

She followed the others up the steps and through the heavy front door held open obsequiously by Sister Jane, a newly professed recently arrived at St. Gertrude's. Once—was it only three years ago?—she herself might have held the door like that, felt it appropriate, be expected to, as the youngest in the house. Not now. Only four years in the house, and here she was, planning a major disobedience, a deception. *Why?*

For there seemed to be no question, she thought, as she took her place beside Sister Patrick and pulled out her sewing box; there seemed to be no doubt she'd try. She'd find a way out, down to the city, to Columbia . . . to meet him. She slipped a wooden darning egg into the stocking and spread the disintegrating fibers of the heel across the rounded head. Then she set to work skillfully weaving. She was thinking . . . *How?*

And why? That, too, she wondered as she lay in her cell that night and listened to her principal, Sister Stephen, on the other side of the curtain, slipping off her headdress, hanging it on the specially bent hanger, kneeling in prayer, climbing into bed. How could she, Sister Claire, lie ten feet away from that squeaking mattress, planning . . . what?

This she wonders, lying there. Is she really motivated by charity? Or is it something else . . . something deeper, a need she cannot even name as she lies listening to Sister Stephen's rhythmic snore.

"Beware of contact with men," Reverend Mother Jerome had told them many times at the house of studies. Constantly, on campus, the young nuns came in contact with men. And ever since then she'd heard it more than once. Familiarity is to be avoided. Friendship is suspect. Of course, even her mother, always given to clichés, had said it years ago: "Familiarity breeds contempt, Claire." Yet—it wasn't as if she were planning to jump into bed with Ted Johnson. But he had reached out to her.

Christ had friends. He responded to their needs. . . . Her own
parents had reveled in the pleasures of good friends.

She misses Sister Hilary, miles away at the college. They might
have talked of these things—did years ago, when they knew
less. Though Sister Mark never gossips and is absolutely discreet,
they do not discuss the Big Questions . . . obedience, cloister.
Sister Mark seems to have made her own permanent peace with
the contradictions of the life.

What then is love?

This she wonders, moving through the routines of the next day.
What is love? Love is answering to the need of another. But—
any other? Why is the chance to visit Sister Clement, eaten by
cancer in the third-floor infirmary, why is this less compelling
than the call to see him? Listen to him? Because, for one thing,
he's intelligent. Sophisticated. And he has reached out to her.
In charity, she should respond.

All this is so much rationalization. She already knows she will.

His letter came Monday. She must find a way.

It is already Tuesday.

And then, at four-thirty that very afternoon, comes the call.

Her bell, five-one, is ringing. She is in chapel making her
afternoon meditation. It has been spliced with scenes from last
summer—scenes as clear to her now as she sits in the darkened
late afternoon chapel, bending over the Bible on her knees,
meditating on St. Paul, as clear to her as a film in Technicolor.

. . . She is leaving class after the fourth day. She is still feeling
self-conscious, but happy, so happy to be there. She has received
back a brief critical paper they were to write on a Wallace Stevens
poem, "The Snow Man." Professor Goldsmith has returned it
that day with public praise. A plus. He has read part of it to the
class. Still flushed with pleasure, she leaves, feeling that now
the summer workshop is possible. Even though she is the only
habit there, perhaps the only Catholic. At least they know she

has a mind. And before the six weeks are over they will discover her other attributes.

Now she is hurrying out of the classroom. The car will be waiting. Every day Sister David and Sister Andrew drive back from their summer course at Hofstra and park out front. As she is leaving the room that day, she hears her name called. "Sister Claire." She turns. Ted Johnson, who has been sitting beside her all week but has exchanged only a few rather witty remarks. He has seemed somewhat shy.

He is by no means handsome. He is balding. Tall. Slender. He has dark eyes that size you up sharply, as if they were trying to look inside, and a dark shaggy beard. He wears T-shirts and jeans. When he is not talking or laughing, his long narrow face looks almost gaunt. This summer he has already acquired a tan. He moves and gestures with a concentrated energy that fascinates her.

"That sounded like a terrific paper," he says, hurrying through the doorway toward her. "I was wondering . . ."

They stand just outside the classroom door. She feels a pleasant rush of heat at his recognition.

"I don't want to annoy you, but . . . would you mind if I looked over your paper? I couldn't make anything out of that poem at all!"

"Fine," she answers instantly, searching through her books to put her hands on the paper. "You're welcome to it."

"This is a whole new ball game for me, you know," he says, taking the paper with a quick nod of thanks. "I spend my days thinking about numbers and formulas."

They laugh and begin to move together down the hall leading to the exit from this old classroom building.

"Are you leaving now?" he asks.

"Yes. I get picked up every day right after the last afternoon class."

They stop by the front door. Through the glass, she can see Sister Andrew talking to a policeman. He'll relent. They always do. She parks in the No Parking spot every afternoon. New York cops love the sisters.

"Well, maybe after I look over your paper we could talk about the poem sometime?" He is looking down at her, into her, with those brown eyes. "At the moment I'm swinging from limb to limb, hanging on by my fingertips." He's glanced out the door, perhaps spotted the car, the companions. "Besides . . . I'd like to know you, Sister."

There is something in his manner—disarming, uncluttered—that wins her.

"I'd like to know you, too," she replies. It is true. A chance to talk to someone outside, not about anything heavy, nothing deeply personal, just talk about the material they are studying—books, poems, stories—talk about things of the mind. Something that isn't the spiritual life, the grade nine syllabus, or provincial gossip.

He holds open the door for her.

She thinks of all this, sees it in replay now as her convent bell is ringing, as St. Paul rests on her knees, as she sets him aside and hurries out of chapel.

Five-one.

Five-one.

And now apparently Ted Johnson wanted to talk to her about things of the body. What does she know about things of the body?

"How are you?" she says when she hears his voice on the phone. The same voice—amused, tolerant. Only now, somehow, more serious sounding.

Old Sister Phillipa is standing two feet away. When she is portress, Sister Phillipa always stands two feet away. She keeps track of all incoming and outgoing calls.

I can't talk to you now, Claire wants to say. How can he guess from the other end?

"I felt so foolish," he is saying. "So I just wrote you another letter to say that."

A stab of fear. This one may not go unslit. Then what?

"But I'd still like to meet you," he says. "Can you get down here on Saturday afternoon, by any chance?"

Ah, such a simple request. Why, when she appeared there so promptly every day for six weeks last summer, why should he suspect the tangle of red tape, spiritual as well as material, this will involve? Saturday afternoon. Sister Phillipa is watching. The simple request. The complexity it unravels.

"Yes," says Claire desperately. "Just say when and where."

"I'll watch for you at the front door," he says. "Hopworth, the building where our classes met. Look for the man in tweed with elbow patches."

"Thank you, Sister." She nods, slipping from the booth and returning to chapel.

Sister Phillipa notes on the record kept at the portress booth that at 4:30 P.M. on Tuesday a call came for Sister Claire. It is unlikely anyone will question this. Parents call to complain, students call to say they're sick, must miss a meeting.

Claire returns to her place, opens the book, sets it on her knees, and stares at the tabernacle. How will she deal with the letter? *Reverend Mother must not get it.*

Their meetings were innocent. Reverend Mother could have sat in on them, except that she wouldn't have understood much. And not understanding would have made her feel threatened. Reverend Mother Constance, their superior since last summer, had a totally literal mind. Her charity in the house, though, was real. She visited the sick daily. She would see any sister anytime. She liked to have them come to her. She was motherly. She had been kind, so far, to Sister Claire, admonishing her only not to get too close to the students. That way dangers lay. She saw life in small units of clearly defined daily acts of virtue. That view had much to commend it.

She kept regular hours in her office on the second floor of the large three-story convent. Finally Sister Claire could see no other way. If Reverend Mother slit this letter she would be (1) disturbed at the level of intimacy it supposed and (2) call in Sister Claire to find out more. One was to trust the superior totally, like the confessor. But trust cannot be commanded. Claire knew that. And hadn't Ted expected her to guard his trust?

Somehow she must intercept that letter. Extract it from the superior's office. It should arrive today, Wednesday. Mail was distributed before noon, left at their places in the refectory. Surely it would be in Reverend Mother's office by, say, ten-thirty. Her door was always open during the day. Nothing else to do, then, but sneak in and hope for the best. Be back late for class, but that could be managed.

All through first and second periods, Claire slammed her spiritual weight against a creeping layer of dread. "How do you understand a noun clause, Mary Lou?" What madness was driving her? Yet she must retract that letter. "Be careful of adjectives, Nancy. They can dilute a narrative." Why must she? Because if she didn't, Ted's situation would be Reverend Mother's knowledge, and maybe Mother Provincial's, and maybe even the subject in some disguised way of a conference. Who knew? And she would face sessions about this—cautions, admonishings, and all the while she would be helpless to convey the truth: that he was simply a friend. Friendship was suspect.

As Claire left the school side of the building, pushed back the heavy fire doors between, and hurried down the quiet corridor of the third floor (the old and sick floor), she prayed no one would intercept her, asking, "Sister Claire, what are you doing over here at this hour?" The infirmarian, for example. Or Sister Phillipa, prowling. "Shouldn't you be at class, Sister?"

She crossed the intersection of corridors at the center of the building directly above chapel and headed onward. No one so far. After the school-day sounds on the other side—girls hurrying through halls, voices penetrating classroom walls, announcements over the P.A.—this side felt funereal. No one around. Floors highly polished. The only light came from the far end, the stairwell just beyond Reverend Mother's office.

She reached the open door. She stopped. What was she contemplating? Her stomach dissolved to slithering jelly. She felt sick. Her palms grew clammy. But she must do it. What if Reverend Mother was in there? She'd quickly invent another excuse. What if Reverend Mother came in and found her there? No excuse then. She can see Reverend Mother's pretty, unlined face—astonished. Hurt.

She knocked against the door frame. Nothing. Not a sound. No one in there.

She peeked around the edge of the door . . . empty . . . then stepped quickly inside. Perfect order. Reverend Mother had opened the slats so that early morning light bathed the office. The desk was almost clear. There, to the right of the green blotter, lay a pile of mail. Unslit. She saw that in a flash.

Terrified, she picked it up. How would she ever explain if she was caught? Would they throw her out? They couldn't, because this sin had no category. It wasn't like violating chastity, say, or obedience. Could one call stealing one's own mail disobedience? The real crime lay (she knew it as she flipped quickly through the letters, half expecting the voice from behind, the shocked tone) in violating the superior's premises. That one was unforgivable. The superior represented God in their midst.

Ah, here it was. *Sister Claire Delaney.* His writing. She slipped it quickly through the side slit of her habit, into the huge underskirt pocket, turned, and left.

Striding down the corridor back to her sophomores, past the closed doors of the old and sick, through the heavy fire door, back into the sanctuary of her own classroom to a hasty, "Good morning, girls, sorry I'm late," she felt she could breathe again. The cloud, that one at least, had been lifted.

But more. How, on a Saturday afternoon in late September, would she get herself into New York City?

She would lie. There was no other way.

When she knelt for Reverend Mother's blessing outside the refectory after breakfast Saturday morning, she felt a bit hypocritical, a bit guilty. More frightened, though, that in some way she couldn't anticipate she might get caught.

And then it was done.

And now who on earth could find her here in Manhattan, Sister Mark safely stowed in the university library, willing to be an accomplice? Claire had claimed she needed books that weren't available in the high school library. A tenable request. Officially, they were encouraged to be serious about teaching, though Reverend Mother no doubt thought this request extreme. Typical of Sister Claire. But she'd blessed her quickly, without a demur, and asked no questions. The lineup for blessings was long that morning.

So here she is, walking briskly with him, passing people who seem not even to notice the long-skirted nun with her oh so secular escort, Ted in a tweed fallish jacket today, patches on the elbows, loafers, tan trousers, and his fedora. His shaggy dark beard has threads of white. He is nervous, she can tell.

"Thought we'd go to lunch in the Student Union," he says. "They've a nice restaurant upstairs."

She moves along beside him quickly. She's already made up her mind. She will eat with him today. Having gone this far, she can hardly back out now, say to him, "But that would be breaking cloister. We're not allowed to eat with seculars." Though once (she knows this) she would have refused. In fact she did—a day not too different from this—February, though—and she at the same university that day but accompanied by her then superior, Reverend Mother Rachel. Sister Claire thinks of it now, of how she felt betrayed that day as Reverend Mother bent a rule and drank coffee surrounded by a bevy of professors while she, Sister Claire, their invited guest, said, "No, no," because she was bound by rule.

What makes a rule bendable, breakable? The previous summer each house in the province gave every nun the opportunity to travel by car to the newly opened World's Fair. They were permitted to eat there, to walk the promenades, visit the pavilions—beginning with the Vatican, of course. How could she claim, then, that *this* is breaking cloister? What invisible circle creates cloister, non-cloister? How absurd can you get?

So she strides alongside him, relishing the clasp of September sun against the crown of her veiled head, trying to push back her own anxieties. She is doing this as an act of love. That she is clear about. Love involves risk, commitment; love is not a safe virtue.

"Here we go," he says, pushing the elevator button, lifting them high above the throbbing, littered street.

Her first impression is of wicker and hangings. Bordered by large windows on two sides, the restaurant is filled with tall wicker chairs and small tables covered with cloth of woven designs in blue and white. On every table including theirs (which is, thank God, in a corner) stands a small vase of fresh flowers. Pastel mums. From the high ceiling hang woven banners with some symbols on them that she cannot read. Indian, maybe. Or maybe not.

In any case, at last they are here. She looks at him as he orders. "Want a drink?" he asks.

She shakes her head. She makes herself very quiet. She is here to listen, to hear what she can hear. She knows already she will have no advice to offer. He doesn't want advice.

"Well," he says, opening his napkin, "you're a good sport."

"I got a friend to come with me," she says. "She's in the library."

He looks knowing. *But,* she thinks, *he isn't. He knows absolutely nothing about my tiptoeing into Reverend Mother's office to get the letter, about Sister Phillipa hovering around the portress booth, about my lying as I knelt for a blessing outside the refectory this morning. He knows nothing. Except that I came. It is enough.*

He leans over the table, his dark eyes alive and quick. "Watch out! Better duck. Here comes His Eminence!"

Her heart leaps. She turns quickly to look, then laughs. His idea of a joke. Maybe he knows more than she thinks.

As they nibble through stacked turkey sandwiches and a salad, he talks. Hesitantly at first, then more confidently. They've been seeing each other since before last summer. It was going on all summer. (She'd never had a clue.) She is young, maybe twelve years younger, beautiful, she understands him, but (and this is the essential thing) with her he has sex in a way he's never been able to have it before. They meet each other. It is wonderful.

She listens carefully. It is a difficult task to pick your way honestly and alertly through this morass. He has a wife. Two small children. But are those the things that matter? He knows those things matter. That's why he's written her. He reads bed-time stories to his five-year-old; his seven-year-old daughter is always after him to make another explosion with the chemistry set.

"I walk through the house at night and look at teacups," he says. "There is no life in teacups. I look at the furniture. No life there." He stirs his coffee.

She cannot mention the barrage of effects straining through her at this moment. The extraordinary sense of exposure, sitting in a public restaurant for the first time since 1954. Eleven years. With a man. And listening to, of all things, his domestic woes. If he weren't so obviously suffering, she might enjoy hearing about this. But he is exposing himself. And for a man shielded in irony this cannot be easy. She listens, summoning to a focus all her powers. This is all she can offer: an understanding ear. She has no advice for him.

Every word he speaks, every depiction of his pain, shows her more clearly how very little she knows.

"I don't expect you to advise me," he says, sensing her feeling. He's done this before, sensed what she was not saying. For that very reason he was, she suspected, a rare teacher.

"I have no advice," she says, stirring her coffee. It is close to two o'clock. They must be home by three forty-five. Reverend Mother had reminded them as they stood for a moment in the hallway after breakfast. Chapter at four. It will take at least an hour to reach the convent by subway and train.

One thing she cannot, will not say. She has resolved that

before she came. She will not say, "Go with her. Leave your family." Perhaps he has expected that nudge. She appears to be a freedom-loving soul, despite the incongruous clothing. They'd all remarked it one way or another during the summer. "You seem so *normal*." Tones of masked surprise, as though a woman clothed as she was must be an exotic fish inhabiting an aquarium of more exotic specimens breathing a different ether. She'd worked to dispel that silent judgment. Outside of class many of them were reading Henry Miller. At break time they often talked of *The Rosy Crucifixion*. She watched them and thought that even if the library at home had Miller's books—which obviously it didn't—they would have nothing to do with her life, and she wouldn't have time to read them anyway. She had five hours of prayer a day, counting Divine Office. Add to that meals, recreation, preparation for class, driving time, and getting to bed by nine-thirty, and what time was left? So she listened and watched. And after a while they were no longer careful, spoke more freely, made jokes back and forth that supposed access to an experience that simply was not hers. That didn't disturb her. To be seen as less than human would have disturbed her.

Suddenly he leans forward, his dark beard dipping toward his plate, and asks, "Tell me, Sister Claire—an irreverent question, perhaps, but I don't think you'll mind—how did they ever get you?"

"They?" She knows what he means. She is stalling. For this she was not prepared. She feels herself growing red.

"The Order. How did you get into this in the first place? You seem so . . . normal." He leans back in his chair.

"Ah . . ." She pauses, momentarily at a loss. She is thinking of her family, Vivien, Burt, the world into which she was born, a world ringed in love and certitudes—family, neighborhood, church . . . a vanished world. "Where to begin? It's complicated, Ted." She looks squarely at him. "But I can tell you it wasn't a case of *their* getting *me*. The big bad nuns. Any more than right now your situation is a case of someone getting *you*." She smiles, toying with her napkin, tempted to tell him how on graduation day itself—when she'd already signed her papers and filled her trunk with convent clothes, Sister Mary Ann, head of Sodality at college, ignorant of Claire Delaney's plans to enter, called her aside and said, "Claire, you'll make a wonderful wife and mother." Would he believe her? See the humor?

"Okay," he acknowledges readily. "You mean you made a choice."

"Yes. I was twenty-one. Out of college. But . . ." Where to begin? How far back to go? College? High school? The womb? "Where shall I start?" How to unwind back to a beginning? She may never see him again. Is it worth it?

"Good question," he says. "Start anywhere you want to. I have time."

His voice is quiet, steady. He sits quite still, as if this matters.

And so she begins. Just why, she later tried to understand. Something in his openness released her, perhaps. He wasn't judging. He had no ulterior motive. He really wanted to hear. He respected her. And she could trust him . . .

She started at random. Once begun, she felt it grow, her story, take a shape within the space created by his quiet attention. She didn't worry about sequence, causal connections. Life was not a filing cabinet. He would see the inner logic. For that is what she sought to convey, perhaps even to discover. And how odd, she thought, to find herself here amid the decorative wicker and forbidden food, here by an act of disobedience, exposing her soul to this man, believing he could hear her, honor her discomfort, her doubt.

". . . and there was Mother Magdalena in high school," she tells him. "And then college nuns who were learned, who were splendid teachers . . ."

"And you wanted to teach?"

"I always wanted to be a teacher."

"But you didn't have to be a nun to teach. What about . . . men?"

Ah . . . men again. She fiddles with her napkin. She wants to be honest. "They were around, Ted. I liked men . . ."

"And?"

She pauses. "It's not so much that I didn't want to marry. I dated. Liked some boys . . . though never *the* one. But I'd always been taught and I believed—perhaps because I breathed it from the time I was born!—that the highest and noblest way for a woman was a religious vocation. You grow up *inside* something and you can't see it from the outside. Even Pope John said being Pope is like being inside a paper bag."

"He's opened a few windows."

"A few. He was in a position to. But it's been tough. And they may not stay open."

His eyes are on her, quiet, attentive. A secular ear. Can he honor this?

"So . . . for years I prayed I'd be found worthy of that high vocation. Every day I prayed. Daily Mass during Lent, Advent. Yearly retreats. Novenas. And after all those years there came a moment when I felt . . . *called.* So I responded."

Nothing more to say.

"And . . . there is no denying experience," he comments.

"No," she says, grateful she hasn't. "There is no denying experience."

"How old are you?" he asks.

"Thirty-two."

"And has . . ." He puts it to her delicately, as though he had already observed, knew her answer. "Has your sense of things changed?"

"My sense of things is . . . changing."

They both knew it was time to stop.

He picked up the check, studied it. Then he looked over at her and said quietly, "Well, Claire. If ever there's anything I can do for you . . . just get in touch. Count me a friend."

He paid the bill. Left a tip.

She observed these maneuvers with subdued fascination. Rituals of self-possession in a secular world. Simple things. She seemed to have forgotten how to do them. He pulled out a plastic card. That she couldn't remember. Her dates seemed always to have paid cash. She'd managed a checking account at college, of course, but nothing major. Sodas at the corner drugstore, trips to town to see a movie, an occasional trip to Manhattan, the train home.

He took her elbow as they left the restaurant, guided her gently toward the elevator. A courtly gesture. It warmed her.

Then they were down, crossing again the sunlit square, heading toward the front door of Hopworth, where she could see Sister Mark waiting, clasping her book. She'd probably made her spiritual reading, poked around in the stacks. She made no pretense of being a scholar. She loved to float, observe, laugh. She seemed untroubled by excessive ambition, though she was a worker. She was smart. And loyal. After St. Bartholomew's closed, they'd made her full-time infirmarian in the house—a wearing assignment.

"I see your friend," he said. "Want me to leave you here and go through the side door? Or do you want me to meet her? How much does she know?"

"Everything," said Claire, then reddened. "No. I didn't mean that. I don't mean about you. I mean she knows I'm meeting you, that we've gone to lunch. She doesn't ask questions."

He nodded. "I'll leave you here," he said definitively. "Might be simpler all around."

He took her hand quickly. "Don't think this didn't mean something." He looked down at her. "And I'll see you again."

He squeezed her hand. Then he turned away, down the street, toward the side entrance. She saw his brown suede elbow patches disappear. She waved toward Sister Mark and hurried forward.

The chapter of faults met on the second floor in the community room usually on Saturday morning, but today, by a stroke of luck for Claire, at four o'clock. She slipped in and took her place on the chair fourth from the back. She was fourth from youngest in this community, age being figured by years in the Order. The youngest accused themselves first, kneeling by their chair, stating aloud the formula: "Reverend Mother, I humbly accuse myself of . . . ," then listing three faults. The guidelines were clear: the faults must be external violations of the rule. She understood the theory behind this but had grown to feel that what she could state had little to do with the realities of possible infraction in this particular aquarium. Wasn't the world of real adventure and transgression, decision and choice, interior? Invisible? Secret? And did naming three external faults really go toward healing rifts growing daily deeper in a community torn with internal conflict, anxious about rumbles of change portended by theologians arguing but not yet finished at Vatican II?

Sister Claire knelt. She barely heard the sisters behind her as they spoke: Sister Jane, Sister Edward, Sister Andrew. She was caught in a sense of contradiction so sharp it shook her whole body, threw a boulder into her throat. She couldn't think, speak. She was next.

She wrenched past the boulder. "Reverend Mother, I humbly accuse myself of—"anything, anything—"failing in silence, mortification, and of having looked curiously about."

She bowed her head—and saw the sun-drenched streets about Columbia, the bag ladies sweeping through trash bins, the drunk lying near the entrance to the Student Union. She saw Ted—his dark beard threaded with white, saw him lighting one cigarette after another, felt again his distress, his struggle.

Someone poked her from behind. "Sit down," whispered a voice.

Her turn was over. As the four youngest sat, the four sisters ahead of them knelt to accuse themselves. So it would move, up through the ranks.

At the end would come Reverend Mother's assignment of a penance—today a rosary to be said for the whole community and for those in the world suffering from an absence of love in their lives. Reverend Mother did not accuse herself in public. She settled herself at her desk and looked down at the paper in front of her.

"Today, Mothers and Sisters, I will speak to you about love."

Reverend Mother's voice sounded light and confident. A pretty voice.

Sister Claire looked about. Down in front, Sister Phillipa's head was drooping. She often slept through conferences. Behind her Sister Gertrude, bent almost in half, dear Sister Gertrude, who saw so much and kept her peace, bent over now with the disease destroying her spine. And then . . . Sister Cletus, Sister Catherine . . . Sister Stephen . . . and the others, rows of black heads whose shapes and angles she could identify even from the back.

"St. Paul tells us charity seeketh not its own," began Reverend Mother serenely. "That if we do not have charity we are as tinkling cymbals. Christ tells us that when we come before Him we will be judged on our charity. I wish to speak to you of charity to our neighbor, Sisters. Our neighbors live in this house. Your neighbor is the sister next to you. The sister who chews too loudly, the sister who annoys you in chapel, this is our God-given arena of charity . . ."

Neighbor. A certain man went up to Jericho . . . Who was one's neighbor? Whatsoever you do unto the least of these . . . Father, forgive them . . . Who was one's neighbor? The drunk lying across their path? Sister Phillipa at the portress booth?

Was this even a useful question?

She saw again the life in his eyes. "Duck. Here comes His Eminence." She felt his hand warm on her elbow.

What had she offered him?

A responsive heart. She had felt his pain, had offered him all she had—an open ear.

Was that charity? Was that what God had called her to, what she had vowed "forever"? Was that the meaning of *agape,* the concept they'd striven so earnestly as young novices to grasp? Something deep inside her had opened that day. She couldn't have named it, described it. Like the pale green lighting trees in early spring, or summer's freshness through an opened door. Like a shift in the weather.

Sister Claire sat surrounded by black, deaf to the pieties of her superior, aware now of a light staccato snore coming from down in front, the vicinity of Sister Phillipa.

At least, she thought (and thank God for it), at least she had not been caught.

Angels of Reality

Rain pounds against the roof as she climbs—one step, another, black slippers sliding tentatively onto each stair—up, up. She knows exactly which steps harbor groans and creaks, which can be relied upon not to betray her. She's learned how to deliver herself by feel through this darkness, almost holding her breath until she reaches the top. She makes her body small, light, compact, mastering stealth. She has been doing this for weeks.

Ah, now, the top.

One window at either end of the long attic. Beneath her, acres of sleeping, dreaming nuns. Above, the heavens—galaxies of light dancing in space, celestial symphony of the spheres. None of this does she hear or see as she pauses at the top of the stairs for a moment, listening. Satisfied, she pulls the string of one light bulb, dousing a sheet of moonlight at the far end of the attic.

About twenty-five steps into the attic (she's counted and does again now) sits a small table in the middle of the floor. She moves gingerly toward the table, sets on it her loose-leaf and heavy hardbacked textbook, eases herself into the chair on the far side of the table . . . and prays.

That tonight she will not be caught.

This is where she prepares for class. The extra class she's agreed to take. And this is the puzzle that stalls her, night after night, until she wills the puzzle aside and forces her mind to absorb the primary exports of the Pacific Northwest, the resources of the Mesabi Range, the why of the ghostly gash in the hillside of Butte, Montana, the wonders of this earthly Eden.

This is the puzzle: Why is she climbing like this, why is she cramming, in the attic of a dark convent on a hillside in Yonkers in fall of the year of Our Lord, 1965? What propels her climbing feet? Her secret sinning? Why has she not said, long before, *It is impossible?*

> *Lucifer failed. He fell from the heavens. He burns in the fiery pit. His light became darkness. He goes about seeking whom he can devour. Therefore, be ye sober and watchful.*

When she was twelve or thirteen, she wanted to look like Elizabeth Taylor, play the piano like Vladimir Horowitz, have a dozen children, and upon dying go straight to heaven among the ranks of the saints. Depending on the day or the hour, one or the other of these ambitions held sway. During retreats she wanted to be a saint. At a concert she longed for keyboard virtuosity. Now, as she opens her book, such dead vanities are no help. She wants only to prove that she has brains.

This is brains?

Sister Stephen sent for her. Sister Stephen, whose personal anxieties generated strategies of supervision in the high school that

irritated everyone. Not all principals in the province were like
Sister Stephen. In Calais, Claire had been initiated into teaching
under an extraordinarily enlightened principal, Sister Isidore.
She would fight for her faculty, her students. She would build
a school. But Sister Stephen is a rubber-stamp principal: whatever Reverend Mother says. And Reverend Mother Constance
on the other side of the heavy fire doors, remote and safe in
her pin-neat office, what can she know of battle scars incurred
daily through wars of love and learning with resistant adolescents? Though this was only her fourth year at St. Gertrude's,
Claire could feel the cancer eating out the communal soul in
this house. And Sister Stephen, imported to help matters, was
only making them worse.

"Sit down, Sister," she said that morning in late October,
pushing aside the one sheet of paper on her desk. "How are
your classes going?"

She had perfected a smile of concern. She wanted her teachers
to know she cared.

"Fine, so far." They were seven weeks into the semester. No
point in stressing the obvious: in a day with seven class periods,
she has five classes of English, one of Latin. The heaviest teaching
load in the school. She is proud of it, doing well. The students
love her. She swings through the halls feeling talented, capable.
Her vows hold her intact; her love makes her whole. Sister Mark
tells her she may be overdoing it, but she relishes the challenge.

"I know you are very busy, Sister. And the reports from all
the students are certainly fine."

Sister Claire suppresses her urge to comment. Sister Stephen
simply would not grasp why such checking on her teachers is
odious.

"I do have a problem, Sister." She pauses, watching Sister
Claire. "You know that our Sister Genevieve is ill."

Claire knows nothing.

"Reverend Mother told me last night that Sister Genevieve
will not be able to return to class this year, Sister. She is too
sick."

Such illness is a mystery. Sister Genevieve is five years ahead
of Claire in religion. They never went through novitiate or juniorate together, experiences that give one a perspective on a
sister. Claire knows only that suddenly Sister Genevieve has
disappeared. The hospital, perhaps. She's been looking drawn,
nervous, downright twitchy. But alluding to personal difficulties
is taboo in the house of God. Unnamed, they will cease to exist.
Only the superior is privy to such secrets. And the infirmarian—
perhaps. One tries to smile.

Sister Stephen is smiling now . . . the same smile she offered
last spring when she counseled Sister Claire to stop playing the
piano on Friday afternoons after school for a few of her friends
among the students. They would stay after classes for an hour
or so, talk, listen to her play. Sister Stephen did not approve.

She presses together the balls of her soft white fingers. "Sister
Genevieve's class in geography has to be covered, Sister. And
I am actually quite perplexed. We simply cannot afford to hire
another part-time teacher . . ."

She picks up the paper from her desk and studies it. "I have
your schedule here, Sister. And I know that already you are
carrying one extra class. That gives you six periods . . ."

Sitting there listening, watching, Sister Claire feels that spot
opening inside her again. It's happened before. It's like a reflex,
a tiny fissure that widens when the invitation is issued—the
challenge, the question. *I can do it. I can do it. The little engine
that could. Let them know.*

She tries to hold that quivering spot still. Sister Stephen wants
a volunteer. It is madness.

". . . and you have five preparations . . ."

"Perhaps I—" She hears herself saying it, the words she
doesn't want. Why do they come again? *Where do they come from?*
"I think I could manage it, Sister."

Sister Stephen smiles more widely, a rubbery smile that re-
veals a jaw filled with large white teeth. "I didn't want to ask
this of you, Sister." She sets down the paper and folds her hands
on top of it. "You are, I know, very capable."

In the attic, by moonlight, Claire does not feel capable. Beneath the rafters, dark cartons cluster, dead furniture crowds: a broken prie-dieu, fractured lamps, the side of a box spring, a mattress. Perhaps this is a tomb. But aren't tombs beneath the earth, not above it? She feels desperate. By the dim light she studies imports and exports, the glacial features of North America, the meaning of watershed, Continental Divide. She must quiz her class each day. They are accommodating, sympathetic perhaps. Surely they guess she is but half a step ahead of them. But they'll get through the year, all of them, and she the only nun who carried seven periods that year, six preparations.

Insane.

"Perhaps you take your schoolwork too seriously," Reverend Mother admonished her when she asked permission to stay up an hour later to prepare.

"What is too seriously?" she'd dared to ask.

"Surely you do not need to prepare every day for every class, Sister."

Reverend Mother Constance had never taught high school, never coped with that volatile mix of wit, intelligence, will, and hormonal buzz.

"I do, Reverend Mother. And I know nothing about economic geography. Sister Stephen needed it covered. I see that with my other classes I will need permission to stay up until ten or ten-thirty during the school week."

She had expected Reverend Mother to understand. It seemed a reasonable request.

Reverend Mother had remained silent for a long instant. Then she'd sighed as she replied. "Yes, Sister. I see you do have a problem. But God will give you the grace. He never abandons us. You were generous enough to agree to take this class. He will not fail you. But you need your sleep, your rest. We have a very full day. We need our nuns in good health. I cannot in conscience grant you this permission."

Pointless to mention that nuns at the college stayed up every night, that she was saving the Order the cost of a part-time teacher. Pointless to argue. Because arguing was a failure in obedience.

And so she climbs nightly. More than her health, she needs peace of mind. She simply cannot get her classes prepared in the leftover time of a day. For two weeks she tried. By then her classes felt like half-settled Jell-O slithering out between her fingers each day, each hour. She could have told Sister Stephen it was impossible, but that would bring other complications, immediate and remote. For one thing, if she stopped now, the class would get its third teacher of the year. If one could be found. More important, if she admitted now her mistake—was it a mistake?—that would be used against her, to her disadvantage, later. Or could be.

An opportunity she couldn't foresee might come along. When she asked permission, the reply would come, "No, Sister. It isn't prudent. You tend to take on too much." Already she'd come perilously close to such denials. It was all too easy to get labeled.

So she will stick out the class in economic geography, get through.

The attic, these winter nights, grows cold.

What happened to the angels who did not remain faithful to God?

The angels who did not remain faithful to God were cast into hell, and these are called bad angels, or devils.

What is the chief way in which the bad angels try to harm us?

The chief way in which the bad angels try to harm us is by tempting us to sin.

Do all temptations come from the bad angels?

Some temptations come from the bad angels; but other temptations come from ourselves and from the persons and things around us.

Why, as she stares at pictures of the Cascade mountain range, do these words return to her? She has not seen the old Baltimore Catechism in almost twenty years. How far she has moved from that world of neat questions and answers, those lessons with the illustrations at the head (mortal sin a milk bottle full of black milk, venial, a milk bottle full of spots!), and those vocabulary lessons whose words many of her students today might not comprehend: *sanctifying . . . indelible . . . sacramental . . . presumption . . . benignity.* The last word, she recalls suddenly, came from the lesson on the virtues and gifts of the Holy Ghost, a wonderful lesson that told her of hidden powers she carried, powers depicted in the drawing of a tree that stood on a small island surrounded by the waters of grace. Springing up from that favored island was the tree of these new powers—hidden powers she could call on in times of stress—wisdom, understanding, counsel, fortitude, knowledge, piety, and fear of the Lord.

She could use a bit of that right now, she thinks, wrapping her seersucker robe about her legs, tucking it in tight. She needs a new sense of understanding. What is wisdom? What is knowledge? She's up on fear of the Lord.

Soon snow. It is mid-December.

*

"In 1823 Giacomo C. Beltrami, a political exile from Italy, joined an expedition to explore the Minnesota and Red River valleys," she tells them.

Another six weeks have passed. She and the class have settled into a tacit understanding that this is a course to be gotten through, that it will contain no electricity from either side. Mary Ellen is, as usual, taking notes in her stuffed notebook. Sarah Greenfield is yawning. Two o'clock sun has struck the green bulletin board at the back of the room. Perhaps it is warming up outside. Soon February thaw. This is their final unit on exploration of the Midwest.

"In Red River country he left the party behind," she continues against the yawn. "He took one guide and two Ojibway Indians. They set out toward the southeast. Eventually he was stranded. Then, guided by Indians, sometimes carrying or towing his canoe, he did come at last to a body of water he called Lake Julia. It was twelve miles north of Bemidji. He gazed at its wide and beautiful blue and believed he'd found the northernmost source of the Mississippi. He was wrong. Afterward, back at his camp on Cass Lake, he learned from Indians about another lake, now named Itasca, the real source of the headwaters. He didn't try to reach it. On his map he described it as the western source of the Mississippi."

She can almost smell their boredom. Who, at sixteen, can take seriously the question of headwaters?

"That's all," she says. "For tomorrow, know how Schoolcraft's expedition to find the headwaters differed from that of Beltrami. Finding the headwaters of the Mississippi has goaded the imaginations of men for decades."

They look at her as if to say, *How could it?*

But it does.

Beneath the light bulb that night she sees him, the deluded explorer, old Giacomo, political exile, yearning for fame, justification in the eyes of his countrymen. "I, Marco Polo; I, Christopher Columbus; I, John Cabot; I, Giacomo Beltrami": his litany, the blessed he longs to join. She sees his flashing dark eyes as he motions stragglers onward, speaking in signs to the Indians, this flamboyant Italian in his leather boots. Leather? Well, boots anyhow. She wants him in a cape with scarlet lining. Highly impractical, but it suits him, her Giacomo.

She studies their maps: Beltrami, Schoolcraft, the meanderings of the old Miss, the tiny puddle of its beginnings that grows and wanders, a blue snake uncoiling across the flat map, dividing America.

Could she map her route to this light bulb, this dark attic, this absurd ascent, what would it show?

Not uncertain meanderings on a flat map, but the steady attempt to rise. This is why she climbs. This is why the innermost spot quivers open, against her will. This is beneath all her yeses.

Does not the greatest and final yes lead up?

Jesus rose.

Mary rose (so they say).

Vapor rises. Must the vapor of her mind, her imagination, also rise?

That night she dreams. It is the peak of summer. She is climbing up, up, up, clad in shorts, sneakers with socks, a cool shirt. She is about eleven, almost too old to climb. Already her mother is after her to stop. Past a certain age it is "unbecoming" to be a tomboy. The tree is in their backyard, a tall leafy maple whose lowest branch can be reached by a tiny leap from the ground. Especially on early summer mornings she loves to do this, go outside after breakfast when the sun, bright but not yet hot, shines through the leaves, patterning the grass in shapes that dance and shimmer. She leaps upward, catches hold, pulls herself into the tree impervious to scratching bark. She is climbing toward the sun. Catch hold of the next branch, now. *Pull.* Through the branches. They scrape at her, tiny twigs threaten the eyes, her arms push through leaves as she climbs up, up. Toward the top. She cannot quite reach the top, although she is not very heavy, ninety-eight pounds at most. She has begun to grow breasts. She is careful of these, lest a twig snap against them. Branches beneath her feet grow slimmer, more delicate. She must pull herself up more gently, test with one foot for the weight, the spring, gradually slide both feet onto the branch, then let go with her full weight before she pulls herself up farther.

From here everything looks different. She hugs the trunk of the tree and sways with it. Back and forth. It's a sturdy tree that accepts her weight and leans with it without cracking.

Finally, when her last foothold tells her this is as high as she can go, she stops and looks out, down, over the backyard with its striped lawn chairs, the purple and white hydrangeas, the brown lilacs, toward the house where meals and homework and bedmaking and dishes and sweeping and dusting and keeping-quiet-because-Daddy-is-resting are sealed inside. And she is on the outside, near the top, quietly swaying with the tree, hugging its warped bark against her, pressing the thin soles of her sneakers down on the gnarled branch beneath.

The bell rings.

She leaps from bed to begin her prayers, brushing leaves from her hair, a residue of bark still clinging to her hands.

Veritas Caput.

She asks that on the quiz next day. "Explain the name of the park which holds the headwaters of the Mississippi." Itasca. End of *veritas,* beginning of *caput.* This they may consider a double-cross, but she's teaching Latin I to the same class.

Afterward, as relief from the quiz, she reads them a brief account of a later exploration of the region leading to the headwaters. "There I was," writes Nicollet, "sweeping aside one by one the branches in my way, sometimes sinking through the mossy crust on which I was treading, plunging knee-deep into water, falling amidst the slimy decay of big trees on which I thought I had sure footing but which completely crumbled under my weight."

She has never had a tree crumble under her weight. The tree in the backyard held her up. Climbing has always appealed to her, the effort and thrill of hoisting oneself up through the leafy arms of nature and grace, aiming for the very top.

Yet now, reading his account to her barely tolerant sophomores, ignoring their boredom, their illicit gum-chewing and covert doodling, she moves alongside the great explorer, feels with him the precariousness of earth itself, solidity turning to mush. She places a wary foot beside his, shares with him the sudden sharp betrayal of what had seemed sure.

Her students are not listening. She doesn't care. These words are not for them but for her. Someone, something has sent them. Could it be the Holy Spirit? They reach deep into her understanding, her experience.

Through them she gasps anew the old lure of adventure, the

desire to chart new paths through the dense and tangled richness of this world. Grasps even more the need to make maps—an activity which before had always seemed to her as dull as the paper on which they'd been written. And finally grasps, anew, what she has long believed . . . that light (sometimes just a sliver) can come from the oddest quarters, even through that horrid hardbacked too-thick book of facts called *Economic Geography,* which she never wanted or needed to know.

As they leave the room that day, the girls are puzzled by Sister Claire's smile.

*

March has come, a cool one, and with it Mrs. Greenfield, mother of Sarah. She comes not to speak of Sarah, but of herself. They will sit in the parlor, though it's close and dark. Mrs. Greenfield has developed the capacity to ignore convent parlors. She comes twice a year to talk to Sister Claire. Today it is too chilly to sit outside.

What ghosts haunt those eyes? Mrs. Greenfield is unhappily married. She is making the best of it. One way to do this, she has discovered, is to travel. After each trip she returns to the convent to talk to Sister Claire. Always she brings back postcards. Today she is full of southern Germany: baroque churches, cathedrals, the Schwarzwald, the Bodensee. She rhapsodizes about the Münster in Freiburg.

"Our guide wanted us to climb to the very top of the tower, Sister," she says. "I tried. Henry went on ahead of me. I stayed at the end of the line. We climbed, around and around, in this narrow stone tower. Finally we came to a small ledge, a kind of resting place. Then we began again. Our guide wanted us to see the view of Freiburg, a beautiful town, from the top. Finally I could go no higher. My stomach was upset, my knees watery, I felt I might keel over. So I backed down, waited on the landing below, where I could look at postcards and buy some descriptive brochures. There I picked this up for you."

She hands Claire a postcard.

"Even though I didn't get all the way up, this shows what I missed. It was the most interesting view: a look up through the tower toward the sky, rather than down toward the town below."

A spiderweb in stone, that's how it looks. Concentric octagons, perfectly symmetrical, gathering to the center, the point, the very top, *die Spitz*. Only it is no longer top, but center. Flattened out. Next to this card, Claire holds another view: the tower seen from the square below, a filigree in stone stretching heavenward, delicate and exalted—the dream of ascent.

"This cathedral wasn't damaged in the war," says Mrs. Greenfield. "Of course, they took out the windows. But it was a miracle the structure was left untouched. The whole square around it was demolished."

A miracle.

Was it a miracle that the bomb did not hit? Or is it a miracle that now, sitting in this dark and stuffy convent parlor, staring at the postcard lying on her virginal knee, Claire sees not a tower chiseled in stone, not a spire, but a web? Who had the idea to look at it that way? Is the actual miracle that now, from this glossy postcard offered her by a dissatisfied woman with sad eyes, she begins to view human aspiration from another angle? Look to the sky through the stone. Discover the spaces.

Simeon Stylites, a fascinating kook, built himself a pillar and ascended. There he stayed for years, a living steeple. He built himself a platform with a balustrade and settled into his elevated hermitage, or so he hoped. Yet, we're told, they climbed up there to bug him, earnest God seekers, to talk to him, even confess, to receive from those holy hands the bread of life. (How did they get *that* up there? Other question: How did he handle bodily functions?)

She thanks Mrs. Greenfield for the card. A place marker for her economic geography text.

Sarah Greenfield is a troubled girl. She wears her pain like a party dress, something that will get her noticed. Once noticed, she shifts her tactic—challenging her audience to justify such attention. Bright, she collects her A's with disdain. She is perhaps embarrassed to suspect her mother wishes she would become a nun.

Sister Claire resolves to pay more careful attention to Sarah. In three months she will leave St. Gertrude's for the summer.

*

Easter has come and gone. Everyone is busy filling out recommendations for the coming general chapter in Rome. Now that Vatican II is over, its decrees promulgated, change is inevitable. Rumor has it that a new habit will be adopted this summer. The change of style will be optional.

Tomorrow is the Feast of the Ascension. Reverend Mother is giving them a conference on this event. The text is convincing as it reads. Claire has always loved especially the part where Christ has just finished scolding the busybody apostles for their curiosity, always wanting to know what's coming, what's in it for them. He tells them off so neatly, succinctly: "It is not for you to know the times or dates which the Father has fixed by His own authority; but you shall receive power when the Holy Spirit comes upon you, and you shall be witnesses for Me in Jerusalem and in all Judea and Samaria and even to the very end of the earth."

Reverend Mother can't let the text be. She's got to make a moral of it. "Live always as if in heaven with the Lord," she tells them. *This,* thinks Claire, is *no* heaven.

"And when He had said this, He was lifted up before their eyes, and a cloud took Him out of their sight."

A compelling picture, and tantalizing. As Reverend Mother drones on, Claire thinks of heaven. Up. And her excursions nightly to the attic. Almost over. But what—still the question troubles her—has made her climb?

Temptation.

What is temptation?

Lucifer, she thinks, as she climbs that night, easing onto each stair. Lucifer, that fallen boob, took Jesus to a mountaintop and showed Him the world. *A mountaintop.* She's seen mountains, though she's never climbed one, literally. From a distance, a moving train, she's felt their presence: Mount Rainier, Mount St. Helens, stalwart greats of the Pacific Northwest, their gleaming snowcapped peaks severed by mist from the land below.

Her parents had taken them both, Paul and Claire, on a train ride across the country when Paul graduated from prep school. "You should see your own country at least once," her father had said. And she'd tried to match vast spaces, deep canyons, and rugged peaks with the flat pink and green and yellow states of their atlas. After a while the distances had tired them. She would have liked to sit on a mountainside and pick wildflowers. She thinks of that trip now as she sits in the attic beneath her light bulb, opening the book. Now she would appreciate it.

Yahweh favored clouds. *Shekinah.* He spoke down from them.

And Jesus spoke *up* to His father.

Then there was Lucifer. "All this will I give you if kneeling down you will adore me," said the boob.

This was temptation. Lucifer . . . the great promoter of ascent. But Jesus' words were clear . . . do not hide your light under a bushel. Set it on a mountain for all to see. When, then, did ambition become temptation?

She flips the pages, glancing at pictures. Soon no more climbs to the attic. Spring has come. The girls will take their exams, pass or fail, run into summer with rippling knees and shorter skirts. If skirts . . . They will find their trees to climb, shed what earth they wish to shed. Climb toward what they desire. It is difficult to assess desire. Once, she had thought it simple.

She opens the book. They are almost done.

*

Can one dream forward? Do our dreams lead us mysteriously to the future?

Five days later she asks Sister Mark. It is Saturday morning and they are in the laundry mixing cleanliness with godliness.

"Do you think you can dream forward?" she asks, rubbing a bar of yellow soap against stained linen. "Last night I dreamed I was climbing a mountain, puffing away, exhausted, my muscles screaming. I thought I'd die in the effort, but I kept going."

"In the habit?"

"Heavens, I don't know." She cannot remember such a detail. The habit is on everyone's mind these days. She remembers only the exertion, the sheer effort of the climb, vision of the top magnetizing desire. Hope, too. Something gave her hope, a nugget warming her heart. I think I can, I think I can. I hope I can.

"I climbed and climbed. The ground was rocky; sometimes I slipped back. I pulled myself forward by weeds and shrubs, tucked my toes into the soft dirt, longed for one of those ski lift affairs, you know what I mean?" (Maybe that's how she used to imagine God: a kind of benevolent ski lift.)

Sister Mark plugs in the mangle.

"Anyhow, I was just about to reach the top and—*powwee!* The whole top blew off, just like that. As if it had been waiting for me to arrive! Terrific blast. I stood there holding my ground, and watched stuff come pouring out—rocks and fire and blue gases and junk. It was crazy, showering all over the place, shooting high into the clouds, blacking out the sky. Then came layers of sticky soot. It fell around me like the residue of a great firework, the ultimate Roman candle. . . . Then I went on climbing. That's the funny thing."

"Why?"

"Because I was just as curious as ever. You'd have thought I'd be afraid, run for my life, give it all up. Not a bit of it. Only now, in some way, everything had changed. It wasn't so much that I wanted to reach the top anymore. I wanted more to find out what was on the inside of the mountain, to peer into that enormous hole, see and explore every last inch of that fabulous crater. Would it be all darkness? What would I find glowing? Would I discover some new element I couldn't have imagined from the outside?"

Sister Mark, sorting the pile of altar cloths beside the mangle, pauses. "Sounds just like you," she says. "I can't imagine you running away. You'd be bound and determined to find out what was on the inside." She takes one damp linen and smooths it out, smiling. "And so . . . what did you discover?"

"Nothing," says Claire. She spots a loose thread on the templet she's been laundering and pulls at it, unraveling the hem. "An unfinished dream. That's all."

"Like most," says Sister Mark dryly, and starts the mangle.

"Men of Galilee, why do you stand looking up to heaven?" asked the mysterious men in white. A perfectly logical question. "This Jesus who has been taken up from you into heaven, shall come in the same way as you have seen Him going up to heaven."

A passage fraught with difficulties, but she understands their question.

She's becoming interested in angels, especially these men in white. They seem so brisk, so matter-of-fact, so get-on-with-your-business-will-you? Stop mooning around.

It is the last night. She has closed her book. Someone was up here today and opened the two windows. All day the smell of lilacs and honeysuckle and mock orange has blown in from below, collected now as a thick, sweet perfume, attic incense.

She's gotten through the course. She feels no more capable than she did in September, but a good deal more tired. Next time she'll conquer the anxious quivering need to say yes, to prove herself. It was stupid.

Angels favor dreams. Joseph, the cuckolded one, was warned in a dream. He took his wife and child and headed for Egypt. And the wise men. They outfoxed Herod, thanks to an angel. Even that other Joseph, remember him? Reading Pharaoh's dream. Let my people go. And Jacob. He wrestled.

Late spring whispers all about her in the attic. She moves to the window now, a pause before she descends.

The full moon pours white light on the jungle of apartment buildings surrounding the hill. The Big Dipper dips over Westchester. Orion straddles Riverdale. That may be the shoulder of Cassiopeia over Manhattan Island.

Sister Claire gazes at rooftops, television aerials, chimneys, fire escapes, stars, the Milky Way, the whole eternal spangled sky.

The two of them are coming slowly toward her. Vapor streams out behind them, wisping into night. What matter if they're vapor? She *sees* them. They leave the stars far behind, intact and glittering. They are coming, coming. Long before they arrive, she feels their breath. It forms no syllables. They hum to her soul a new song . . . that climbing leads not heavenward, that maps chart only that which has already been found.

She rests her head against the window frame and breathes deep the lavender air.

They come like clouds against the evening sky. Of buried moments they sing, breathing half-acknowledged desire. Imperceptibly they slip within. She remembers now: angels have that special quality. They can pass through doors, walls, even the wall of the heart.

She opens herself to them, welcoming. These are the angels of reality. She knows them already, always has. They will cool her against scorchings to come, sing her songs half familiar, half strange, melodies of beauty and pain.

Let them come, then, secrets of this spring night, floating on the fragrance of earth, hymning that which has been, that which is to be. Let them come and rest in her heart.

Jubilee

When Sister Gertrude tapped her way slowly into her superior's office, she was told immediately to sit. Both understood this was in no way to deny the presence of God in her superior—a presence usually acknowledged by kneeling and asking a blessing—but simply to deal with facts: a bent back, arthritic knees, and failing eyesight made kneeling difficult. Moreover, unreliable vision sometimes affected her judgment of distances.

"How are you, Sister?"

The aged nun wedged her cane between her chair and the side of the superior's desk.

"Fine, thank you, Reverend Mother."

The usual answer. Despite obvious physical sufferings, Sister Gertrude managed a certain opaqueness about her health that more subtle superiors found disconcerting. This one took her at her word.

"Perhaps you shouldn't be coming to all the hours of Office, Sister. Save your strength for your jubilee celebration on Sunday. Not many of us are fortunate enough to reach such a day, you know. Keep up your strength so you can enjoy it."

On the surface all the words worked together, but they pulled against the clear sense Reverend Mother conveyed of being preoccupied with other things.

Words at odds with facts caused Sister Gertrude little surprise. She knew life seldom delivers what it promises. It would take more than that to anger her now. Though there had been days— back when her veiled hair was still red and she charged about the house (noisily, it was pointed out) rather than crept—when she felt choked and breakable, like a fragile cylinder full of explosive gas. Corked. Sealed. Labeled, even. Dangerous. But explosion cost more than control, she'd learned. And got nowhere. Eventually practice turned silence from an obligation of rule to a form of self-protection. And so a precarious synthesis was wrung out of passing years: the outer decorum habit required, the inner self relatively intact. Compassion was there to be tapped, yet also an eye alert to manipulative nuance, the religious masks of power. She was no fool.

These days she lived in dread. Not so much of death, inevitable, as of surrender to nostalgia. That she might turn into what she looked like: a relic. Dated and bent. Left over. Stuck forever in the past. So she was watchful. Wary of memory's seductive power, she steeled herself to face the present wide-awake. But that, too, could betray: you know not the moment or the hour.

So at seventy-five Sister Gertrude held an odd place in the community—an old religious, dying by inches, who preferred *The New York Times* to the *Review for Religious,* yet never missed her daily rosary. Her blend of alertness and decrepitude sometimes baffled others. Over the years many had claimed her affection, but she was not easy to know. Though smaller minds failed to grasp her synthesis, they sensed that even now, *especially now,* she fought feebleness and scorned quaintness—refused, in short, to be written off as a character.

And now she had reached the crowning point of her religious life, her golden jubilee.

"Have you drawn up a list of those you would like invited, Sister?" Reverend Mother was poised, expectant.

"Really, Reverend Mother, I would be happy to have just the members of the community there."

"But surely, Sister, there are members of your family . . ."

Always the push toward the outside now. Once, the religious community had been considered family. And the other? Mother, father? Luminous dust at memory's rim: a sudden flare, then shadow. She would see them all before long.

"Only Gloria, my grand-niece, Reverend Mother, and I don't believe she'd even know the significance of a golden jubilee."

Gloria sprang from the Protestant side, daughter of the brother who married out of the Church and raised a family of religious nondescripts.

"Well, then, Sister, are there any friends on the outside you would like to invite?"

More promising. All those years of teaching at St. Gertrude's, first in primary, then as the only piano teacher for the whole school, elementary and high. Droves of pupils. The specials who came back after school to soak up music, learned to play four-hand with her: Clementi, Mozart, Brahms, Weber. Still thought of her, came to see her when they were in town—mothers now, dragging their children for review, having them play a tune for her. *Plinka-plinka-plink.* Rigid dressed-up bodies. Instructed on decorum. Pigtails. Barrettes. Always a sonata, usually the first movement. Anxious mothers swollen with pride.

Yes, they remembered her, sent Christmas cards, birth and death announcements, wedding invitations. How many dozen bootees had she crocheted till aching fingers refused first that, then even the sympathy notes?

Yet when all was said and done, her touch with their rituals of life and death was peripheral. What did they know about her—*now?* And what did she know about them? How *could* they participate in her triumph? Too personal, too precarious. She would renew her vows before the assembled community at Mass on Sunday morning. Need there be more?

She peered up through thick lenses at the pink-complexioned face half-smiling at her. Pretty. In a baby-doll way. Unlike some, still in the modified headdress. It became her. A consideration, no doubt.

Gracious, chatty, charming in small doses, this superior relished celebrations. Attention. Operating the strings of pleasure. Her prettiness and surface charm caught the eye. Parents responded enthusiastically to her at their periodic gatherings. She might have fluttered effectively as the wife of a small business executive. Instead she bubbled whenever possible, turned sharing a box of chocolates into a giggling flourish of magnanimity, and hogged with disarming charm the trivial stages of daily life.

Sister Gertrude breathed deep against the pain of lifting her head. The back, the neck were alarmingly worse. The disease eating straightness from her spine threatened to fold her in half before they boxed her.

O death, here is thy sting: decay before dust. It would have been easier to go ten years ago.

"Reverend Mother, I've been thinking about this. I've spent fifty years of my life in this house. The size of the celebration doesn't matter to me. I would be grateful for a simple ceremony. Not a solemn high Mass. Just the usual. And no outsiders, at least not by special invitation."

Disappointment darkened the eyes.

"That will be fine, Sister. After all, it is your day. I have, of course, let Sister Andrew put a notice of it in the last Alumnae Newsletter. Perhaps you saw . . . there must be old students who would want to know. We owe it to them."

Typical. Let it pass. Of course I didn't see it.

"I do have one request, though, Reverend Mother."

A gleam.

"You know how good Sister Claire has been to me for the

past three years." Seeing to all sorts of details: telling her of schedule changes, carrying up her laundry and mail, delivering her notes to Reverend Mother's box, answering her bell. Even— emptying the commode. Changing the sheets. More often lately. Humiliating. They never spoke of it.

"Indeed, Sister. But then you know Sister Claire is happy to do it for you."

A lie. Less than the truth, at least. Who was proof against the unpleasantness of age—leaking, smelling, creeping, clinging age?

"Anyway, Reverend Mother, I would like to have Sister Claire play the organ at Mass that morning and then sit at head table for breakfast with us."

She caught the sudden intake of breath, felt her superior's hesitation. Searching for an answer. Delicate matter. Only the jubilarian sat with the superior and her assistant at head table.

"You know I hesitate to meddle in Sister Hildegarde's domain. She asked to play your jubilee Mass."

Sister Hildegarde had inherited choir from Sister Gertrude when arthritis finally had made playing the organ impossible. Tenacious and cranky, she was a formidable adversary. She resented Sister Claire's appointment as "helper" and rightly perceived this move as a not-so-discreet nudge toward retirement. Superiors interfered with her as little as possible as she scowled and hacked her way through the thicket of liturgical pluralism after Vatican II. Stay Gregorian or go folk? They had gone folk for the most part—for the sake of the girls—but, loath to let everything go at once after generations of training, they hung onto Gregorian for themselves, bringing it out and polishing it up for special occasions within the community. Sister Gertrude was a special occasion.

"But surely, Reverend Mother, she could let Sister Claire play this one morning."

"Have you mentioned this to Sister Claire?"

"Not yet, Reverend Mother. I thought you should be the one to arrange it with Sister Hildegarde." Even this superior would see the point.

"I can understand that having this would mean something to you . . ."

Sister Hildegarde kept Claire as far from the locked organ as she could.

"As for sitting at head table, I'm afraid I'll have to say no to that, Sister. It pains me to have to."

"Is it that you're afraid to break precedent, Reverend Mother?" An argument that carried little weight these days, especially when the superior was pleading to make her jubilarian happy.

"No, it isn't that."

The quick answer carried a ring of truth. Reverend Mother looked genuinely troubled. Sister Gertrude sensed distress. A fool she had been, perhaps, to raise the whole question. Yet it mattered.

How else to acknowledge a rarity in these times—a younger nun who cared and noticed, refused to skimp where others had and might?

Reverend Mother picked up a letter opener and ran the point along the grooved edge of the blotter holder.

"I think, Sister, that I should perhaps break some news to you now. You will have a Day of Recollection tomorrow before renovation of vows. This will give you time to pray quietly. I would not tell you this if I didn't know I could count absolutely on your discretion. I must ask you to speak of it to no one."

Sister Gertrude tensed herself.

Don't let her see you're already worried sick. Friendship is friendship. Never easy to come by, especially here.

But she was old. Age had some advantages, among them release from the impossible pressure to be all things to all men. Enough to be *something* to someone.

"Sister Claire is leaving us."

Pain speared her. She stared down at blurring black and fought to meet these words with the right face. Clearly a response was expected. What *was* the right face?

"Sister Claire has been disturbed for some time. You know

she is a sensitive person. I've encouraged her to seek help within the Order, even arranged several permissions, including time with Father Callaghan, but she has refused. I tried to persuade her to wait until Mother General comes from Rome"—her visitation would begin in two weeks—"but she insists she doesn't wish to wait any longer. Finally she had decided to ask for immediate exclaustration. I feel I must respect her wishes."

Exclaustration. Fancy word for the first step. Out. Like Sister Charles last year, disappearing one night. Or the other two, Edmund and Celia, setting out to do good among the poor, finding an apartment in the lower Bronx, armed with permissions. Going to the people. Then, first thing you knew, getting a dispensation. Out. For good. Soon the house will be empty but for tapping canes and wheelchairs. A few pinch-faced superiors.

But Claire.

She shifted her hip cautiously and straightened a fraction of an inch. Pain stabbed. She resented her superior's confidence, an unwanted burden. What could she say to Claire now? They were to meet in a few minutes after high school dismissal. The masquerade was on. Unless Claire herself opened up. Maybe . . .

"I know Sister Claire wouldn't want me to spoil your jubilee, Sister. But there are reasons why she has to go before that day, and perhaps it is better that you know so you can pray for her. She has not been well for some weeks."

Comfort in a formula. Fury raged deep within her at her superior's complacency, her comfortable sense that life would go on as it had. Let her live a bit longer: the inevitable would come.

"She is leaving before Sunday, Reverend Mother?"

"It was the only arrangement she could make. She will leave us tomorrow."

"Arrange Sunday as you wish, Reverend Mother," she heard her voice saying as she thought desperately: *I must get out of here.*

"Of course I've given her the best to read." There they were, piled high on one corner of the desk—Kung, Rahner, Baum, Chardin—potpourri of the most advanced thinking in the

Church. "I've tried to point out exciting new waves of thought. The Church is so *alive* now." She beamed. "A pity, really, that we must lose some of our best."

Words and facts again. The effort to look comprehending and compassionate strained her face into ripples of vague distress.

"Thank you, Reverend Mother." Pushing herself toward the edge of her chair, she reached for her cane.

"Pray for her, Sister. I know you'll remember her tomorrow. The prayers of a jubilarian have special efficacy, you know."

Sister Gertrude gagged. Planting her cane before her, she inched her way out of her superior's office, unable to speak.

Hammers of pain throbbed relentlessly behind her eyes. Linoleum blurred beneath the tapping cane, and she surrendered unconsciously to the head tremor that bobbed her uncontrollably as she crept ahead, praying to meet no one.

Past the elevator. In use. Down the long hall. Tap. Tap. Through the swinging doors into the foyer. Toward the portress's booth. "Good afternoon, Convent of St. Gertrude, may I help you?" Sister Jennifer on duty, knitting. *Jennifer.* Back to her old name. It suited less in late middle age.

Through the large inlaid front hall. Tap. Tap. Someone silently pulled the heavy front door open for her. Who? Too painful to look up. Brown canvas . . . wedgies, did they call them? "Thank you, Sister."

Out. Sunshine spilled through crowding maples in front, checkering the asphalt drive that circled up the hill past the front door of the convent. Once a pasture. Then a dirt path, from feet of early students trudging here. Gravel then, finally asphalt. Some students drove to school now.

Down the grooved steps to the landing. She straightened slightly to look. Empty. Sun blinding, easier to stay bent. Down the last steps, tap, tap, and she crept toward the green park bench under the elm. Hers. Paint-flaked, bird-stained—her place where the seat groove exactly fit her shape and let her fold over in peace. Soon it would be too cold to sit out here. It had been an unusually warm fall.

High school students streamed out the main door of the
school, straggled past her, unseeing. Bare legs. Not like the old
days of stockings, pale faces, and uniforms. Attractive uniforms:
plaid pleated skirts, plain green blazers with the crest of St.
Gertrude's. Such an achievement, the day they first came in
uniforms looking—classy. And liking it.

Only vaguely at the edges of her mind did the sense of that
loss play. Trivial, finally. What was eating at the center now was
baffling, unspeakable. Claire would be out to see her as soon as
her class was gone, staff meeting over. Friendship, yes. But her
charge, as well. The world shifted when you became someone
else's charge. For three years now . . . Who would have her
next? Would they run out of nuns? Hire nurses? Everyone was
waiting these days to hear the verdict on St. Gertrude's. The
Academy elementary school and St. Bartholomew's had already
been closed and the younger nuns who taught in them sent
elsewhere. Mother General would arrive before long and deliver
in person the verdict of last summer's general chapter. Everyone
in the house felt it; few spoke of it. St. Gertrude's was the oldest
house in the province, its very origins tied up with the coming
of the nuns to this country. Those who had spent their religious
lives there took deep pride in the house. Sister Gertrude's guess
was that eventually the place would become an old folks' home.
In time. These things took time. It would come too late for her
to be their star boarder.

Pounding from the chapel drummed into the throb of her
head. Hammering. The renovations would be completed by Sunday, the last bit of liturgical updating to bring it in line with the
requirements of Vatican II. They had taken their time. Too many
old nuns around to protest. She would miss the comfortable
dark old chapel, bleeding Jesus and all. Little left.

She reached automatically for a bead. Little thought required—the mind hovered while the lips moved. It brought
quiet comfort, a sense of release. A dead devotion many had
claimed, then recanted unconvincingly when they discovered
John XXIII said his daily rosary. She loved him for it.

Then Claire was hurrying down the path toward her, short skirt swinging, laughing with a few students. She wore stockings, sandal-type shoes, a plain blue skirt, a bulky sweater. The lively small-boned face with vivid dark eyes was framed by dark wavy hair. Beautiful hair. When she'd finally uncovered it just last summer, her face had seemed to recover its old softness. More feminine-looking now.

Sister Gertrude struggled for composure as she surveyed the young nun chatting animatedly with students. Surely that age would be harder, she thought. How did Reverend Mother so glibly put it?—"In the world but not of it"—cautioning them against seeking popularity with students, outsiders. ("You know who she means," Claire grimaced later.) "Open to change, yet committed." Reverend Mother's matchbox mind stored neat summary statements that encompassed paradox. But, thought Sister Gertrude, change can be a bore. Trapped at times in nit-picking conversations about changes in habit and custom, she rejoiced perversely that her own bent shape made redecorating useless. She would go out like the picture postcard of the old nun.

Claire plopped down beside her, puffing.

"How *are* you?" said Sister Gertrude.

Don't sound anxious.

"Glad it's Friday. Another week done! Did you get to see Reverend Mother?"

"Just a little while ago to settle things for Sunday."

"Does she want a big party?"

"Well, yes, I suppose, but I asked her to keep it simple. Easier on all of us."

"Gregorian or folk?"

"Gregorian."

"Good. Somehow I didn't feature the guitar combo at your Jubilee Mass. Who's officiating? Is it settled?"

"She didn't say and I didn't ask. Father Callaghan, I suppose, though I'd hoped for one of the others."

Father Callaghan was their regular confessor from the Jesuit scholasticate nearby. For two years he was replacing their regular confessor, Father Purcell, who was in Spain studying. A short paunchy man with rosy cheeks and the manner of a disappointed tenor, Father Callaghan lamented the attenuated liturgy and made the most of a chance to officiate at formal functions. Before these he warmed up his *solemnior tonus* in the sacristy, to the secret amusement of those outside. Most of the nuns preferred one of the less pretentious second stringers—Father Mooney, tone-deaf but ingratiatingly earnest, studying for his doctorate in classics; or better yet, Father O'Neill, a lean-faced scholar in religious studies who occasionally fired them with brief memorable homilies at morning Mass and was a great favorite with the high school students. He said Mass for the students once a week and often stayed around talking with the high school nuns afterward. He missed teaching and was eager to finish his studies and return to the classroom. Often Claire filled in Sister Gertrude on her latest conversation with Father O'Neill.

But Reverend Mother catered to Father Callaghan. Understandable. He would undoubtedly be called in to chat with Mother General when she came to assess the spiritual health of the house. The Order held Jesuitical opinion in great respect.

"I bet Hildegarde is thrilled about that! Has she seen you?"

"No. No need." Sister Gertrude let the beads slip and gripped her hands tight in her lap.

"Well, is there anything special I can do for you today or tomorrow?"

A subtle pressure in her tone. Wants a part in my jubilee, thought Sister Gertrude.

"I'll need a clean veil and habit. And would you check discreetly that Hildy picks out decent hymns? Nothing lugubrious or sentimental. Even though she misses the pedals, I want 'Jesu, Joy of Man's Desiring' at Communion. You pick the recessional."

"I don't want to bother you tomorrow." Claire paused, looking carefully at Sister Gertrude, whose face was partly hidden. "I may have to miss Sunday."

Dead center—the words sliced into the festering sore she had circled in her mind for weeks as she watched Claire's war of nerves and prayed she misread symptoms. She should be inured by now; the exodus was on.

Did one ever grow inured? In so many ways she saw her earlier self in this younger nun—not so young if you looked at it straight. Young only by crazy convent timing. Thirty-three. The perfect age, they used to be told.

And tempted.

Succumbing.

That would be the official version.

Reverend Mother would tell them all in a tone that tried to balance understanding and certitude. Or maybe just a cold note on the bulletin board when Claire was safely gone. That had been the way lately: more efficient, less threatening.

"How was it today?"

Suppress pain, shift focus, ignore her surprise at your seeming lack of response. If she wants to explain, she will.

"The same only worse. Esmerelda ran the meeting, decided the biggest problems are our inaccurate attendance books and how to fit in three Regents cram sessions."

"How was 2A?"

Her best class. Sister Gertrude knew the hierarchy of students, kept up on the readings so they could talk about them.

"Terrific. Linda Coughlan was high on Dickens. Unbelievable. She saw the *humor*—fancy that? Read a part on the trip to see the Aged. The class loved it. I didn't expect anyone to connect with Dickens." They were finishing *Great Expectations*.

"How about *Henry the Fifth?*"

Reverend Mother had given them all permission to stay up for the special television series on the history plays these past few weeks. Most of the older nuns declined and headed wearily off to bed at the usual hour, but she had stayed up till midnight—partly out of desire, largely to keep up with Claire. She was doing the plays with her Senior Honors groups.

"They liked *Richard the Second* better. Though not all . . ." She seemed disinclined to enlarge.

"Any clues on your assignment for next year?"

Not fair, perhaps. There had been troubles with this principal, minor skirmishes until Sister Stephen tried to adjust Claire's grades to fit the school curve. Then *war*. Scars ran deep on both sides; it had seemed possible Claire might be transferred.

"Not a word. But let's not go into that now. I've got to help out in the caf, getting things ready for the parents' meeting tonight. Just wanted to check with you before you go into retreat. If I can do anything else, just leave a note at my place."

"You'll let me know about Sunday then?" Immediately she regretted her pressure as distress shadowed the dark eyes.

"For sure. I'll leave you a note. You're going to stay out here awhile?" She was already on her feet, anxious, it seemed, to go.

Sister Gertrude picked up her beads. "Can't go into chapel until late tomorrow when the work's done. An exile in God's house!" She managed a wry smile, felt it twist crooked.

Claire was hurrying back up the path.

Haste in her step, thought Sister Gertrude, watching the figure blur. *Wants to be done with this. Doesn't know whether or how to tell me. Maybe won't.*

She often had trouble sleeping, and lately the problem had grown worse. She envied those who could fall asleep anytime, anywhere—at weekly conference, in chapel, in line for confession, on portress duty. Sister Alphonse's snores during afternoon meditation had been a joke in the house for years. "Meditation Morse Code," Claire called it, "tapping our messages from the other world." Sister Cletus could hardly make it through one psalm at Office before her head began to droop. But Sister Gertrude lay in bed night after night shifting and twisting. Such straight beds were not for bending bodies like hers.

Sometimes she read—novels Claire brought, poetry, the Bible, anything. But her sight was going rapidly, so more often she spent nights like this—standing at her third-floor cell window, looking out over the moat of lights surrounding St. Gertrude's dark hill, mesmerized by the play of moving headlights and neon signs. She drew strange comfort from the sense of all those lives out there hidden behind flickering windows of dark apartment buildings lining the streets around the hill.

Once she had looked out at a stretch of almost total darkness. . . . How many years ago now? Over half a century! The hill, the house—so proudly theirs—separated from other lights by acres of pasture. The students, a hardy lot, trekked in from miles around; some rode horses. Then gradually the lights came closer. First, little houses, then clusters, then whole streets, apartments, stores, theaters. Grass was swallowed by concrete. The old careless woods shrank to a neatly spaced border between sidewalk and street that said you were now in a town.

Enrollments multiplied—first the Academy, then the offshoot parochial schools. Yearly registers were crammed with familiar names: O'Grady, Sheehan, Coughlan, McGrory—put there by parents determined to pay a little extra and send their hordes to the good sisters, who would fortify them for the new world.

I wouldn't know any of them now, she thought. Bare legs. Lipstick. New world indeed.

What's in a name? she thought vaguely.

Her first surging sense of loss had waned, leaving behind an aching undertow that dragged at spent emotions.

Claire out there, soon. *Into that darkness. Tomorrow?*

She stared into the play of light and dark before her and felt disinclined to pray. Numb. Weary to a point of vacancy, more than anything—vacancy. A hollowness spread through her as if an invisible force had siphoned off not only strength but desire. *The way Papa blew out Easter eggs,* she thought. *One pinprick. Puff! A shell left. Now paint it. Decorate it. Child's play.* "It takes a man for blowing," he'd boast, and hand her the shell intact every Easter, surprising her eager palm with its lightness. Fragile unbroken shell.

That's it, she thought, *the final pain. A relic now. The empty egg. Decorated. Hollow. What breath blew me out? They knelt around the Little Flower's deathbed and clipped her nails as she gasped her last. Relic hounds. Odd I remember that now. So bizarre, I thought it. Now I see.* She didn't care at all. There comes a point when it doesn't matter.

Beneath the scooped-out places within her stirred a lethal fear that snaked around raw hollows, licking compassion dry, secretly hissing resentment.

She still has her life. Out there. Something in me has died.

"Not many of us are fortunate enough to reach such a day, you know. Keep up your strength so you can enjoy it."

Wasn't that how Reverend Mother put it?

Claire might come back a few times. Bring her children. *Plinka-plinka-plink.* What could it possibly mean?

At last—dawn. The faint mist shrouding apartment buildings rose wispily into cool pink streaks of early light. Gripping the bed rail, she turned back into her cell. It was four-thirty when she finally arranged aching bones on the bed and dozed fitfully into her Day of Recollection.

Not recollection at all, but torture. Not that any external irritation was added to the usual routine. No one was checking. Those days were gone forever, thank God. That she even persisted in putting herself through that routine—strict silence, reading, Rosary, three meditations—was no longer expected. Individuality was the fashion. "Reverence for the movement of the Spirit within each individual—that is the deepest and oldest tradition of Holy Mother Church," declaimed the letters from Mother General still read aloud periodically in the refectory.

Some chose other forms of piety these days. After all, might you not reach the Spirit through the communal experience of shared insights, reflections? Spontaneous prayer, original liturgies, mime, dance, poetry? What resources of the human spirit could be considered taboo in the Church newly alive to the meaning of incarnation? Claire had described for her with a mixture of irony and sympathy the last profession she'd seen. Gone the candle, wreath, ring: no more Roman Rite for the

Consecration of a Virgin. Poof! Dancing now, a jubilant song, a meaningful liturgy devised by the novice herself. "Swinging," Claire said. Not unmoving. "Did she say 'forever'?" Sister Gertrude had asked. "No, she made up her own formula." They both agreed it left something to be desired. At least Claire had agreed then. Humoring her? What happened, she had wondered but not said, when the springs of spontaneity dried up? Empty cisterns, broken wells. The silver cord broken . . .

But grooves of habit and need run deep. She pulled tight the sweater-shawl Claire had knit for her and tried to focus on the Last Judgment—this afternoon's meditation. Coldness fingered her bones, though early afternoon sun streamed through the window, hitting the crucifix, gleaming the golden figure to life. A dying God there—unlike the plainer symbol many now wore around their necks—dull pewter cross, no corpus.

Sterile, she thought, but kept her mouth shut. What difference did a symbol make, anyway? The new crucifix in chapel would be the glorified Christ resplendently robed. Father Callaghan rhapsodized about the appropriateness of a risen figure. After all, wasn't resurrection their hope? Wasn't one mistake of the past all this emphasis on suffering, the bleeding Jesus—as if that were an end in itself? *"Not so!"* He hoisted his paunch emphatically as he explained how the renovated chapel would be a liturgical gem, a pleasure to pray in—"uplifting," he said. No wonder outsiders had never understood, judged them. At last Pope John has opened the windows of the Church! ("All the easier to jump out," Claire quipped later. Sister Gertrude laughed appreciatively, but her heart dipped. She was already anxious then, and that was more than a month ago.)

What time was she leaving? Today, Reverend Mother said. This very moment she might be stepping outside. Into a car? Whose?

Three o'clock.

She could still be here—apparently had been at noon, for who else would have spread habit and veil on the bed during lunch? No note.

Steps outside the door.

Sit still. Hopeless to try to get there in time.

A long pause.

No knock. Then the footsteps tapped away down the empty corridor in the Saturday afternoon silence.

Claire? Come to say good-bye? Changing her mind? Not wanting to ruin her retreat? Not wanting to leave without good-bye at least? Torn?

Urgency erupted deep within.

I will find her. One last chance to make things clear. This at least I can do.

A creaking heap I am, she thought, grunting herself out of the faded green chair. With a final massive effort she stood almost upright. How could such a little pile of bones take so much energy to raise? Clutching the bed rail, then leaning against the side of her mattress, she inched past the commode toward the corner where her cane stood.

Check Claire's cell first.

At the end of the corridor (so vacant—many went out on Saturdays now, visiting, shopping) she struggled with the heavy metal grate and, finally inside, pushed the four button, but the elevator went down. At the second floor Sister Dominic stepped on and slammed the gate shut.

"Heard about Sister Claire?" she asked as she pushed the button.

She sniffed out the most secret items in the community and conveyed them by some sure instinct to the worst audiences at the worst moments.

Sister Gertrude pretended deafness.

"A scandal! What will the students think? Worse than that—the parents!"

She stared at the ragged hemline in front of her and focused contempt on the wide beige columns planted in sensible shoes. Invisible ankles.

Will I be given over to her? The thought shot panic through her. *Spend my last days in the mud? My mind would crumble.*

She dragged herself in desperate silence past the thick figure and got out at four.

Now to the dormitory.

Empty cell. One bed stripped: Claire's. No other sign. Naked mattress ticking on the small metal bed broke the perfect symmetry of ten white beds in ten small cubicles.

Back at the elevator, Sister Augustine was waiting. A kind, unobtrusive figure in the community, she had opted for secular dress in middle age and now wore a turquoise print with long sleeves and a soft bow collar. Not all had caught on to the art of dressing to advantage. Sister Gertrude noted the rubber-heeled low shoes: considerate. Sister Augustine clucked and herded her fifth-grade class in an atmosphere of bosomy solicitude and faintly perfumed powder and always brought to evening recreation at least one "charming" episode from the day. Unaware now of her sister's recollection, she chattered about the coming fifth-grade promotion exercises.

"This year we've done away with long dresses for the little girls. Too much expense, Reverend Mother said. But we'll still have the same basic program; the parents expect it. The children are getting all excited. Getting out on one?"

She pulled back the grate at Sister Gertrude's nod. On the first floor there was a sense of stir. Passing the guest pantry, she was bumped into by a flustered Sister Agnes nervously balancing a stack of china. They exchanged silent nods.

Party mania, she thought. *I asked to have it simple.*

I can tell by the refectory lists. Claire always serves on Monday nights.

Her cane thumped a steady echo down the deserted corridor. In the pantry by the dishwashers she strained upward. Pain gripped her. Impossible.

"Can I help you, Sister Gertrude?"

Harold, the cook, obliging as ever in his smeared apron and flour-sprinkled shoes. Nothing the sisters asked surprised Harold now, after seven years in the house. In the old days he used to kid with them evenings when the younger ones came down for dishes in his enormous kitchen below. Life was different now; some of his favorites gone, died off or left.

"Harold, just tell me if any names are crossed off the servers' list, would you please?"

"Sure thing, Sister. Workin' hard for your big day tomorrow. Isn't often we get a *golden,* you know. First one since poor old Sister Carmelita." (She'd died five years before, contorted in cancer, screaming at the end.) "Got a triple-layer surprise comin' up for you. Wait'll you see!" He scanned the list. "One name— begins with *C.* Can't quite make it out, it's scratched out so heavy. Monday night server. Claire? Catherine?"

"Thank you, Harold."

Why do I feel nothing?

"Anythin' else, Sister?"

"No thanks, Harold." *Rise to it. He cares.* "Don't work too hard, now. I can't eat much cake, you know."

"Okay. But they'll all enjoy it." Harold was irrepressible. "Put in a good word for me, eh, Sister? Good ole Harold, sluggin' it out down below."

He grinned affectionately after her as she tapped back down the hall.

Chapel then. Where else? I'll find my way around now. Tap the distance between front pew and sanctuary. Better than a bellyflop tomorrow. Sister Gertrude, our golden jubilarian, flat on her face before the altar of God. Possible. Resurrexit. *Easier not to fall.*

The workmen were just leaving, lugging out things. One held the door for her as she stepped into the cool dark.

To sound unmistakable. Pedals, too. "Jesu, Joy of Man's Desiring."

Only Claire gets pedals like that! Playing her way through God knows what state of soul?

Climb up there, see her. Easier than yesterday. She'll see I can understand—at least that.

As she dragged herself upward, she listened automatically for pedals, noting the occasional slip. A vision of Sister Claire De-laney rose before her—younger, fresher, arriving at St. Gertrude's more than five years ago, anxious about fitting into the community—for around the province it was known as a difficult community. Then, after a year or so, finding time on the occasional Sunday for a treat—a trip with Sister Gertrude to the high school auditorium, where they'd play four-hand on the grand piano there. Or, later yet, meeting in Sister Gertrude's cell, tuning in the Met on the little radio Reverend Mother had given her when all other ways of making music were failing. Bones too stiff. "You can still turn a knob, Sister," Reverend Mother Dolores had said. She'd handed Sister Gertrude the radio with a flourish and a smile.

Claire coming every morning, faithfully for the past three years. Discreet. Attentive. Helping her out of bed lately, helping her dress. Emptying. Fixing her liber. Bringing copies of hymns for Mass, books from the high school library. Talking about her classes.

Sound filled the chapel now. Diapason open. Too heavy for Bach, really, but the soul has needs, she thought.

At the top step finally, she forced a look straight at Claire's back. Same becoming blue skirt. Then, in the tilted organist's mirror, their eyes met. Silence abrupt: like sound turned inside out, vast spaces of silence around them echoed the hollowness inside Sister Gertrude.

Why don't I feel more? Something has died.

She crept forward.

This I can do; show her.

Then Claire swung around on the organ bench, short dark skirt lifted above the knees, legs swinging gently.

Waiting. Unlike her. Must be steeling herself.

"I've been looking for you." As she whispered, Sister Gertrude saw the grip on the organ bench—knuckles white—the flushed face, guarded eyes. A telltale pulse in the center of the forehead.

"Did you get your habit and veil?"

"Thanks. Did you come to my cell this afternoon?" *Say yes.*

Claire paused. "No. Not since I left your things."

The footsteps . . . pressure mounted within her. The throb began behind her eyes. The burden was on her then. She was too old . . .

But Claire saved her, blurting it out in incoherent whispers as she helped her over to a chair near the organ bench. Half choking, between heavy breaths.

"I've wanted all day to see you, or yesterday—but she warned me . . . I didn't want to be the one." She looked at Sister Gertrude anxiously. "You all right?"

Am I all right? A bag of bones. Is she afraid I'll collapse?

"Of course."

Good she can't see my face.

"I know you've suspected—I've wanted to be discreet. It is hard, girls all around, friends to hurt."

They heard movements in the chapel below, and she dropped her voice even more. Sister Gertrude strained to hear.

"I pleaded with Reverend Mother to let me stay just till early next week at least."

Sister Gertrude felt her heart turn. Once.

"You pleaded?"

"You know how she is. I felt sure I could appeal to that. Help the party along. I had plans for tomorrow, too."

"Don't think of tomorrow."

What tier are you on, Harold?

Tiny pains darted at the back of her head, her scalp tingled, seemed to shrink. *A skull in the making here,* she thought.

"But I did." Claire spoke with more control now. Gulps subsided. "I even wanted to play the organ. Would have faced up to Hildy for the occasion. No go. Reverend Mother's more nervous about the visitation than I'd suspected. Either I go right away—*today*—or wait till after Mother General's visit. But that's still weeks away, and I couldn't . . . She put the pressure on for a fast exit. I called my father. Smoother that way. The surface will be smooth again by the time Mother General gets here. If I wait too long—more talk."

"But why today?" She got that out reluctantly.

"Last day Mother Provincial could see me with the papers before she starts her retreat. Afterward, too close to the visitation. So—she glanced at Sister Gertrude ruefully—"you were the expendable one."

Surprise, thought Sister Gertrude. *Hold yourself still. Don't show it. She's told you at least. That much.*

Suddenly, silently, another pair of shoes were a few inches from her own, black low-heeled pumps with bows. Reverend Mother had come in from the second floor to check on chapel.

"Do you need anything, Sister Gertrude? I never expected to find you here!" An oblique reminder that she was breaking retreat. Then realism prevailed. "I'm sorry to find you upset the day before your jubilee."

Choke. *The day before my jubilee.*

"I wanted to see Sister Claire before she left, Reverend Mother." Why lie now? "I heard the organ and found her here."

"Yes, I got the key for her . . . it seemed the least." Porcelain compassion, smooth, painted.

Reverend Mother turned toward Claire, who was standing rigidly by Sister Gertrude, an arm about the bent old nun's shoulders. "Are you nearly ready, Sister? Mother Provincial plans to see you immediately. She's already come and is getting papers ready in the priests' dining room. Her train leaves soon."

"I thought Sister Claire had come to my cell, Reverend Mother, and I couldn't get to the door quickly enough so I've come looking for her." True enough.

"That was me, Sister. I wanted to see if you objected if a few of your old music students come tomorrow. I'd had a call and was sure it didn't matter to you, but I thought maybe you'd like me to fix up a little reception for them afterward in the parlor."

Party party. Why didn't I bump Sister Agnes harder, smash the china? Jubilee.

The secret pressure of unsuspected anger hissed within, filling her emptiness, heaving against inner and outer control, furious, insistent—a demonic surge blasting reserves of hard-won peace. *I haven't the strength to blow her hollow,* she thought. *Find the pin. Dear God, let me find the pin. Something must scratch that surface.*

"Reverend Mother, Sister Claire said you made her promise not to speak to me before she left. That she *wanted* to be here for the jubilee."

A slow flush spread over her superior's features.

How beautiful she can look, thought Sister Gertrude, blurred with anger, hating age. Tears of rage soaked her withering cheeks. Her head bobbed relentlessly.

Do they know I'm angry? What do they see?

Reverend Mother seemed to measure them both with her quick glance. How long had they been there together? What had been said?

"And did she tell you why we agreed she should leave, Sister?"

The arm behind Sister Gertrude stiffened.

"Reverend Mother—" Claire sounded choked.

Let them worry, thought Sister Gertrude. *Strength in this bag of bones yet.*

"The sooner Sister Claire removes herself from contact with the girls the better, Sister. I would have chosen not to tell you this today, but her decision does not involve her alone. Father—"

"Reverend Mother!" Claire's voice had become a muffled gasp.

Sister Gertrude sensed in a moment a subtle complicity between them. Was there something she did not understand?

"I will write, I will write." Claire hugged her hastily and bolted past.

"Perhaps you can now understand my hesitation a little, Sister. Sister Claire has not been discreet. We live in a changing Church, a changing world. But to have something like this going on before the eyes of our students—both Mother Provincial and I agreed when Sister Claire decided to go that it should be promptly. She has notified her father. He'll be here shortly. No doubt she will find her way. We must try to excite her as little as possible. She is disturbed."

"I don't understand, Reverend Mother." Her voice thinned to a small whisper.

"What I am saying, Sister, is that Sister Claire and Father O'Neill have . . . they have been together perhaps too much this year . . . time will tell . . . and now— Try not to think of this, Sister. It is better to put some things out of our minds. You must save your strength for tomorrow. With God all things are possible. You can best help Sister Claire by your prayers."

Reverend Mother left quickly, touching the old nun's shoulder in a light gesture of compassion as she turned away.

Even anger died now, its last tremors subsiding to ash as she knelt and faced the renovated altar, recognizing nothing. The bare spaces of the stripped sanctuary seemed to mock the shaking figure who searched wordlessly for a sign, a link with the place she found herself in. But it was all strange, all gone utterly strange—no faintly smiling Queen to the left, no faded stations regularly spaced on the walls, no comforting vigil lights flickering hope, gone the oversize bleeding corpus—replaced by a gleam of gold she could scarcely make out in the distance.

It did no good to look; the new chapel failed the needs of her spirit. Yielding to a tide of pain, she let her head fall and, eyes shut, sought within herself another way to pray.

A golden jubilee was still a big event in the community, even these days when many moments that once seemed major had shrunk or disappeared.

"Daisy, Daisy, give me your answer trooo—" crooned Harold as he moved about the kitchen before Mass and shot the final frosting into place. Humming, he bent over in concentration— patting here, smoothing there, carefully squeezing out ripples of yellow-gold for the crowning detail, a cross on top. Finally sighing relief, he stood back to admire.

"Some beaut!" An aside to his helper, who came in for big occasions, a silent little man who swept and peeled and watched all with an expression of secret amusement. "Think Jesus ever had such a bee-oo-ti-ful cross, Jerry?"

"Yeah, boss. Neat." Jerry paused in licking beaters. "Do we get a piece?"

"Depends. Probably. They always eat a lot at jubilees, though. Don't imagine she'll have family comin'. But Reverend Mother's got some little party goin' in the parlor afterward, Sister Agnes tells me. Didn't know it till this mornin', man, so we'd better get started on them eggs!"

Upstairs the refectorian scurried around, wishing Reverend Mother had made up her mind earlier what holy cards to give whom for the occasion. Hard to know the right thing these days—a picture? A text? Latin? English? Traditional? But Sister Richard felt small sympathy for the complexities of taste brought on by *aggiornamento* as she ran around in stiff new pumps to distribute each at the right place. Then she put the finishing touches on the small dish of pansies at each table, checked and double-checked the three places at head table: holy cards, special card for the jubilarian, gleaming arrangement of late tulips in the center. Suddenly she remembered and ran to get a cushion for Sister Gertrude's chair.

Nearly Mass time, and Sister Agnes was still fussing in the large parlor. These affairs made her jittery—details, details. Butter knife on each small plate, goblets—Reverend Mother had insisted, though it didn't seem proper for breakfast—small salt and pepper sets at every other place for eggs. It wasn't so easy to have everything set up presto for a party of ten. Especially when you got word at the last minute that there would be three priests instead of one. It meant juggling patterns: only two complete sets in Wedgwood. Fortunately she'd taken down all the Limoges from the guest closet yesterday and washed each piece, just in case. She studied the large oval table, warming to the subtle blend of silver against damask, sparkling Waterford, daintily floral-patterned dishes, yellow rose centerpiece.

In the organ loft Sister Hildegarde was furious; she'd found the organ unlocked. Not only that—choir had been only so-so at practice, too many absent yesterday. This Offertory was full of episemas, and they weren't up on their Gregorian. She'd peeked over the edge and seen former students down there, probably expecting to hear things the way they used to be. She slid her feet around silently on the pedals, tentatively locating "Jesu, Joy of Man's Desiring" as she waited for the signal to start.

The sacristans were already exhausted. All was to be in gold today. On Saturday afternoon Sister Joan had taken a cool iron to the gold silk chasuble with its heavily embroidered cross, and all the linens were fresh—just in case.

Good thing. "Father just called." Reverend Mother caught her on her way to the sacristy before Mass. "Two other priests are coming to help concelebrate. Not a solemn high since Sister Gertrude didn't want that, but they'll stay on the altar. Lovely for our first Mass in the new chapel!" Purring out, she left Sister Joan to cope.

"Everything in the new sanctuary is exactly in accord with directives," she whispered to Father Callaghan as he checked the Ordo. "Renovation of vows comes right at the Communion. When the choir starts singing, Sister Gertrude will come up the center where the prie-dieu is set."

"Do I have to say anything?" He turned his sharp blue eyes on her and stared with the intensity of a committed liturgist.

"No, Father. She may be slow in getting there. But then she just renews her vows out loud, receives Holy Communion, and returns to her seat. After that the community receives as usual."

He turned back to the Ordo.

The guests sat in the back pews, and Reverend Mother, radiant, bustled in to hand them libers and hymn sheets just as things were about to begin, then hurried back to her place at the head of the line of nuns carrying lighted tapers. They would proceed in the old manner even though the old symmetry was gone: here a short skirt, there a long; here a veil, there none. They entered slowly from the rear and moved two by two down the center aisle, bowed in turn toward the renovated sanctuary and then toward each other, genuflected, and took their places—six to a pew to help the singing.

As solemn entrance was executed to the grand harmonic strains of "Now That We All Our God," Sister Gertrude sat bent over in the first pew, hugging her shawl against chill. She felt numb and confused—only vaguely aware of the bodies behind her. Nothing felt familiar this morning. But for Dominic (rescuing her from the commode, sent by Reverend Mother as time for Mass grew uncomfortably near and their jubilarian hadn't yet appeared) she might never have made it. As the chant curved high behind her, she stared vaguely at three swishing white skirts, three pairs of black shoes moving on the marble sanctuary floor ahead of her.

I asked for one, she thought indifferently. *One priest.*

Incense swirled past and around her, the voices of celebrant and choir engaged in harmonious exchange above her. Then—the Easter sermon of St. Peter. She knew it by heart, and the words slid off her mind as if it were waxed.

"Do not return evil for evil, or insult for insult; on the contrary, return a blessing because it is a blessing you have been called to inherit."

Inherit. I am at the end, she thought. *Blown out.*

Gripping the polished maple pew to raise herself for the Gospel, she half heard the familiar words about presenting her offering at the altar: Leave if you remember your brother has something against you. Be reconciled.

Impossible. Faces, hundreds, a procession of students, sisters, friends flickered before her briefly—merging into one: Claire's. Others thinned to ghosts already, Claire not quite gone. Only a matter of time.

The Communion antiphon—her cue.

I forgot to measure the distance, she realized suddenly, desperately. Panic seized her. *Will I make it?* She grasped the pew with one hand, clutched her cane with the other.

The distance to the sanctuary seemed endless. Behind her,

rising above her *tap tap tap,* her sisters' voices merged exquisitely in one of her favorite antiphons: *"One thing I have asked of the Lord, this will I seek that I may dwell in the house of the Lord all the days of my life."*

May they be few. I am a relic.

She inched ahead, feeling dead inside.

Inchworm Gertrude.

Tap. Tap.

Let the rubber tip hold on this polished surface. Will I fall? Not here, dear God, not here. In private at least. Better the commode. But here . . . I will become a legend.

She moved ahead grimly, forcing a steady creep across the smooth, gleaming surface that dwarfed her.

Finally the prie-dieu. A spasm of pain caught her as she knelt awkwardly beneath the host Father Callaghan held high above her. He was flanked by his second stringers, Fathers Mooney and O'Neill.

They counted on my not knowing, she thought distractedly.

Now: focus. The final test. Head raised, she narrowed mind and memory to a fine point, searching for the words of renewal. How many times had she repeated this formula over the past fifty years!

Dear God, let me remember.

The voices behind spiraled rhythmically down the subtly cadenced *vitae meae.*

Almost finished.

Silence.

Struggling to sustain her faltering head, she looked at the gold embroidered bulge before her that promised resurrection.

Searching. At last they came.

Softly but firmly she began to speak the familiar words memory found.

The Perils
of Translation

Since novitiate days, she'd loved the *Te Deum*. Other hymns—
the *Magnificat, Nunc Dimittis, Pange Lingua*—she'd heard before, in college. The *Te Deum*, however, was new to her, in days
of making all things new. Daily, at the end of Matins, it rose
heavenward, incorruptible, offering cosmic praise, asking nothing in return except for the plea of its final cadence: *in te, Domine,
speravi, non confundar in aeternum.*

More than the others, it resisted the vernacular. Take the line
*tu ad liberandum suscepturus hominem, non horruisti virginis
uterum.* The new breviary read: "When you were to become man
so as to save mankind you did not shrink back from the chaste
Virgin's womb." Wordy. Diluted. No longer could the tongue
roll over that *horruisti,* savor the r's, then spit out the *-isti,* or

linger in the sustained abasement of *suscepturus*. Something had been lost.

Twelve years beyond the novitiate now, she still felt that about the *Te Deum*. At four-fifty in the afternoon she'd dash into chapel exhausted from a day of managing adolescents with braces and breasts. Imperceptibly, as the chant began, she crossed a threshold. Mundane concerns were submerged in the ancient cry of God's exiled people. She carried all the same old baggage into chapel—aching body or head, simmering disagreements, struggles with students—but once there she let it go, relinquished what she could of it, to join herself body and soul with the voice of prayer rising eternally from earth. And whenever she thought of leaving the Order (the thought was now a dark thread woven through the tangled skein of her days), she anticipated the loss of this great prayer, of participating in it, like a death.

Then the pain started.

It caught her first as she was talking to Marie Calchas, a sophomore who was failing all her Latin vocabulary quizzes.

"I don't know why, Sister," the girl almost whimpered as she stood, frizzy-haired and pale, by Sister Claire's desk. "I just can't get it. I study every night, and my mother hears my vocabulary. By next morning it's gone."

She was about to reply when the small deep pain cut through her. Exactly where, she couldn't have said. She held her breath and tried to look thoughtful.

"Keep trying, Marie," she said, more sympathetic than she'd intended. The pain left a strange interior quivering, like custard slit by a clean knife. "I'm sure you'll get it before long." She turned to clear her desk, and the girl left.

All week the pain attacked when she least expected—as she knelt in chapel or at chapter, once even as she served at table. That night she almost dumped tomato soup all over poor old Sister Gertrude's trembling hands, extended for the bowl. Fighting for composure, Sister Claire watched the orange puddle slide around on the dark plastic tray and strained not to spill more.

Gradually she became clearer about the pain's location. It struck somewhere between neck and waist, left of center.

"It seems to go straight through my heart," she admitted to Sister Mark. "I know that sounds silly, but that's how it feels."

"Gas?"

"No, it's not like that."

Sister Mark nodded. In addition to her duties as infirmarian, Sister Mark had this year been given one freshman English class. "For a bit of relief," Reverend Mother Constance had told her. So many in the house were old and sick that being infirmarian was taxing. Stable and reliable, at forty-five, Sister Mark seemed to have resolved the contradictions of community life in 1966 to her own tolerance, if not satisfaction.

"If it keeps up," she said, "you'd better speak to Reverend Mother. I wouldn't want to give you the wrong thing."

It kept up.

She tried, finally, to explain to Reverend Mother.

"It may be nothing, Reverend Mother, but I thought I should say something." If only the pain would strike now, thought Claire. When you wanted proof, it never came.

"I've felt it off and on for over a month, but just this week it's grown worse in the morning."

This superior, Reverend Mother Constance, was kind to the sick. Difficult to deal with on school matters, she showed un-failing compassion toward those in physical pain. She ap-proached life with a literal mind, found relief in dealing with an immediate practical problem she could name.

"If you feel pain at meditation, Sister, why don't you go to your cell and rest there? There's no rule that says we must meditate sitting in a pew, you know."

She herself, surely fifteen years older than Claire, knelt up-right, morning after morning.

"Let me know how you feel in two weeks, Sister."

.   .   .

The pain continued.

Sometimes Claire awoke to its stab with the rising bell. It would spear her as she jumped from bed, or impale her half-bent over the sink, brushing her teeth.

In the novitiate she'd been able to meditate with her eyes shut. Now, no sooner would she sit back in the pew than her head would begin to grow heavy. Sometime later she'd awaken with a start to find herself slack-jawed and drooling. How long had she been asleep? Behind her, Reverend Mother knelt upright.

At least, when it came, the pain kept her awake. She'd will her eyes open and stare at the tabernacle, trying, as they'd been trained, to see the scene of her meditation. But pain, she learned, wipes the imagination clean. When it struck it obliterated all, reducing her inner life to blank.

Finally she began to do what Reverend Mother had suggested.

How odd to walk back through the empty house, past Father's dining room, past closed parlor doors, the hall shrine to St. Joseph, up the staircase to the young nuns' dormitory. She was an intruder exploring emptiness; surfaces had gone mute. Later they would again speak: dishes clink, telephones ring, mops glide, doors open and close.

In her cell she closed the curtains, slipped off her short veil, and flopped on the bed, arranging her skirt for minimum wrinkling. She closed her eyes again and tried to concentrate. But she feared falling sleep, so she opened them and stared at the curtain.

The second morning, just after she'd arranged herself on the bed, she heard the dormitory door open, footsteps approach her closed curtains.

In slipped Sister Mark, finger to her lips.

"Need anything?" she whispered.

Embarrassed, Sister Claire shook her head.

Sister Mark lifted the chair next to the nightstand and brought it over beside the bed.

"I'll stay awhile in case there's anything I can do."

Sister Claire could see only the edge of a black knee.

Outside, a radiant autumn maple flamed by early morning sun sent shafts of pink light through the large windows. The warm light played against the inside of her curtains.

She tried to picture a tired and thirsty Jesus with the Samaritan woman at the well. "You are right to say, 'I have no husband,' although you have had five and the one you now have is not your husband." How calmly he nailed her lie, even as he continued to offer her life. "Woman, I am thirsty. Draw water from the well."

Suddenly pain.

"Oh," she gasped, and shutting her eyes tight, drew her shoulders together as if to make it stop.

On her forehead she felt the light cool pressure of a hand. "Where is it?"

The chair was pulled closer to the head of the bed, and a strong arm slipped beneath her shoulders.

Something deeper than pain shot through her, liquid and electrifying. The cool hand remained on her forehead. She clenched her body again, then released it. The pain left. Sister Mark's arm remained.

Half an hour later they returned to chapel.

Morning after morning that fall the bedroom scene was repeated. Pain attacked, Sister Claire left the chapel. Once she had reached her cell and was on the bed, Sister Mark knocked, entered, and took up her station. If pain came, she was there to help catch it, clasping her friend in an embrace at once strong and simple. Sometimes, when the attack was severe, Sister Mark's plastic guimpe (she still wore the old habit) would bend as she held the young nun to her.

Imperceptibly, shadow began to trail Sister Claire's pain. It wasn't about Sister Mark. She trusted her implicitly. It was about herself. As she left chapel these mornings, there grew in her a secret yearning for the hour of communion to follow. In the quiet of the morning, as light filtered through the dormitory and Sister Mark held her, she felt something new. She couldn't have named it. It was like walking into a place you'd expected to find cold and empty and discovering a fire crackling on the hearth and a cushiony chair made ready for you. Only those metaphors wouldn't have occurred to her. It was twelve years since she'd sat on a soft chair.

When the bell rang for the end of meditation, the infirmarian would rise, lift the chair back to its place, and leave quickly so Sister Claire would have time to put on her veil and get to chapel for Mass.

One morning late in October, Sister Claire left chapel, went to her bed, and waited. The dormitory was chilly and still quite dark. Though the pain had yet to strike, she was certain it would.

She lay there listening, watching the curtain, imagining John the Baptist in the desert. Soon Advent would begin. Prepare a way for the Lord, make straight His paths. Though she tried to conjure up the great precursor—the desert, the crowds, the camel's hair, the leather cincture—she knew what she was really doing: distracting herself. The locusts and honey of her penitential imagination failed the desires of her heart, and she knew it. The more she struggled to see that gaunt selfless prophet and hear his words, the more she felt herself adrift on a moving sea with invisible shores, unfathomable depths.

That morning Sister Mark did not come.

Later she explained. "Sister Cletus fainted in her stall right at the beginning of meditation. You'd just gone out. We had a hard time bringing her to. Sorry I couldn't get up to be with you. Were you okay?"

They were standing in the hallway between classes. Girls brushed by them, whispering and giggling. In two minutes the buzzer for the next class would sound. How to expose one's heart in the bustle of a high school hallway?

Sister Claire looked at her friend. Small dark circles showed beneath Sister Mark's eyes. Lately she'd been less patient with the students.

"It's okay," she managed. "It wasn't bad this morning."

In truth, the pain had never come. At least not that one. As she lay on her bed, the blankness of the dormitory, the stillness of the white curtain, the nakedness of her own heart had rent her with terror. What was happening to her? This was nothing she could speak of at 10 A.M. in a crowded high school corridor.

Perhaps never.

Sister Mark continued to come. During the day they never spoke of it. It did not cure the pain, which plagued her all fall. Finally Reverend Mother suggested she go in for tests.

"It's the only sensible thing, Sister. This has been troubling you too long. We must get to the bottom of it."

She agreed reluctantly. It meant getting someone to take care of Sister Gertrude for three days, and covering her classes. But it meant also time away. She needed that—to think, three days at least.

The hospital room: white walls, white bed, white table, one spot of green—the vinyl chair in the corner. The window overlooked a paved parking lot, but she spent little time looking out, for she'd been instructed to stay in bed. They were to do something called an upper G.I.

"If you don't mind, Sister, would you put this on?" urged Mrs. Cassidy, head nurse on the floor, who bustled in the first afternoon.

She produced a white hospital gown and left.

If she didn't mind! Mortified, Claire struggled with it. The stiff, too-short sleeves left her elbows cold and exposed; her wrists looked all bone. Air tickled her bare back. Stretching her arms around, she found strings in back and tied them. Quickly she climbed into the high bed and pulled the light covers over her chest.

Hospital beds dissolve the will to work. How, in such a setting, could she get serious about *The Mill on the Floss,* the fourth conjugation, or even the breviary? She stared at the cheap cru-

cifix at the foot of her bed, the cracking plaster over the bathroom door. Voices twanged on the intercom. "Calling Dr.
Morrissey, emergency." "Would Miss Ryan please come to outpatients immediately." "Dr. Kramer is needed in surgery. Would
Dr. Kramer go to surgery immediately."

Hours passed. She began to grasp the hospital's internal geography: outpatients, emergency, obstetrics, cardiac, surgery.
Thank God she wasn't in for surgery. Throughout supper hour
carts rattled by her door and nurses chattered outside in low
voices. She was not to eat anything.

She swiveled the bedside tray table over the bed and set her
breviary on it. No excuse not to pray. The tissue-thin pages
stuck to her fingers, but she got through the *Te Deum.* Then
she closed the book, shoved the table away, sank back on her
pillow, and stared at the wall.

That night she slept poorly.

"Now, Sister, how are you this morning? Had a good night, did
you?" Mrs. Cassidy popped the thermometer into Claire's mouth
and held her wrist. Moments later she held the thermometer to
the light, then shook it down with a satisfied nod. "Fine, dear.
All's fine."

Next she wheeled a small machine into the room.

"Now don't be nervous, Sister. We're going to take an electrocardiogram this morning. Dr. Kramer's orders. It doesn't hurt
at all, dear. Just a precautionary measure."

Claire watched as Mrs. Cassidy, efficient and motherly, grew
busy turning nobs and arranging dials.

"Now, dear, this won't take long. We'll have to turn down
the covers a bit." She whipped back the bedclothes and folded
them at the bottom of the bed. "There." She beamed at Claire.
"Now we'll have to ask you to lift your top."

Mortification. Shame.

At the touch of the cool air on her nipples, she shivered.

"Now, dear, we have to apply this gel where we'll attach the
electrodes. It may feel a bit cold."

Electrodes! She saw herself frizzled, zapped to a strip of curled pious bacon and returned to Reverend Mother.

Cold thick goo, like Vaseline, was anointing her ankles and wrists. She kept her eyes shut.

"Now just relax. It will all be over in a few minutes."

At the shock of the cold around her left breast she opened her eyes and watched Mrs. Cassidy's cool, clean fingers. Once, long ago, Vicks VapoRub had burned her chest beneath flannel. Then her chest had been flat.

Curious items, these small, pale, exposed breasts. She hadn't really observed them in years. Not since she'd dared a half-naked swim in the lake at Shadowbrook. The air made the nipples go hard and pointed. Tiny goose bumps rimmed the pink hills. Quick and clinical, the nurse seemed to notice none of this. In no time she'd hooked Claire to the machine. A small needle jiggled back and forth.

This bizarre pattern of squiggles was her heart? What be-spectacled, white-coated doctor in what remote laboratory would decipher this code?

The tiny needle stopped.

"There!" Mrs. Cassidy detached her.

During the next two days the pain caught Claire only once or twice. She listened to doctors, buzzers, rattling carts; she smiled at nurses, fingered her beads, and tried to think. Away from students. Away from Sister Gertrude, Sister Mark. All the others. Away from everything but the inner need to decide—would she stay? But even when she put the question that way, she felt beneath it a deeper question: How *could* she stay?

For although she loved her teaching, cherished friends in the community, the school, although she could find moments of peace in prayer and she responded to the liturgy (some of it, at least)—*she no longer believed in the life.*

It was as simple as that.

Who was she to judge a way of life that had withstood the tempests of four hundred years of history?

Yet, deeper than that, how (and why) should she use history alone to justify violating her own mind, her own sensibility, limited though they were?

She knew why she had entered. Just the night before she came to the hospital she'd written it out for herself, a statement to study, refine, here in the sterile wasteland of her hospital room. She looked at the words now on the sheet of paper she'd tucked into her breviary for just this moment.

When I entered, I thought it was the truest way I could bear witness to what I believed . . .

She might have liked to talk to someone. Who? The closest she'd come was last week, after Father O'Neill's high school Mass, as he had his coffee in the teachers' room. Just the two of them. She happened to be free. He'd stayed on and on, evidently lonely, describing for her his own perplexities in these Vatican II days. They had often talked, but never had he been so open. Was there such a thing as a "temporary vocation" as some now claimed? But one couldn't be a "temporary priest." Once a priest always a priest. They'd had that drilled into them since childhood. Nonetheless, he was going to leave, he told her. *Soon.*

She'd listened to him with a full heart, thinking of her own "forever" at final profession. Yet, facing his confusion and pain, she felt somehow lucky—for growing within her now for weeks, months, had been the sense that when the moment came she could, she *would,* decide. Freely. On her own. So she didn't speak too much that day about her own feelings. He needed an understanding ear.

Later Reverend Mother had sent for her and said several nuns had felt that her being alone with Father O'Neill for so long behind closed doors had given bad example to the students.

She watched Mrs. Cassidy move about the room, always cheerful, bustling. Somehow Sister Claire's questions seemed self-indulgent beside the busy, generous labor of the hospital nurses, the groans of the sick and dying. Maybe Mrs. Cassidy had an alcoholic husband, a retarded child. Maybe she got through her day by sheer grit. Who could tell? In any case, she never forgot to take Claire's pulse and inquire after her bowels.

One thing gave Claire comfort during those days: the rosary. Not a fashionable devotion any longer. It was strange to discover that the hard black beads slipping through her fingers, and the small silver crucifix pressing against her palm, felt more real than print on a page.

It was a Catholic hospital. The staff was at home with nuns. In the X-ray room the technician, a young glossy-haired man with bulging eyes, patted her shoulder. "So you've got a problem, huh? Guess no one's immune." He disappeared behind the machine. "Breathe in, Sister."

She pressed her breasts against the flat cold surface and inhaled.

"Hold it. Good. Exhale."

After three days the tests were over. Barium, X-rays, heart squiggles had revealed nothing. "Perfectly normal," said Dr. Kramer, standing by her bed. This failed cherub with his rosy cheeks, curly white hair, bloodshot eyes, and tobacco-stained teeth seemed preoccupied. Clearly, he would have preferred a more exotic challenge than a nun with a pain.

On her last morning the door of her room opened noiselessly and in came a man and a woman. They stood by the bottom of her bed.

"Well, now, Sister Claire, how are we feeling this morning?" He was small, thin, and pale. Beneath his white coat he wore a white shirt and a black string tie. His fine white hair, combed straight back, was evenly distributed over a pink scalp, and his smoothly shaven cheeks were bluish, almost transparent. In one temple a blue vein showed. His heavy eyebrows overhung eyes that seemed to fade as he looked at her. His voice was oily.

"Fine, thank you, Doctor."

"I am Dr. Seamen, Sister, and this is Dr. Seamen, my wife." He nodded toward the woman beside him. She held a pen and clipboard and seemed to be copying something from Claire's chart. "We are feeling better now?"

She stifled the urge to retort, "What is this papal 'we'?" Pressing the sheet tight against her chest, she managed a nunlike "Fine, thank you." She regretted not having on her night veil. Something about this man made her want to be covered.

"Now, Sister, we would like to ask you a few questions."

Female Dr. Seamen wore a white jacket, and her very black hair was piled in an intricate shiny coil. Glasses on a black cord rested against her flat chest, and her nails glistened pink.

"Now, Sister, you seem to have been suffering from an unidentifiable pain for some weeks?"

She nodded.

"Can you locate it? Just point, if you would."

She pointed to her stomach. She could have pointed anywhere.

"Ah. Do you have any other physical complaints?"

She shook her head. Better to be dumb, neutral, colorless.

"Now then, Sister, how long have you been in religious life?"

"Twelve years."

Female Dr. Seamen was writing.

"And how old were you, Sister, when you entered? You still seem quite young."

"Twenty-one, Doctor."

The light in his eyes faded. "You came from Washington?"

"No, Doctor. Hawaii."

He'd write her off as a loony now, for sure. She'd never even been to Hawaii. His dead eyes betrayed nothing.

"Ah, Sister." He took a deep breath and moved in closer. She longed to shove him away. "Is there anything you would like to mention in connection with—this pain?"

She saw the white hairs inside his nostrils, the pale half moons on his thumbs.

"Not really, Doctor. It hasn't bothered me lately, to tell the truth." Could he absorb the truth?

"You've had it quite some time?"

"Since school started in the fall."

"And you've been careful about diet?"

"We are all well fed. The four major food groups each day."

In his temple the blue vein moved. "Very well, I'm sure. And now a few more questions. Could you tell me a bit about your life before you entered?"

She saw what he wanted. "If you're asking did I date, yes. I considered marriage." He would imagine a warped childhood. Should she make one up?

A glimmer in his eyes. "And?"

"I never found *the* man." That should shut him up.

"I see. Yes." He nodded toward his wife. She made a note. "And now, Sister, do you have any problems in the life you've chosen that you'd care to talk about?"

Idiocy. She wanted to spit at him the same question. Do you have any problems in your life that you'd care to talk about? With that giant of a wife? Or just with getting through a day? Would you expose this to a complete stranger? In a hospital room?

His wife dyed her hair. Claire was conscious of her own uneven cut, gray at the temples.

She knew what he meant. Sex. Or maybe obedience. Having been disappointed about the warped childhood.

"I have an excellent superior," she said. She intended to call Reverend Mother after they left the room.

"I see. Is there anything else you wish to talk about?"

He was slimy and relentless. She looked at his pale eyes. There was something ineffably dehydrated about the man, as if he'd looked into people's souls—no, he wouldn't say *souls* but *psyches*—so long and hard that he'd stopped existing.

"Certainly," she said. "Tell me, Dr. Seamen, do you believe in the immortality of the soul?"

"Well, now, Sister—"

"Or the grace of God?"

His wife glanced at him as she put her hand to her hair.

"That, Sister, is hardly my—"

"Have you heard the latest, Doctor? That God is dead?"

"Now, Sister Claire . . ." He fingered the end of his black string tie. "God is not my field."

"Ah," she replied. "Then what are you doing in here? For I am a woman of God, Dr. Seamen."

"But your pain, Sister—"

"It's you," she said shortly. She looked at his dying gray eyes. "There's nothing I wish to talk to you about. What troubles me is a pain in the gut." She was suddenly weary. "I don't know why they sent in a psychiatrist."

"Standard procedure." He backed away from the bed. "Very well, Sister. I hope you feel better."

Later, on the phone, Reverend Mother said she didn't know why the doctors had been sent in.

But Sister Claire knew why, though she could never have explained to Reverend Mother. He'd been sent, that creep, to bring her light.

She watched the door close behind their white backs that day with something akin to glee.

Indeed, she did feel better. He could never know how much. For during that crazy interview, fending off his obscene probing, she'd found, at last, words for herself. Not for him. (And later, looking back on it all, she realized that during that half hour she'd been living through some high cosmic joke only a god could have invented.) While she parried that obnoxious psychiatrist and hid behind words, she was secretly discovering her answer. Now she knew. When the door closed behind them, she knew. Even as he was speaking, she knew. No matter the pain, the loss, no matter the friends she must hurt or disappoint (and this would cost her dearly), her way of affirming life must be to seek a new one.

She would act. Soon. On her own. No being sent off to consult a priest. She'd seen what that did to others. He'd double-talk her into guilt. She'd return a subdued, compliant dishrag. No being sent off to a shrink. She'd seen that one, too. Sister Genevieve had returned from her mysterious absence an altered being. Someone else. According to the rumor, the Order still dealt with a hospital that gave shock treatments. Hilary had told her. Two nuns at the college had been sent to that hospital.

No. She would act freely, on her own. Moreover, she had no intention of returning to the world a washed-out ex-nun. If it was possible to return in style, she'd do it. Trade black-and-white for Technicolor. Where could you get a tan in November? She'd borrow money from her parents, go to Florida.

She had stayed more than twelve years. Vatican II was over. She'd studied the kerygma, was up on Kung and Rahner and Schillebeeckx and Baum. She'd weathered interminable community discussions, orgies of self-examination, tempests of doubt. She'd sought in prayer to uncover the secrets of her own soul.

Yet nothing, absolutely nothing, had so effectively freed her from the final vanity as her encounter with absurd Dr. Seaman.

She must finish writing out her statement now, a kind of insurance against later, when words might again fail her.

She reached for her breviary, found her pen. She took the paper on which she'd begun her statement before she came to the hospital. She wrote:

I no longer believe that religious life can speak effectively to this world of the love of Christ. Therefore, I, Claire Delaney, freely choose to leave it.

The truth of Christ, as I understand it, is one of love for men that is unmistakably human and forgiving, incarnating an absolute respect for the sacredness of the person.

She slipped the paper back into her breviary and began to get dressed.

*

Florida burns the body, washes the mind.

For this, ten days later, she was not prepared, although she'd tried to prepare for many things, imagining what a freshly sprung nun would need to survive three days of adjustment to the world. She had a brain, a tongue, all the usual equipment. She didn't worry about the sun's effect on her skin.

Her mother, more sensitive to wrinkles now than twelve years ago, warned her. "Be careful, Claire. The sun ages your skin."

And her father dryly concurred: "Better take care of yourself. Don't want to be zapped to a crisp on your first exposure."

They were nervous with her, disoriented. As if someone set in a frame on the mantel had suddenly stepped out of it. She understood. Her one night back in their house had felt barely tolerable: rooms too small, too close together. They'd tiptoed around each other. She'd grown accustomed to some kinds of space.

That would all be worked out. For now—she was resurrecting Claire Delaney, thirty-three, beneath Florida sun.

When she collected her mother's gray suitcase at the airport baggage claim, hailed the limousine to the Hilton, stepped out and walked in the hotel lobby, she half expected people to stare. Surely, before the day was over, she'd do something odd, forget to tip, tip too little. Yet no one seemed to notice her.

Palm trees bordered the check-in desk. A fountain in the center of the black-and-green lobby spilled azure foam over gold-and-silver fish. Uniformed clerks, tanned women in white, men in sneakers and shorts moved through the lobby like assured extras in some show to which she'd found a ticket but not the script.

She brushed against a palm tree and checked in—"Miss Delaney, oh, yes"—found her way to the elevator without help, hummed up to the fifteenth floor, and walked the long, carpeted hall to her room.

Airy and clean, it looked out to sea. A huge picture window bordered by green flowered drapes framed blue ocean, blue sky. At first the brightness hurt her eyes, but she squinted and kept looking. Fifteen stories below, white sand stretched for miles in either direction. Gaily striped umbrellas sheltered sunbathers, and white bathing caps dotted waves in near shore. Streaks of purple-blue darkened the water farther out. In one of these three sailboats dipped.

It was two in the afternoon. She kicked off her shoes, surveyed the huge double bed with its hideous carmine flowers, the over-size TV, the large gilt-framed mirror at the foot of the bed. She plopped down on the soft mattress and stared at the ivory telephone.

Perhaps he would call her. She was in no hurry.

"My brother Bob would at least take you out to dinner," Hilary had said. "He'd love any excuse."

From her parents' home she'd called Hilary at the college. It was easy to get through to her. The main switchboard rang her office and there she was. When Claire told her she was home, Hilary was muted. "Look, I'm not surprised," she said. And then tried to think if there was something she could offer.

What could you offer a freshly sprung friend? Her brother's gesture.

"He's down there alone, waiting for his family to come," she said. "A new job. I'll send him a note about you. Here's his telephone number, just in case." Then, after giving the number, "Look, as far as I know that's what he's doing down there. That's the official public line. But tread carefully. He's a great guy. I just don't know that much about his private life." They talked a few minutes before Hilary finally concluded, "And don't worry, Claire. We'll see each other again!"

And now—here she was in the world of sun and sky to re-discover herself.

Above the dresser a picture of surf bathers and sailboats du-plicated the view from the window. Was this the right place to have come? She had to start somewhere. She'd wanted a place where no one knew her, where she could rediscover her own skin unobserved.

She pulled herself together, checked her face (not bad), left the room. If Bob Raleigh hadn't called by tomorrow night, she'd call him. By then she might feel up to it.

She retraced her steps past fountains and palm trees, left the hotel, and headed toward what must be town. Small expensive-looking shops lined the streets, their windows exploding with color—turquoise, fuchsia, yellow, everything. The few young women who passed her seemed perfectly tanned and painted. She was overdressed and undercolored, a bland fish in exotic seas. The sky was too blue, the sun too bright, she too—dull. She wore a white skirt, an orange-and-white blouse, purchased quickly under her mother's careful (and dated) eye.

She turned into a small store, hoping to browse unobserved.

"Can I help you, Madam?"

The slender saleswoman with crimson lips, a hot-pink dress, and eyelashes at least half an inch long, waited.

"I—I wanted some lipstick."

"Yes, Madam. Over here."

They moved toward a glass case. The woman captured a gold-framed mirror and set it near Claire, tipping it toward her.

"Now, what shade do you usually wear, Madam?" She slid open the case from behind the counter and suspended her hand inside while she parted an encouraging smile over large white teeth.

"Well, I—" Black, silver, gold, topaz, emerald: rows of lipstick cylinders, colors from the Book of Revelation. Revlon, Max Factor, Elizabeth Arden, Helena Rubinstein. *Ask me to reel off the gifts of the Holy Ghost,* she thought.

"We have a special on Revlon products this week, Madam."

She could have recited the twenty-two verses of the *Stabat Mater.*

The saleswoman pulled her hand from the case and straightened up. She closed her lips.

"Perhaps you could advise me?" said Claire.

"For evening, Madam? Or daytime?" Her folded hands rested on the glass case.

"Daytime."

"Let's see . . ." She bent forward, the edge of the display case pressing against her silver belt. "You have rather light coloring, Madam. And"—here a slight intake of concerned breath—"if

236

you do not mind my saying so, your eyelids are already beginning to crack. You must be careful of the sun, you know. Did you just arrive?"

"Yes." *Lizard lids on this hick. Only thirty-three and already a hag.*

"I would say your coloring would benefit by something with a rosy tone. That depends, of course, on what colors you usually wear."

I'm a stunner in black and white.

The freckled hand began exploring treasures under glass, setting lipsticks on the counter.

"Now, this is Pink Delight." She uncovered a silver stick and rolled out a pink cylinder. She spread a narrow line of pink on the back of her left hand. "This might do, Madam, quite nicely. It would bring out some of your highlights, but I'd recommend our new color for fall, Elfin Cerise." She opened the black lipstick case and rubbed a thick streak of deeper red beside the pink. "What do you think?"

Even Solomon in all his glory was not arrayed like one of these. "And the others?"

"Ah, this is quite a bit darker. Suitable, I think, for evening. Particularly if you have complementary eye shadow." She opened the last tube. An even darker red rolled forth. "This is Cool Carmine." She smiled. "I'm particularly fond of this, myself. It's luminescent."

She might have been naming the eighth wonder.

"Luminescent?"

"Yes, it shines a bit in the dark. Lovely for evening."

"And does the darkness comprehend it?" This time she *said* it. "Thank you. I'll take Elfin Cerise and Cool Carmine."

Back at her hotel room, she dropped her purchases on the dresser, stretched out on the bed, and slept instantly.

In her dream she lay in a huge green room beneath a glass dome. White-haired Dr. Seamen stood beside the bed. Above her, through the glass, she saw blue sky and slowly shifting clouds. Farther distant, behind the clouds, a brilliant blue-and-red bird flew. It dipped and swerved, disappearing, reappearing in a swoosh of color. Dr. Seamen held a gigantic thing like a magnifying glass. He extended it over her entirely, covering her face. "Ah," he breathed, leaning forward and peering through, "you've made the right choice, Sister. Cool Carmine." She could no longer see the bird. Through the oddly blurred perspective of the curved glass, she saw only the enormous blue vein in Dr. Seamen's temple throbbing, like the pulse in a lizard's belly.

She awoke exhausted.

For a few moments she lay staring at pictured surf, then glanced at the travel alarm. Five-thirty. She got up, washed, put on the blue linen dress, yellow shoes, and yellow beads she and her mother had found just yesterday. She was very hungry.

The dining room was a large, cool room overlooking the patio. At the doorway she stopped. Almost empty. Perhaps it was too early, only six o'clock, convent dinner hour. At a table for two near the door a tanned man in a light-blue suit sat reading the paper as he sipped a drink. He glanced up at her.

The tall dark-haired man in a tuxedo who stood near the doorway nodded toward her and stepped forward. "Would you care to be seated, Madam?"

"No, no, thank you. Just looking for someone. He isn't here yet."

The tuxedo bowed and turned discreetly away.

She returned to the lobby and punched the elevator button, mortified. Had he seen her embarrassment? Her downright fear? Absurd. What was there to be afraid of? She wasn't two.

She arrived at the fifteenth floor, found her room, went in, and looked carefully in the mirror. The lizard lids didn't show. She still looked good. Maybe no one would have noticed her.

She slipped out of the dress, put on navy shorts and a white T-shirt, and headed back downstairs and out the front door.

It was still warm. The soft evening air comforted her skin, touching it lightly. Would she ever grow used to this?

Three blocks from the hotel she found a chicken take-out place, bought three pieces, and headed for the beach.

She would walk. To her right the gleaming hotels of the Gold Coast blocked the city from view. Warm evening air stroked her legs, her arms. She gnawed a chicken wing, dropped the bones back in the bag, and licked the salt from her fingers.

She passed hotels set back from the beach and fronted by shuffleboard patios and kidney-shaped pools. The mingled sounds of laughing voices and the clink of glasses floated past her toward the sea. Finished with the chicken, she took off her shoes and walked along the edge of the water. Waves licked her toes. A ridge of white foam lined the soft white sand. Now and then she disturbed a rainbow of bubbles and watched as sand sucked them slowly away.

She should have gone someplace less tropical, less absolute. But where?

She thought of old Sister Gertrude, whose jubilee was over now. Who would be wondering where Claire was. Somehow, soon, she'd find a way to let her know. . . . And Sister Mark. There had been time for no good-byes. Perhaps that was the better way. Why should she by her words cast doubt on the rightness of their choice?

And Hilary. They would meet again before long. Claire felt that. In what costumes, what place? It didn't matter. The world opened before her.

She walked for a long time that evening, thinking, remembering, praying, until the orange disk sank against a cobalt horizon and stars winked fitfully above. The sand beneath her feet turned cool, and rows of hotels became flickering shafts of light along the darkening beach.

She thought of Father O'Neill, his troubled face that day in the staff room, the depth of his pain. He would be leaving soon. Reverend Mother insisted on linking the two of them. Perhaps that would make her explanation to Mother Provincial, to Mother General, all the easier. What did it matter?

She did not expect ever to see him again.

As if from afar, from some other planet wheeling through space, she remembered the old familiar pain, saw again the white curtains of her cell, the black edge of Sister Mark's knee. The pain had left as suddenly as it had come.

She bent down to scoop fine, soft sand with a fluted pink shell. The shells along this beach were pink, pearly, opalescent—unlike the sharp razor clam shells of her childhood beaches. As she walked again along the water's edge, she listened. Forever, the *lap lap lap* of water arriving, departing. Maybe on the other side of the world someone at this very moment stood listening, thinking the same thought. She heard the light whir of a motor and saw the outline of a boat dipping past.

Farther out, from some invisible point of origin, a searchlight flared yellow beams across the sky. She almost expected a shape to emerge from the black water, moon-ridged now in silver. Nothing spoke. Everything spoke. Unbidden, those ancient, timeless words arose within her as she watched the arching columns of light . . . *tibi omnes angeli, tibi caeli et universae potestates, tibi cherubim et seraphim incessabili voce proclamant . . . in te, Domine, speravi, non confundar in aeternum . . .*

It was almost midnight when she returned to her room, took a shower, and went to bed. She would call Bob Raleigh the next evening, after a day of swimming.

On her last evening in Florida, Claire Delaney went with Bob Raleigh to a restaurant called the Bird of Paradise. Her three-day rite of passage had worked: she Cool Carmined her lips with a steady hand and threaded the hotel lobby with confidence, walking her tender sunburn toward the pudgy balding man in a white suit waiting for her by the palm tree. He was deeply tanned, wore no wedding ring, and was, she quickly saw, shy. Probably leery of an ex-nun. Nonetheless, she felt his approving eye.

The restaurant was just outside Fort Lauderdale. He drove her there in a low dark blue car whose front seats could be individually adjusted. She was dying to experiment with them, push them up and down, back and forward, but she restrained herself and crossed her legs, secretly admiring her bright yellow shoes. The hair on the back of his tanned hand shifting gears was bleached golden.

"One of my favorite spots," he said. "I don't often get to come here these days."

They were driving up a winding road bordered by swaying palms. Inside, he nodded to the host and led her to a small dining room. Their reserved table for two was beside a large sunken garden, rampant smoldering foliage and exotic flowers. She tried not to stare.

"A drink?"

"A daiquiri," she said smoothly, noticing his small ears. Her mother had liked a daiquiri.

It was altogether easier than she'd expected. She could study a menu without feeling theatrical. In the hotel shop she'd found yellow earrings to match her yellow beads. She held her smarting back away from the chair.

"Got quite a burn, did you?"

"Yes. My parents tried to warn me about Florida sun."

"It's deceptive. When I came down here last June, I was a mess. One big peel."

The thin stem of her cocktail glass felt cool and smooth, the tart sweetness of the drink soothed and excited her. She looked at the menu, intrigued. Chicken Bombay, sauteed bananas, coconut, toasted almonds, rice pilaf; Stuffed Baked Grouper with lobster sauce; Broiled Red Snapper Almondine . . .

"What's good?" she asked.

He, the worldly one, took pleasure in explaining each dish. They settled for lobster tails broiled with garlic butter. More than twelve years since she'd tasted lobster. Her father had taken them out for lobster before she entered.

Bob had gone to see Hilary in October.

"She told me you were ill."

"Yes. A mysterious pain." She sipped her daiquiri. How much

to say? Mrs. Cassidy, Dr. Seamen, the solace of Sister Mark, the strength of her arm, her love. "It came and went. In the end, Reverend Mother told me it was all in my head." She was beyond bitterness. Surely he too had lived.

He snorted. The hands fingering his fork were manicured and firm. He worked for a corporation she'd never heard of.

"I've heard that one before." He was good at sympathy.

"Did you visit her often?" Large red flowers yawned near their table. Somewhere a bird trilled, a high quivery song, pure and sweet.

"In the beginning not at all. I couldn't stand the thought of it. She's my only sibling. She'd buried herself, and that was that. Then, after a few years—" He stopped, busy with lobster tail and drawn butter. "Well, it began to seem not all that important, what she'd chosen to do. I wanted to be in touch. What business was it of mine if she wanted that life? So I looked her up, just like that. Appeared two years ago at college and asked to see Sister Hilary. There she was, in black and white. That was all it took. Blood's thicker than water." He swirled pale meat in melted yellow. "So I've seen her just a couple of times since. Though, to tell you the truth, Claire"—he eyed her and popped the lobster piece into his mouth—"I still find the atmosphere hard to take."

"I can imagine." John the Baptist, the desert, locusts and honey. A faint shadow of the old pain grazed her heart. *Distract.* "Do you know the name of that red flower over there?"

"Hibiscus. Originally from Hawaii. Sometimes called Shoe Black Plant or Chinese Rose."

The bird continued to trill, shifting keys.

"You've studied botany? I thought you were a businessman."

"A hobby. It gets me through long weekends."

He had a wife, two children, somewhere up North. At first the situation was unclear to her. Then she deduced he was alone, separated or divorced. They skirted the topic.

He was peeling an avocado. She memorized his moves. Her future might include an avocado. A whole avocado ranch, for that matter. She knew so little, or had forgotten it . . . children doing homework, dishes, candlelight, arguments, love-making in a shared bed. . . . What pain shrouded his breakup? Or was it relief? Did he want her to ask, or was it enough to sit here with a woman he'd never see again and buy her dinner as a favor to his sister? When would he tell Hilary? What did he have in mind? Was this generosity, pure and simple?

"Do you know the names of the other flowers?" She glanced toward blossoms in the center of the garden—orange, purple, yellow, turquoise, red—mostly red. They jostled each other, throats open, yellow and heavy, stems tangled in a brown and green jungle. She remembered the lovely daisy, Queen Anne's lace, the blushing pansies of her childhood. These were from some other continent, some other world.

"Lots of them. Do you want Latin or English?"

"English. My Latin's good for only a few things."

"That one over there with the orange blossoms is Mexican Fire Vine, and next to it is the flower that gives this restaurant its name, Bird of Paradise."

Bright orange petals and a tongue of deep blue trembled above its long green bract, edged in red.

"Then there's Elephant Ear, Cathedral Bells, and guess what that low plant over there is with the magenta undersides of leaves?"

"What?" She saw he enjoyed showing off. Maybe this was the secret with men: just get them started.

"Moses in the Bulrushes. Then there's Angel's Trumpet, and all along that border Devil's Backbone."

"Enough." She laughed. "I can absorb only so much."

They worked their way through Southern pecan pie with mounds of whipped cream. People filled up the tables nearby. Low voices, clinking silver, the brisk movements of waiters: it all comforted her. From somewhere came strains of music—strings, a piano, a drum, something else, a horn she couldn't identify.

"I should have warned you." He was offering the waiter a plastic card. "Do you dance?"

He was checking the bill again. She watched his square fingertips, the golden hairs. He was preoccupied, adding. She saw the refectory, the chapel, Sister Hilary—his sister.

He looked up. "I wanted to dance tonight. Haven't had a chance since last Christmas. I didn't want to say anything until we'd met. Of course . . . if you'd rather we can just sit and watch."

Deference to the ex-nun, defrosting virgin. The bird trilled again.

"Is that a real bird?" She stalled.

"Copied from the bird sanctuary at Disneyland. They've put three birds in that garden that can trill and call and make all the authentic sounds. Pure fake, but quite a feat." He nodded the waiter away, put his napkin on the table. "Well?"

"I'm out of practice. Haven't exactly been dancing lately."

He grinned and took her elbow as they left the table. They moved around the edge of the sunken garden, making their way toward the music.

They passed a stuffed alligator. "Incredible," she murmured. His hand grew warm on her flesh.

"This is Florida."

They took a table near the already crowded dance floor. Blue and red globes revolved about the floor, strewing circles of shattered light.

She watched the hot twisting bodies in silence.

"I've only danced ballroom," she said, fascinated by liquid knees and shoulders. At dancing school they'd worn white gloves to protect against perspiration. Near her, a woman in cerise ruffles swayed and rotated, elbows flickering. She wore silver shoes and a huge silver flower in her black hair.

"They might play a fox-trot or rumba later," he said.

"What're they playing now?"

"Don't know the name." He tapped his fingers against the tabletop. "You just get out and move with it."

"I've never done it."

"You might be surprised. You can't make a mistake. Want to watch for a while, or would you like to try it?"

She saw the lust in his eyes. Or was it lust? The driving rhythms cut through her, into her, unlocking. Strings, sharp and sweet, pulled at her. Her throat grew dry with desire.

"Watch?" She smiled and pushed back her chair. "Not on your life. Let's dance."

*How shall we sing the song of the Lord
in a strange land?*

Psalm 136

At Peace

It was sheer accident that I happened to be passing through
Calais, Maine, when the obituary columns listed Barney's death.
Even more accidental that I happened to pick up a paper that
night and read of it. But for an engine breakdown, I'd have
charged right through that godforsaken town and left it behind
forever. As luck would have it, though, our ailing train gasped
to a halt about twenty miles outside town. After the usual apol-
ogies, reassurances, official explanations, and unofficial speculations, they hauled us off, baggage and all, and left us huffing
and puffing in the frost, a band of about fifty derailed passengers
thrust on the bleak bosom of a November night by the Canadian
border.

It was every bit as chilling as I remembered it. Small pockets
of human frustration clustered alongside the track, here and

there a cigarette lighter briefly illuminating anxious eyes or a stoic jaw, intermittent mutters uselessly rehearsing our impotence as we waited to be rescued. The surge of rhythmic power that had so effortlessly borne us past hamlets, shacks, straggling ends of villages, vacant sagging barns, wintering maple and evergreen forests, miles of unpeopled marsh, standing cows, and scattered workhorses—was still. For hours we had sat in the overheated cars staring vaguely out at the darkening landscape that passed us, lulled and rocked by the mechanical song of our train, or we had turned away from that mesmerizing window to the comforts of the inside: a drink, dinner, conversation, a snooze. But now our instinctive balances of cold observed and warmth enjoyed had been exploded: we were on the other side of that glass, we were out there, ourselves impossibly part of the desolate landscape with which we had felt so tenuously connected, if connected at all. *We* were in the moving picture, but we weren't even moving.

There was no inside to turn to, no way to shut this out, turn it off. The best distraction I could find from gradually numbing toes and buzzing irritation all around me was to stare straight up. I could remember that from before. It wasn't the old cliché of finding solace in the sky. Not that sky. It was simply that there was no sky like it anywhere else I'd been. There was nothing else to do with it but look. It was a sky that reduced one to staring. Going blank. A sky whose vast darkness somehow inverted and restated those vacant stretches of landscape it shrouded by day. Neither a pillar of fire nor a manned rocket seemed to have anything to do with those heavens. Stars were everywhere in the black, patterned holes cutting through—to what? No trace of that pinkish rainbow that arches over a large city at night, the almost sickening glow of darkness's covenant with urban hustle-bustle. I can remember seeing, once, the night sky over the steel works in Gary, Indiana—puffed with swiftly merging forms of billowing gray-yellow above belching flames: gorgeous. Faced with that, one might come to believe in apocalypse. But this sky yielded nothing to human desires; it remained barren and silent even with studding stars and subtle wisps of whiteness graining through its black. I stared and felt again what I remembered feeling long before about the marsh sky: it was neither reassuring nor warming. It was silencing.

Eventually we were taken care of. They stuffed us all into a bus and transported us to a Holiday Inn just outside town, from which they would collect us next morning and put us on the ten o'clock train they promised would leave promptly. When I finally lugged my loaded suitcase and parcels into that plastic world, even the blank surfaces of chartreuse and mauve in the predictable lobby and the equally opaque surface of the desk clerk were welcome. At times vacuity disguised as the familiar can seem to give warmth. This was such a time. I was relieved to be inside. In no time I had squared away my belongings, freshened up, picked up a paper in the lobby, and headed for the dining room. One thing I remembered about Maine food: their fish chowder was usually fabulous. This was the perfect night for a bowl of it.

When the waitress disappeared with my order, I settled down with the paper. I'd had enough of enforced socializing and people-watching for that night, and soon enough I'd be back in my own nest of domestic wear and tear. For those few final hours, at least, I cherished my solitude. And so the unfailing defense: I folded back the evening paper and began to read.

By the time dessert came, I was to the obituary page. It didn't take long to reach the obits; papers in that section of the country are notoriously slim. And then, there it was:

Died

Sister Barnabas MacLean, 74, daughter of Angus and Genevieve MacLean of Scotland, coadjutrix sister of the Order of St. Agnes. Funeral from the Church of Our Redeemer, Saturday, November 28. Friends may call at the convent between the hours of 3:00 and 5:00 and 7:00 and 9:00 on November 27. Donations may be made to the Heart Fund.

Barney. It had to be Barney. There could be only one lay sister in northern Maine named Sister Barnabas MacLean. Reading that notice seemed to paralyze all my responses momentarily. I didn't want Barney to be dead. Not, mind you, that I'd seen her in twenty or more years. But Barney had a corner in my consciousness that was carpeted, furnished, mythologized, and turned to in moments both secret and articulate. I had told many stories about her to dear friends. There were others I would tell no one because she trusted me not to. There was a pact of secrecy and trust between Barney and me, had been since I left the Order and even well before that. Barney belonged to life, the life of memory and mind that was mine. I didn't want her buried.

I remembered our first encounter still with a spasm of discomfort. I was new to Our Redeemer's community, fresh from the Washington house of studies, impressionable, earnest, conscientious—not to say scrupulous—about keeping untarnished and pure the vows I had just made. I realize now how hard it is to convey to an outsider what strange beings we were when we finally completed our three years of novitiate training and two years of juniorate and went to live in a community. We were filled with ideals, many as yet untested, schooled to the observance of details we believed would become the measure of sanctity in a world that denied us more obvious martyrdom, committed to a daily round of prayer and meditation that was taxing, time-consuming, and, we fervently hoped, eternally efficacious. Anyhow, there I was, assigned that first year to help Sister Barnabas in the kitchen during my "free time"—of which there was none. I had some vague notion that I was a victim. When I'd innocently told a few sisters what charge Reverend Mother had given me for the year, they rolled their eyes expressively, charity notwithstanding, and wished me luck.

So I found my way to the kitchen on my third day in the community. There she was, Sister Barnabas, puttering slowly around. It was ten o'clock in the morning, a Saturday.

"Good morning, Sister Barnabas," I said from the doorway, timid of crossing the premises without her clear sanction.

"Hrumph." It was barely audible. She kept moving about, grunting and sniffing, opening the refrigerator, shuffling to the sink, slamming cupboard doors, effectively communicating to me without so much as a word that she wished I were at the opposite end of the house, if not of the world.

"Reverend Mother told me I might be of some help to you in the kitchen."

She stopped dead. Then she looked at me, scowled, and snorted. "Help! So that's her idea, is it? Never *has* liked the way I run this kitchen. So she sent a spy, eh?"

She slammed the drawer behind her with her broad rump and grabbed the broom. Sister Barnabas was lame, but she compensated amazingly well. When she really wanted to move quickly, she did. Now she hobbled over to about two inches in front of me.

"Well, you can get right out o' here an' find yerself somethin' else to do to pass yer Saturday mornin's more in keepin' with the education the likes o' you has had." She started to sweep vigorously, covering my feet with the broom, forcing me back out of the doorway. "An' that's that!"

I left.

Something kept me from telling anyone about it. I held my peace and mentioned nothing to Reverend Mother. Not that I wanted to conceal; it was some deeper instinct I couldn't name that said: let her be. So I did. But the next Saturday morning, promptly at ten, I appeared again in the doorway. This time I saw that the kitchen floor had been scrubbed and was glistening wet. Sister Barnabas was nowhere to be seen. It was understood that one didn't disturb her in her room, a tiny cell just across the hall from the kitchen. That week again I felt a bit guilty but decided nonetheless to leave her a note that I'd been there, let time pass, and try just once more.

At ten o'clock the next Saturday I appeared. There she was, hobbling about. Grumbling. Apparently oblivious that I was in the doorway. I waited. Then cleared my throat. She turned immediately, but it was clear she was not about to help me.

"Good morning, Sister Barnabas."

She scowled at me once more. "Well, I got yer note." Not another word. No indication of how she felt. No explanation.

"Is there anything I could do to help you this morning, Sister?"

"Wash the floor." She pointed silently to the mop and pail she had left in the corner by the doorway. As she did that, she was loosening her apron, obviously not intending to be around while I helped.

"Fine." I held my tone as absolutely neutral as I could. Perhaps I did have a charge, after all.

She left and I moved about, sloshing the linoleum and hoping it would suit her. One thing worked in my favor: I knew she was not a fussy housekeeper. In fact, the prioress at that time kept away from the kitchen just because she couldn't stand the mess. The food Sister Barnabas fed us was excellent, the best in the province, I later realized, after I'd moved around a bit. But the kitchen—a god-awful mess. Pots within pots, nothing sized, jars and containers here and there with leftovers and preparations dripping or hardening in various colors and shapes, a conglomeration only she could keep straight. Thick greasy dust coated the top of the refrigerator. The oven window was crusted with a baked glaze that resisted repeated applications of Easy-Off. I learned that later, when the oven came to be my special task, one I loathe even now.

And plants. Where there wasn't dirt or pots and pans or food, there was a plant. Counter space seemed to disappear almost before it existed. Ivy trailing all over the kitchen windows, even though the convent was poorly insulated and the windows were frosty. A jade tree growing from a sodded wash basin in the corner, impatiens blooming fiery red on the edge of the butcher block in the center of the kitchen, a tuberous begonia on the flour barrel, shifted about during the day as baking proceeded. And, who would believe it, African violets thriving on the corner of the kitchen counter.

It made no sense; her plants were always in danger. But they were a precious part of her mess, and she was scrupulous about their care. Talked to them, long before plant nuts were telling us that was the secret. Vented her spleen on them, too. Perhaps it was simply that she had no one else living with whom she felt she could communicate. So the plants got it—whole. And she had spleen aplenty. But they rooted and grew and flowered and trailed in that atmosphere of hostility and harangue. To this day I can't keep an ivy from dying, not even with the advantages of mild climate, peat moss, plant food, sun, water, and a library of how-to books. All she did was mutter and growl, and this in a part of the world whose climate spoke of death. My milder skies of the Pacific Northwest, the long growing season, the abundant rain—none of this has made my thumb green. But nothing green seemed to wither in Barney's kingdom.

Apparently my floor passed muster, for she let me in each Saturday morning thereafter, usually muttering some direction to me and leaving immediately for her room. When I left the kitchen and headed down the hall an hour or so later, I'd often hear her cell door click as she shuffled back to inspect. We went on like this for some time.

Then one Saturday morning she paused as she was leaving the kitchen. She seemed to be making a more elaborate knot in the apron strings she was about to dangle from the hook behind the door.

"Sister," she grunted in my direction. I was busy pouring water into a pail and turned off the tap quickly to hear. "How come you never told Reverend Mother I wouldn't let you in my kitchen?"

"Because I figured you must have your own good reasons." The answer was true, as well as uncalculated. It went right to the mark, but she didn't let on then.

"Hrumph." She hung up the apron and hobbled out. The next Saturday, though, before I started my work, she offered a comment, as if a whole week hadn't intervened, as if we were just continuing our conversation. "Yer the first one has ever done that fer me here." She jabbed the apron onto the hook and left. I mopped away that morning with the distinct sense that in some queer way I'd made a difference in her feeling about the place, about me, or about something else I had yet to discover.

I did discover that something, as the months passed and our weekly punctuated exchanges grew into what couldn't properly be called conversations, ever, but limping dialogues that seemed to erupt, almost unwilled, out of some inexpressible need in her. For my part, I came to see certain things about Sister Barnabas.

First of all, somewhere, somehow, and it was probably many years before, she had been badly hurt. I was never sure just how. I could read the many subsequent hurts that resulted from her being the only lay sister in an order of highly educated women who willed to deal charitably with her but found it hard to absorb her thorns without the flower of articulate acknowledgment. For Sister Barnabas never admitted guilt. Nor did she speak easily or grammatically—or even, sometimes, coherently. Before she could get a statement out, she had to feel she could trust you. Most of the time she made do with monosyllables and grunts delivered with a scowl. By the time I met her she trusted literally no one. Except, for some strange reason as our history bore out, me.

Secondly, she was basically bright. She had had no schooling to speak of—just first and second grade in a little country schoolhouse. (I observed with fascination her self-taught methods of calculating proportions for enlarging recipes.) Then, when she was eight, she had lost both parents: first her father was killed in a freak accident by his own tractor, then her mother, a month later, died in childbirth. She was farmed out to a distant uncle who was none too happy to have another mouth to feed and body to clothe, but saw to it that she redeemed the burden on him by taking care of his four children, all younger than she.

She had known little about the sisters when she first came to them, had merely passed their convent whenever she went into the nearest town, some fifteen miles from her uncle's farm. As she grew older she occasionally saw them moving about in town, and she understood—because she had her depths of uneducated piety—that they lived for God. She was about seventeen when her uncle told her one day that the sisters were looking for someone to help with the work in their convent. She took the hint, went timidly to investigate, and shortly thereafter went to live with the sisters. She had a place and she had a job.

"I felt I'd found a home." She put it to me simply, in one of her many narrations about life in the old days. "They needed an' wanted me. There wasn't many of 'em, but some very good souls. As well as one or two *divils!*" With this, she'd swat an invisible fly or rub her hands energetically against her crusty apron for emphasis and relief, her dark eyes snapping beneath heavy, disorderly brows. "But most of us got along real well. The superior fer years was Sister Alphonsus. She didn't put on airs." Here, a pause with a meaningful sniff. "None o' this bowin' an' scrapin' from here to eternity. We showed her proper respect, but she was one of us. Did the dishes, taught in the classroom like the rest. No stayin' in her office, seein' people an' hearin' their reports on others from dawn to dusk." Again she would italicize her complaint with a physical gesture—kick a box, slam a drawer, or perhaps, if we were chatting in her cell as later came to be our habit, she'd just slap her knee hard once or twice.

It was a particularly sore point with Barney while I was there that our prioress, as the superior was then called, was somewhat reserved and set great store by her dignity. She made no attempt to hide her disapproval of the way Barney kept, or didn't keep, her kitchen. She despised mess; her own office seemed dust-resistant, the top of her desk tediously neat. She and Barney lived in a state of cold war. But meals must go on: the *status quo* was maintained.

In any case, when Barney first went to live with the sisters in town, she found one substantial change in her lot: she felt valued. There was no great change in her material situation. As she herself put it, "We was all from that area, an' most of us already knew what poor farm livin' was all about. So we worked hard an' didn't think much about it. Got mighty cold sometimes, though, in midwinter. That's always what bothered me most. *Cold.*"

Then the world began to change, even that world we may think of as so unchanging. Their convent grew poorer and poorer. In the late twenties and thirties they were largely dependent on alms, their school income having dropped to virtually nothing. They skimped and prayed—and went on teaching.

"We'd peel an orange for breakfast," she told me, "an' even that was an effort, our hands would be so cold. After breakfast I went 'round and started the wood stoves in the three classrooms so by the time the children arrived, those rooms, the kitchen, an' the little chapel would be warm." To me, her kitchen in Calais was always stifling.

When Barney told them to me, I heard stories of those days with the fascination that attaches to some far-distant era, for in my time we were snug in a convent that was spacious, orderly, and well-appointed if plain. In the fifties the superiors could afford to debate whether floors in a new convent would be hard wood or linoleum, whether the chapel would have a pipe organ or an electric one. But the times Barney spoke of were long before such affluence, and the nuns in that little community came to know the meaning of the poverty they had vowed. Barney cooked for them as best she could, gradually mastering the secrets of kitchen and soil. Her hands, swollen with arthritis when I knew her, had the look of hands that were friends of earth.

"I'd always grown vegetables, even as a child," she boasted early one summer morning in Calais, when she took me out behind our convent to admire her flourishing garden. "I surprised 'em all when I managed to stock enough vegetables to take us clear through the winter."

Her secret was a method of storing in shallow holes out behind the convent, lined and covered with hay. It was in one of her early morning trips out to such a hole that she caught her foot in a crevice hidden by snow and turned her ankle badly. It never healed properly. She tried to keep the pain to herself; there was enough to worry about without doctors' bills. Somehow she hobbled about and managed to borrow first crutches, then a cane. When I came to know her in Calais years later, she still had that same cane, worn smooth with use.

Their little group managed to survive in that state for several years, perplexed as to their future but, one supposes, living day by day and pluckily trusting to Providence. I see them in my own imagination as a small band of valiant women committed to the task of hanging on. They were receiving no subjects. Except for Sister Barnabas, as she came to be called, after she finally decided to become one of the group at the age of twenty-six or so.

"I wasn't so sure they'd take me," she admitted to me once in a rare show of humility. "Especially since I couldn't help out in the school. Most of 'em had been through the sixth grade at least. But they liked my cookin', an' they'd grown used to my ways. I felt right good they was so pleased to have me."

She always felt her lack of education. Even when I was in Calais, I'd come upon her trying furtively to improve herself. She kept a tattered pocket dictionary on a secret shelf, and eventually she asked me to read and correct any notes she sent to Reverend Mother. For their communication was chiefly by notes, even though they lived in the same house.

So that was how she spent her early years in the convent. Her job was to scrape the pot as creatively as she could, but the bottom looked emptier and emptier. Their end seemed inevitable: gradual extinction. They were an autonomous house in the rural periphery of a particularly slack diocese. Times were hard all over, and little help was forthcoming from ecclesiastical authorities, who no doubt saw the hopelessness of wasting resources on a dying group.

Chance rescued them. I was on the other side of that chance.

Ann Copeland

But for the improbable, I would never have met Barney. As it turned out, my own Order—highly organized, international, strictly monastic as it was—reached out the sisterly hand. Officially it was called amalgamation. Perhaps interment would have been a more accurate term. Anyhow, Barney's little group of nuns was absorbed by us.

"No way we could know what we was in fer," she'd ruminate as she poked around the kitchen after our work was done, shifting the arbutus, checking the violets, or easing herself onto the rickety high stool near the sink. "But I'm tellin' you, Sister, I'm tellin' you—I never wants to live through seein' a house closed again. Not one I've been livin' in and thinkin' of as home. Not one I knows like the back o' my hand an' loves. It was awful, it was awful." She'd be intense in memory for a moment; then she'd shuffle off, jostling herself back to present practicalities.

I could imagine the world she had left. It's the same today, only more so. This was an early version of the very scene I'd stared at for hours through the train window that late November night. But in her time the whole area was just *beginning* to depopulate, people moving away to greener pastures, someplace where they felt they'd have a chance. Farms—always a precarious source of livelihood in this rugged area of the country—were straggling into anonymous dereliction. The sagging gray barn with loose siding was becoming a landmark everywhere. Wherever you turned, there were signs of village life that once had been but now was gone: vacant buildings with broken windows, abandoned tarpaper shacks, junked wagons, rusting car parts, mounds of debris, litter. Stragglers lingered on—the old-timers who blended tobacco, tall stories, and repetitive wit as they stood staring out at the vacant landscape; the lounging adolescents. It was improbable that any ambitious school would stand a chance of success here. And our Order was committed to education.

"We gathered fer one final party in the old house," Barney told me. "Even the old students, many of 'em now grown with children of their own, came. I made a great cake—we all sang, then ended with Benediction together fer the last time. We had it outdoors, the chapel was too small fer the crowd. I'll never forget the final hymn. 'Holy God,' it was. Next morning they split us up an' shipped us out to the communities that had agreed to take us, by twos and threes. Sister Alphonsus and I came here. I wanted to bring my mutt, but they said no." I thought of her kitten litter at the back door.

"Here," just outside Calais, was where the Order had a flourishing elementary school and was about to start the private girls' high school to which I was assigned. Thus—chance. There were about twenty-five in the community when she came. They desperately needed a cook; there were no lay sisters in this Order. The job was hers. They soon saw, I'm sure, that she had already developed her quirks, but she was tolerated easily since the convent was large enough that they could leave her alone.

That was just it; they could leave her alone. From my perspective, Barney had come from a world one might almost call cozy: where convent and school were in one building, where in the midst of the morning a youngster from the third grade might run into her kitchen to sneak a fresh doughnut if their pungent odor had seeped down the hallway toward the classrooms. Occasionally, even in their hardest days, Barney would prepare a treat for one of the primary grades, and the children would greet her appearance at the classroom door with a cheer, for they knew it meant doughnuts, candy, or the succulent candied cherries she turned out by the dozens at Christmastime. When she went to town, limping along with her perpetual frown, people nodded, or children darted up to her to introduce their parents. She was an institution. I'm not minimizing the hardships she must have known, but it was all within a context that had some human warmth for her. She knew where she fit.

Now all that was gone. There was *no* going to town: these nuns were strictly cloistered. The school itself was an acre away. She saw the children only in the distance, lining up for classes or at recess time. They had never heard of her, much less smelled her doughnuts or tasted her candied cherries. Parents Day was catered and held in the school; she never met the families. The convent itself was shaped like a Y: refectory and kitchen in one wing, chapel in the other, nuns' cells and community room in the third. In chapel the nuns chanted the Divine Office in Latin. To her it might as well have been Hindustani.

She fit in only one place: the kitchen. And that place was cut off from the others. Seculars were not allowed within the cloister; the sisters stayed away from the kitchen. So she was structurally cut off from the others, to say nothing of the fact that she had no history or training in common with the rest of us. Everyone in the Order had at least a B.A. and, as the years passed and our training was upgraded, the younger nuns were sent on to graduate school. Sister Barnabas might have pronounced the same vows we had, but in terms of everyday living that language of shared aspiration was delusion. All the tongues we spoke in the course of a day were to her foreign, even threatening: it was a living babel called community life.

Just about that time I came to the house and went through my Saturday morning trial period before gradual acceptance came. Just why it came was never clear to me. Maybe not to her. Perhaps it was just that conjunction of person, need, and time in one's life that worked, as it sometimes can, for the most unlikely reasons.

"Sister," she'd say to me as I was about to leave on Saturday morning, "do you have a minute?" I dared not say I was pressed, had to prepare a class, had papers to do. Instead we'd go across the hall to her small cell, the only one in that wing. Outside— the silent polished corridors, glistening formica-topped tables in the long refectory, the spotless community room, the tidy cells of the older nuns. Everywhere the house reflected order, an order understood to mirror timeless higher realities. Inside Sister Barnabas's room—clutter, glorious clutter. I understood why she never let anyone in.

First of all, the bed had on it no standard white cotton spread of the kind that reduced our cells to facelessness. Her bed was covered with an old quilt carefully patched in places.

"A variation on the Dresden Plate," she told me, patting it

with her swollen hands and then plopping down in the middle of it as she motioned me to the one small chair. "In the old days we spent winter evenin's workin' quilts with pieces o' cotton the parishioners brought us. Turned out 'bout two a winter— mostly local favorites: Dresden Plate, the Bear's Paw. Double Irish Chain, Maltese Cross. They brought patterens with 'em from their families." ("Patterens," she said, I can still remember.) Her words conjured up a homey rural scene to my stereotyping imagination: a group of nuns gathered around the quilting frame by the Franklin stove. Snow outside. Currier and Ives. No doubt there was tedium in it, I thought, but there must have been steady delight, as well, in working with such beautiful designs and colors. Once a year, for their bazaar, they always raffled one or two quilts.

"One year Orville Landry took a chance in my name," she gleamed. "He was our jack-of-all-trades, a handyman. Loved my cookin'. I used to send him home with a batch o' fresh doughnuts every Saturday night. Anyhow, didn't he win the quilt an' give it to me."

It may sound like a trifle, but just such a detail represented the gulf between these two worlds: her old convent world and the one she and I were now in, the only model I had known, in fact, until I met Barney. For we, trained—with some pride, I always felt—to revere the austerities of monastic observance, had eliminated color from the mind's horizon. And gifts. Whatever we received we turned in to the superior, and we soon learned to warn family and friends not to give anything that was colorful. I can still remember the gaily striped towels I brought with me to the novitiate. On my second day there they disappeared and were quietly replaced by thin white ones. Towels in the convent were white, bedspreads were white, nightgowns were white, one is tempted to say now that the mind went white. The possibility of snuggling down under a colorful quilt that was your very own, a gift from someone you knew, was simply anathema to our highly conditioned virginal imaginations.

The abundance of things to look at in her room! Tacked to her walls was a hodgepodge of fraying snapshots, all from the past: squinting, squatting youngsters crowded together in a photo that was all background and taken on the slant; an aging tintype glued to cardboard backing of a broad-bosomed woman sitting sternly in front of her little cottage.

"My grandmother," she told me, "on my mother's side."

A dog, several shots of the dog, the cheerful mutt who had his own warm spot next to the wood stove in the kitchen of the old house. Her walls were covered with these photos larded in between with holy cards of the saints: Saint Teresa of Avila in ecstasy; Saint Joseph holding a lamb and a staff; the Child Jesus, heart and halo glowing; Mary, decorous in blue and white, grinding the serpent; Blessed Margaret Mary Alacoque receiving the promises; and, of course, the children of Fatima. The small table by her bed held a plastic madonna that lighted in the dark. Sister Barnabas couldn't stand the modern austere decor of our chapel. She loved plaster statues, vigil lights, tabernacles decorated in gold leaf with little doors that opened, processions with strewers, the Lourdes hymn: that whole world of comforting Catholicism we had been trained to regard as theologically and aesthetically suspect. Her thumb-worn *Imitation of Christ* was there on the desk, next to the piled-high travel magazines the milkman brought her.

That first day my initiation into her world of clutter and comfort brought me a feeling of release tinged with guilt: guilt because we chatted away in her cell, which was forbidden by the rule of silence, guilt because we stood in a world of clips from the past and I had been trained to let that past go, to forget or suppress or sublimate—whatever word a more sophisticated secular analyst might apply—the strands that had brought us to where we were. Leaving home meant to me *leaving* home: "No one having put his hand to the plow, and looking back . . ." We accepted, with some perverse pride, the cold absolute that we never would see home again. "Not even if there is a death in the family." That was the way they put it to us. Such a peak of detachment from home represented to us an achievement.

Yet there we stood surrounded, held, and (I felt it consciously even then) warmed by colorful fraying strands from a past of hardship that were gathered as best they could be into a whole skein of life: the effort to hold what had spoken, warmed, and comforted her in a world that was obviously now for Sister Barnabas cold, austere, and fundamentally incomprehensible. I began to understand the litter of her kitchen; I began not to see litter so much as composition, to grasp why she worked so hard at each original piece she produced.

For that was special about Barney. She had in her a touch of the artist. It showed in a variety of unexpected turns: she baked gorgeous, extravagant birthday cakes, quite unasked, and sent them into the refectory on the appropriate day for Sister So-and-so. The prioress disapproved visibly (we were not to celebrate birthdays but baptismal days) but found it futile to argue. Barney assigned me to keep track of the birthdays, to discover them by some means and let her know. She usually got a thank-you. She was wounded to the quick if she didn't, though she'd never let on to the sister in question.

When I came into the kitchen one Saturday morning, I found her muttering and kicking an empty carton about fiercely. I waited a moment, wondering whether I ought just to leave (she valued her privacy passionately), then said as if I'd noticed nothing, "Anything special for me to do today?"

She booted the carton a good six feet till it struck a wall and, turning, she slammed in an offensive drawer.

"Think all that matters 'round here is sayin' yer prayers, sayin' yer prayers, doin' yer work. Can't tell me God Hisself don't like birthday cakes!"

She had just received a note from Reverend Mother urging that she at least adopt more religious motifs for her cakes, not the usual dogs, cats, houses, flowers, etc. The one the evening before had been particularly offensive, it seemed. So Sister Barnabas growled and kicked and scowled her way through the next twenty-four hours, simmering with resentment. The next sister to be so honored got a cake with a bleeding heart on it.

She made her own Christmas cards. I don't think Reverend Mother ever knew. It was quite possible she didn't, for Sister Barnabas, down there in her wing of the convent, had her own world. She kept kittens out near the back door, and her Christmas cards were rough drawings of a kitten or two with a red ribbon, carefully colored, a conventional little message written inside. These she started to create in her spare hours sometime in October, and she would give them to the milkman, the deliveryman, the bread man, the garbage collector, the string of people who came to her back door during the year. I liked to think of the circuit of relationships that emanated from Sister Barnabas's back door: a network of people who spoke her language and read her scowls, were not put off, brought her little treats and favors that she never turned in but hoarded in her cell. She had her favorites, and she played them. What I got from her treasure hoard on my birthday was positively embarrassing, but there was no way of getting around it.

It is extremely difficult to try to re-create now the texture of our relationship during those two years I spent at Our Redeemer's. It settled into a kind of tacit complicity which she herself never fully understood as complicity, for she simply disregarded impossible restrictions she couldn't see the sense of, and went her way. I was of a different breed; I had to balance two kinds of consciousness. Trained to much more rigid ideals, I had my twinges. But through it all, Sister Barnabas's obdurateness, her persistent, passionate grasp at the bits of life she could still hold, her rage at what had been lost and her inability to say what—for in some ways she had never even known what, she could only feel its loss—these realities touched me more deeply than the hours of teaching, of living with that community, of doing what was expected and trying to fathom its meaning.

When I left Our Redeemer's, having been transferred to St. Gertrude's, a house several hundred miles away, Sister Barnabas wept. She did it in the privacy of her room; she was nowhere in evidence the next morning when I left officially, the whole community standing around outside the front door to say the prayers for travelers and then say good-bye.

At supper the night before, she sent me a note by the server, scrawled on the back of an envelope in her childish hand:

Come see me after nite prayer.
B.

There was no denying it. Great Silence or not, she would have her private farewell.

So, after night prayer, when the others were padding off to study hour or to get ready for bed, I went to Sister Barnabas's cell and knocked.

"Sister?" A whisper from behind the door.

"It's me."

She opened the door. Inside seemed strangely dim and shadowy. Then I saw what she had done. The cluttered little cell was aglow with dozens of candle stubs, sacristy butts, no doubt, lighted and stuck anywhere she could perch them. I suppressed my instant urge to warn against fire: the holy cards, photos, papers, old magazines seemed to be leaping toward the flames in my excited imagination. She took my hand and pulled me inside.

Sister Barnabas (Barney I called her to myself even then) had prepared for me a party. Her own kind of party. It was like a child's birthday party. Red, pink, and purple balloons hovered up against the ceiling. Flickering candles cast huge blobs of dancing shadows on her white walls. The house outside her room was absolutely still. She had her small transistor radio that the garbage man had given her three Christmases before going softly on FM. By some miraculous effort she had cleared her desk and set on it a masterpiece. On the cake, built high above the top layer, stood a replica of the convent we were in. A light on in one window, the kitchen. And underneath the replica, "Good-bye." Sister Barnabas was almost speechless herself at the effect of her efforts on me.

That passed quickly, however, and we settled down to cake and Coke. I asked no questions. She had her ways. Her gesture made me want to cry, but I didn't. There was some steel impulse in me that said, "Hold on, it will be too much." It would have been. Instead, we gorged ourselves on Barney's seven-layer cake. She had wrapped several small presents for me, and I was expected to open these, one by one.

"Do you like it?" she asked with childlike eagerness as I'd barely finished opening the can of Johnson's Baby Powder. Then the new toothbrush. Then a little box of Christmas cards she had saved for me. And the most touching perhaps, a bookmark for my Office book: the cutout head of the Virgin pasted on a small strip of leather she had found somewhere and trimmed with pinking shears. I still have it.

Our party lasted about an hour. That was all the time I could manage, with packing yet to finish. But Barney had made her point. At the door to her cell she hugged me and bristled her black whiskers against my cheek, then turned brusquely back into her cell, hiding tears.

Life has a way of simply going on. The large hurdles like good-byes are risen to and then gradually fade before the onslaught of daily tasks, deadlines, and expectations to be met in the or-dinary business of getting through twenty-four hours. It was the same in the convent, only perhaps more so for us, for we never had those upholstered pauses I now recognize as part of a normal rhythm of day-to-day living "outside": the evening when you choose to forget the outer world and curl up before the fire once the children are in bed and the latch is on the door. In the convent as I knew it, there were no such pauses. We moved from task to task; recreation itself was a task, staying awake in chapel could be a task, trusting the validity of one's own re-sponses became a task—especially when they were at variance with what was expected. Days passed. Years passed. We worked. We prayed. We did our best to survive intact.

Through those years I never once heard from Barney. Of her I would hear periodically, just enough—usually conveyed in guardedly judgmental words—to convince me that her life went on as I had known it, fringed with dust and decaying strands, built of the bits of human contact she could elicit in an environment that was basically hostile to her. And to which she herself was hostile. Now and then a friend who had spent time at Our Redeemer's would mention some anecdote about Barney. I gleaned that she was still cooking creations for birthdays, that her kitchen was still messy beyond description, that she was still so grouchy that the prioress found it virtually impossible to assign anyone to help her—that she was still, that is, herself as life had made her.

Five years passed before I decided to leave the Order for good. That is not part of this story really, except that my leave-taking made possible our final meeting. I left, moved far away, worked, eventually married. The shape and feeling of different periods of our lives is mysterious. I passed through several phases of feeling about that chunk of my life, but ultimately came to hold it all at a distance. It ceased to be as living or as painful as it once had been, before the growing realities of husband, family, time passing, gray hairs, and all that whispers to us that regrets are a waste of time. Still, somewhere quite alive in my fading memory of detail there was a stumpy, grouchy, affectionate face and figure: Barney.

I didn't know how alive that figure was until her letter came. The first one arrived shortly after my second baby was born. We were still in the welter of two sets of diapers, sibling jealousy, and house clutter that says life has exploded in colossal disregard for order. It was fitting that into this world of fraying nerves and sharp edges muted by the welcome of loving affection that underlay our fatigue, Barney's letter came. She would have understood and responded to the mess. I remember sitting down in the midst of unfolded diapers, a mountain of them, while Jeffrey finally settled into Play-Doh and the baby was building up for a good yell. I wanted to indulge immediately the unexpected surge of feeling that had risen at this sudden link with a world that had seemed so far-off. I hadn't known I would be so glad to hear. I had spoken often of Barney, and with affection. But I had *placed* her in my imagination; her spot was fixed in my memory. Now she was dislodging herself, refusing to be put away neatly, asserting her living right to be as she wanted to be.

"Dear One," it began. I had to struggle to make out that childish scrawl, large letters on small pages of what looked like her own card, a kitten on the front.

I have not forgot u, u no I did luv u. Life here is worse than it was tho i no u suffered. i did see it even tho i never sed so. i no u have a good husband now and a baby. [She had not heard of the recent addition.] i want u to no i still think of u. if i cud i wud send u sweets. think of me.

B.

Then began our correspondence. It had the same character as our old Saturday morning eruptions had had. I tried to write regularly over the next four years, despite our many moves, our growing family, and my own work. She awakened some sense of loyalty that I wanted to keep alive. Her notes came spasmodically, almost as if some moment in her life that laid claim on her with a particular stranglehold forced her to choke out a letter to a faraway friend. One came, two years ago now, which read in part: "u no, dear one, that if i cud, i wud have left myself. but where wud I go?"

It saddened me. Where would she go? She could never at this point—for she was over seventy, I thought—go anywhere. And she suffered so there. That was clear from her notes, almost illegible and illiterate as they were.

. . .

Then this. "Sister Barnabas MacLean."

There was something offensive and compelling in it. I had had no plan ever to revisit that convent. I had been going to pass right through Maine with no train stop at all that night because I was at that point of fatigue that leaves the traveler with only one desire: to get back to the warm comforts of home. I still had a distance to go. At Montreal Tom would meet me, and we would fly from there back to Vancouver to collect the children from the grandparents before heading home. Home. Somehow, sitting over the last of the chocolate sundae in the Holiday Inn that night in November, I wanted desperately to be back home, fast.

But first this. Barney. I reread the notice several times. There was no way around it. If I chose to, thanks to the breakdown, I could see Barney for one last time. If I chose to. That was the hitch. There wasn't likely to be anyone there that I knew except Barney. What kept me sitting over the second and then the third cup of coffee that night was not any fear that familiar faces would awaken old discomforts: it was simply a question of whether I wanted to see Barney that way.

But there was something else that stirred me, that finally made me gather up the check and head for the room to ready myself and call a cab. It wasn't quite the banality of paying one's last respects but, to be honest, it had something of that in it. Mixed with the need, perhaps, to confirm in my own sensibilities the fact that Barney was dead. My going had something to do with her and something to do with me. For her it seemed somehow right, foolish as it is to suppose our visits of final deference have a thing to do with the dead themselves. But what exactly was that feeling? That someone coming, someone from the outside who had known her on the inside, who had understood her own alienation and perhaps reenacted it in another way, that my coming was—what is the word—"fitting"? Somehow a circle come complete. For me the meaning was clear. It cut a continuity. Not at all a physical continuity like the loss of a child or a parent. A spiritual continuity. That point of common understanding in this world was gone. Just that. Gone. I had to be sure. And honor its reality.

So I went. The taxi was about five minutes late, time enough for me to stand in front of the Holiday Inn stamping my feet as I tensed myself against that November air, time enough to lose myself for a few moments in that resplendent sky. There really is nothing like it elsewhere; of that I'm convinced. By day the scenery there would have to be called bleak: the long, low marshes, few sloping hills, forests of evergreens, stubby farmlands, gray barns—a littered landscape of indigence and lack of imagination. But by night that disappears. It was years—twenty-one, to be exact—since I had felt my neck grow stiff as I strained to follow this design, then that, in the fluffing Milky Way. Orion. The Big Dipper. A night world of pattern revealed by depthless black. The world above. Barney up there?

The taxi came and I slammed in, gathering my inner forces for this last visit. It had about it that character, and I was sensitive to it. How often in this life was I likely to find myself alone, traveling, away from family and friends, driving through a landscape that once had held me, revisiting it almost as if I were someone else? It was a privileged moment. I felt that.

I asked the taxi driver to wait. The convent was the same. I could just make out the familiar dimensions in the darkness: the heavy front door, the wing with the cells and the community room in it to the left, the chapel wing to the right. Extending out back, invisible from the front, would be Barney's wing, the kitchen. Who, I wondered, took over?

"Good evening." The sister was politely inquiring as she opened the door and held it ajar for me to explain myself. She was middle-aged, rather nondescript. Her face had that blond look that ages poorly, pale shading into paler. Her modernized habit was unflattering.

"Good evening. I've come to pay my respects to Sister Barnabas." I didn't even stumble over the formula. It came with the mechanicalness that gets us through some of life's worst moments. I was caught up in a sensation I hadn't expected: utter familiarity. For one brief instant I had the urge to say to the sister: "And if you'll just stand aside, I'll find my way to her cell and the kitchen." But I didn't. I behaved. There was something indescribably strange in that moment of unintended masquerade. Strange—and comic.

"Come in." She smiled faintly, then turned wordlessly as I shut the door behind me and, ignoring the heavy inner doors that read CLOISTER, led me through another door to the right into a small parlor. Of course. I had forgotten that. They would wake her in one of the outside rooms so the public could come. *The public.* The garbage man? The milkman? I wondered who had come. That barrier outside had been so thoroughly obscured in my mind that it was a momentary shock to come smack up against it. The Cloister Door. I had lived on the other side of that. But here Barney and I remet on the outside. Had we been there all along?

There was no one in the visitors' parlor except the casket with Barney in it and one nun praying. This I dreaded. I hate corpses. I hate going to look. Why on earth this compulsion to see Barney again? Then, steeling inner responses, I walked over and knelt automatically at the prie-dieu before her.

It wasn't Barney. Of course it was, but it wasn't Barney. She was in the habit, hands folded, rosary through them. I had never seen her look neat. Her headdress was straight. Her whiskers were gone. Whoever prepared the corpse had shaved the chin smooth, removing one of Barney's most characteristic marks. She was smiling—that pasty, waxen smile meant to reassure us that wherever she was, things weren't that bad. I have never seen that smile on Barney. Her forehead was smooth. No scowl. She lay in a simple box, as was the custom, with a white lining. There were no flowers. Those I didn't miss. But I wanted ivy, arbutus, philodendron, African violets, impatiens—the plant that always seemed to fit Barney. I wanted them all there, surrounding her indiscriminately. I wanted the scowl. Maybe a big cake on the casket saying "Good-bye" with a kitten on the top. Something irreverent. Something imaginative. Something col-

orful. The quilt as a lining for the casket. I didn't want this effigy
of nunhood, of dedication and service. I wanted the real thing:
screaming dissonances in that sterile setting.

Nowhere could I find it. I could imagine her kitchen. Someone would have cleaned it already. Of her room I hated to think.
What had happened to the bosomy lady in front of her cottage?
Was the plastic madonna already at the dump? The nun behind
me went on praying. The silence was oppressive. A tall beeswax
taper at the end of the bier sent flickers of shadow across the
still form. It wasn't Barney.

I nodded to the sister and headed for the door. There, Sister
Poker-Face was waiting for me, and she noiselessly opened the
outer door. I could see the exhaust from the taxi billowing pale
gray in the darkness. He had kept the engine idling against the
cold.

"Thank you for coming. She is at peace."

I nodded. I wanted to rage. I wanted to scream. "You don't
know me, but I know you. You didn't know Barney, but I knew
her!" What was the point? There was no way. Could any scream
penetrate it?

As I walked down the path, I heard the heavy door click
behind me. Then one look up. I was grateful for the cold air.
And stars. The vast Milky Way. The sky that turned all this dark
and illumined its own shuddering spaces with something not
warm but clear. Cold. It cleansed. I breathed deep and looked,
for a long moment. Good-bye sky. Then I heard the motor
revving. The cabbie leaned over and opened my door.

At first in halting spasms, then with that satisfying surge of
power that says all connections have been made, our engine
built up to a steady rhythm. Spent, I leaned back against the
seat and closed my eyes, grateful to be borne away in the dark.